Leader of Men

Book 4 in the Sir John Hawkwood Series

By

Griff Hosker

Contents

Leader of Men..i
Prologue...3
Chapter 1..9
Chapter 2..19
Chapter 3..28
Chapter 4..41
Chapter 5..50
Chapter 6..66
Chapter 7..77
Chapter 8..85
Chapter 9..98
Chapter 10...108
Chapter 11...117
Chapter 12...128
Chapter 13...140
Chapter 14...152
Chapter 15...163
Chapter 16...172
Chapter 17...185
Chapter 18...200
Chapter 19...209
Chapter 20...219
Chapter 21...232
Epilogue..240
Glossary...242
Historical note...244
Other books by Griff Hosker.......................................246

Published by Sword Books Ltd 2022

Copyright ©Griff Hosker First Edition

*The author has asserted their moral right under the Copyright, Designs and Patents Act, 1988, to be identified as the author of this work.
All Rights reserved. No part of this publication may be reproduced, copied, stored in a retrieval system, or transmitted, in any form or by any means, without the prior written consent of the copyright holder, nor be otherwise circulated in any form of binding or cover other than that in which it is published and without a similar condition being imposed on the subsequent purchaser.
A CIP catalogue record for this title is available from the British Library.
Cover by Design for Writers*

Dedication

Dedicated to Major Richard Saphore a true officer and a gentleman and someone I would like to think of as a friend. Thank you for all the research you have done for me. You have helped me tremendously and I do appreciate all that you do for me.

Real People Used in The Book

Sir John Hawkwood- Captain of the White Company
King Edward Plantagenet
Prince Edward of Wales and Duke of Cornwall- his son (The Black Prince)
Arnaud de Cervole- Mercenary Captain
King John II of France
Crown Prince Charles, the Dauphin of France
Pope Urban Vth
Phillip the Bold, Duke of Burgundy
Queen Joan (Joanna)I - Queen of Naples, and Countess of Provence and Forcalquier
John II - Marquis of Montferrat
Amadeus - Count of Savoy, known as the Green Count
Bernabò Visconti - Lord of Milan
Ambrogio Visconti - his son and leader of the Company of Ambrogio
Galeazzo Visconti - Duke of Milan and brother of Bernabò
Pellario Griffo - Chamberlain of Pisa
Luca di Totti de'Firidolfi da Panzano - Florentine warrior
Ranuccio Farnese - Florentine leader
Andrew de Belmonte- an English adventurer
Heinrich Paer – German Mercenary leader
Malatesta Malatesta- Florentine general
Galeotto Malatesta - brother of Malatesta Malatesta
Giovanni Agnello – Merchant and doge of Pisa
Enrico Montforte – Florentine Mercenary
Ricceri Grimaldi – Genoese mercenary
Albert Sterz - one-time captain of the White Company
Annechin Baumgarten – Leader of the Star Company
Cardinal Gil Álvarez Carrillo de Albornoz – Papal envoy

Prologue

Montferrat 1361

The town square we were using to recruit more lances for the company was packed, for it was market day. William, who was responsible for the day to day running of The White Company, had a clerk to assist him these days but he still ensured that every contract that was signed was also signed by him. The young man I had found in France all those years ago was now as valuable to me as my captains, Robin, Martin, Giovanni and Eoin. I simply could not do without him. In theory, I could have let my captains scrutinise the new men who wished to join what was becoming the most successful mercenary company in Northern Italy but I had learned that I was the best judge of men. I had developed an ability to see whom I could not trust. Albert Sterz and Arnaud de Cervole had both been leaders and warriors with whom I had served. Neither were the kinds of men I would choose to serve with me.

These recruiting days followed a pattern. The leaders of each company came with me and spent the day as both guards and observers. They had become bored and were sparring with each other. We were a professional company and not a moment in the day was wasted. We trained every day as often as we could. We had almost recovered all the Montferrat land taken by the Count of Savoy and that was down to our discipline. Of course, the duke was just one of the men who sought to control this part of Italy. The Visconti brothers, Bernabò and Galeazzo controlled Milan and Pavia and it was they who were the real enemies of Montferrat for they had used Savoy to attack the tiny Montferrat.

Michael who, along with Dai, acted as my squire, brought me a fresh pitcher of wine. Considering that it was spring it was still too hot for Englishmen born in the colder north. The line of men wishing to join us was a long one. I spied many Englishmen amongst them. They were mainly archers but there were some billmen. Uniquely English, they could be trained to fight with halberds. There were others who were foreigners: Swabians, Flemish, Spanish and even some Portuguese. Each brought a particular skill and I had learned that a balanced company was the best. The main parts would be my English archers and English men at arms. I had fought alongside such men at my first battles: Crécy and Poitiers, and I was English. I now chose to fight abroad and for money but that was because I had been used and undervalued by the Plantagenet rulers of England. My men fought in lances made up of a man at arms, squire, archer, heavy infantryman and either a crossbowman or hand gunner. I was not convinced about these men who fought with the newest weapon on the battlefield but I kept an open mind. Most of the men who were lined up were in such groups. The squire would stand with the two horses that the man at arms owned and the archer, heavy infantryman and second missile man would stand behind. There were some who came in pairs and even singly. My captains and my friends, Giovanni d'Azzo and Sir Eoin would organise them into new lances. I was above such things for I was captain of the White Company.

It was a good morning. A young English man at arms, Andrew de Belmonte turned up with his squire, three archers and a billman. I was already willing to sign him up even before he spoke. He was a handsome young man and I wondered why he was not a knight. Robin and Sir Eoin nodded their approval and William happily gave him a contract to sign. As soon as it was signed, I said, "I am curious sir, why you are not a knight for you seem to have every attribute you might need except for a title."

He smiled, "I am the youngest brother of three and our manor is a poor one. The most impressive thing about it is the name. I chose the life of a sword for hire but I have hopes that I may earn my spurs while I am here. I was brought up to believe that chivalry and honour are the most important things in life."

"For all that I said I was surprised you were not a knight. I confess that here titles mean nothing, at least not to me and my men. Perform well on the battlefield and you will earn more than any English knight would."

He seemed surprised, "Do we not all earn the same?"

William shook his head, "There is a basic fee that we pay to all men but performance on the field can earn more."

"Thank you, then I will try to earn it." Taking his pile of coins, he and his men left. The laughter as they left told me that they got on. That was not always true of lances.

The next Englishman, John Dobson, was also a good choice but as he turned to leave he leaned in and said, "You know that there is a rumour that the man called Andrew de Belmonte whom you just signed is a bastard of the English royal family?" I had learned that most mercenaries do not gossip and I guessed there might be some truth in the rumour. It would make sense if some royal prince had ploughed a lady's furrow that he might be brought up differently. It was interesting but that was all. I had earned a title but it was largely irrelevant. I wanted men who could fight. Andrew would soon learn to forget his chivalric ideals.

There were two more who signed up after the Englishmen. Both were Hungarians and I knew how doughty they were. I was quite happy for them to join. One, Lazlo Kaepernick looked to be a potential leader. I had many Hungarians under my command and having a leader of the same nationality often helped with communication. The next man was a huge German who swaggered up and he looked as though he thought this was a mere formality. He was wrong. He had with him a squire who was almost as big. He carried the two-handed sword favoured by Swabians and Germans. "Karl von Sturmz, where do I sign?"

I did not like him from the moment he spoke. I had endured enough of arrogant Germans and I was tempted to dismiss him out of hand. William looked first at me and then back at the German. "Have you any horses?"

He snorted with derision, "Why should I need a horse? With this sword I can hew down any rider who comes close to me."

He was right, of course, and we did have men at arms who fought on foot. I glanced over at my captains who, hearing the loud voice had stopped their sparring and were now looking over at me. Robin was an archer but I trusted his judgement more than any other man. He gave a slow and clear shake of the head.

I looked up at the German and smiled, "Thank you for your offer but we have no need of you at this time."

He turned to look at me as though I was the village idiot who had asked the most ridiculous of questions, "You know who I am? I am the butcher of Nissa and any Captain of Condottiere would be lucky to have me! Most would make me a captain."

I smiled, "Then you should have no trouble finding another to take you on."

William said, dismissively, "Next."

The German backhanded William hard across the face and the man who was responsible for my money was hurled to the ground. When I had been younger, I had been handy with my fists. I knew how to brawl. As I stood to face and punish this arrogant German, I knew I had to win. The German wore plate and I had on a perpunto tunic. Although padded it would only soften a blow while his plate would stop my blows from hurting him. He was bigger than I was and, taking the initiative, I punched hard at his chin. When I struck the blow I almost launched myself at him and used my weight to make the greatest impact. I had been right not to hire him. A good warrior has a sixth sense about danger but the German was looking gleefully at William when the blow struck. A tooth flew from his mouth and he reeled as blood spurted from his mouth. He was angry and that never helped. Regaining his balance he pulled back his right hand and I knew exactly what he intended. He would return the blow and smack me hard in the face. I ducked to my left and his hand hit my right shoulder. It hurt. My left hand struck him hard on the side of his head, close to his ear. It was not a blow that he had expected. I had used it before and knew that it not only made his ears ring but also disorientated him.

Just behind the German, I saw his squire's hand go to his sword. If he drew the weapon then this would be a bloodbath. I hooked my leg around the German knight's leg and pushed as he swung a flailing fist at the space I had just occupied. As he fell, I saw Dai with his dagger at the German's squire's throat, "Keep your sword sheathed, eh?"

The German lay on the ground, winded by the fall. I made no attempt to help him to his feet and Dai kept the squire occupied. There were many men watching the German as he attempted to stand and they laughed at his attempts. He had plate armour and he had been hurt, both made him grow angrier and when he finally made his feet he roared and ran at me like an enraged bull. I spun around and hit him hard on the other side of the head as he passed. He turned and looked for me. I walked up to him and before he could do anything I hit him on both ears so hard that blood came from them. I pulled back my fist and ended the fight with a punch to the unprotected face. The blow hurt my fist for it broke his nose which began to pour blood as he fell back, unconscious. The Montferratians who were interested bystanders all cheered at the outcome.

Rubbing my bruised knuckles I said to the squire, "Take your master and quit this town. The next time that I see him I will use a sword and not my fists."

The squire nodded and headed for a tired-looking sumpter that carried the rest of their gear. The poor animal would struggle to carry the German and his mail. No one made any attempt to help the squire as he struggled to load the knight onto the sumpter's back. The jeering crowds did not make it any easier.

As they disappeared, I turned and saw that William had recovered enough to sit at the table once more. My captains were grinning and I smiled as I said to the waiting would-be recruits, "Does anyone else wish to challenge my right to choose my own men?"

The ones waiting to sign all shook their heads and one English man at arms said, "No, my lord, I came here to serve Sir John Hawkwood the hero of Poitiers and you have confirmed that the White Company is the one for my lance!"

I sat and drank some of the wine, "Good, then all is well."

Chapter 1

In our campaigns thus far we had hurt not only Amadeus, the Green Count of Savoy but also Count Luchino Novello Visconti and his cousins Bernabò and Galeazzo. The rulers of Milan would wish to have revenge. The Lord of Milan, Bernabò Visconti was, some said, the most powerful man in Italy. So far I had not had to take him on and I was not sure if I was ready to yet. However, with the new men attracted by our last victory over them, it was time to end this war. I wanted winter to train the new men properly and to find another paymaster away from Milan. Montferrat was not the richest part of Italy and I wanted to defeat the Count of Savoy and have him pay us off. Once we had reclaimed the land he had taken from the Marquis of Montferrat then the balance of power would shift. I gathered my captains in the hall we used at the manor loaned to us by the Marquis. The estate was as large as a county in England and we were not only safe there but well fed.

"We now have a force that should be able to defeat the Savoyards. William, the map."

William was my crutch. He paid my armies and made money for me. He also organised my intelligence in the form of maps and spies he paid. When merchants took goods from us to sell they also undertook to tell us of the lands through which they passed. William was clever and it was a good system. He laid out the map he had drawn of this part of Italy. He had a neat hand. I think he could have earned a good living copying books. I was just glad that he had chosen to serve me. His sister was the mother of my two boys and she lived in Bordeaux with the man at arms who had once served me. There was no animosity for we were all practical people.

I jabbed a finger at Nissa. "The count values this part of his land greatly. It is his major port and gives him access to the east and its attendant trade. I wish to make him fear that we intend to attack it by marching to Saviliagno."

My captains all looked at the place that William had circled in red ink. Giovanni nodded and said, "Almost sixty miles. Three days?"

I shook my head, "Two for I will mount archers. We have six hundred English archers and we have that number of horses. While we ride there then I will have you, Giovanni, lead the rest of the lances and the men on foot along the Po Valley and then the Orco to wait close to Lanzo, north-west of Torino. You will do so secretly. It is Montferrat land but you will need to ensure no spies observe your progress. We will join you there."

Sir Eoin asked, "You are so confident that we will win at Saviliagno?"

"Have you seen any who can stand in our way?" We had won every battle in which we had fought. "I am not arrogant enough to believe that there are no warriors out there who can beat us but if there are then they are not from Savoy or Torino. We use speed and surprise to take Saviliagno and that will make the Green Count come south to protect his port for he will expect us to head there. We will march north and with your men approaching from the east, we will have Amadeus between our nutcrackers." The Green Count was the nickname for the ruler of Savoy.

"But Sir John, it is winter."

"I know, Giovanni, and there is snow on the mountains but there is always snow on the mountains and so far there is no sign of it falling on the plain. We move quickly and, hopefully, create surprise. We ride to war and if nature upsets my plans then we fall back and wait for the spring. This way we have a chance to end this war before winter. Would you not rather spend the winter behind these walls instead of worrying if the Milanese and Savoyards are planning an attack? We defeat the Savoyards and then worry about the Milanese after winter."

I knew that it was a bold plan and that was why it might succeed for no one would expect it. We would be flirting with Torino and the Visconti family but as I had already bloodied their noses, I hoped that they would still be reeling from their last defeat at our hands. I gave my men a week to prepare. We could have left the next day but I wanted nothing to mar our chances of victory.

My captains and I were all rich men and that meant we had the best plate and mail that could be bought. Most of the lances who had served with us since we had been in Burgundy were also well off. I suppose some could have retired back to England but we were successful and the money we took was relatively easy to come by and they used it to make them better warriors. The Marquis paid me and I paid my men but once we won, and we usually did, then we not only took the spoils of war from the battlefield but also the money we were usually paid to leave their land. The result was that the plate armour we wore over our polished mail, was the best and we kept it highly polished to reinforce our name, The White Company. Dai was still my squire but the plate he wore was the equal of any knight's. I had offered to knight him but he seemed happy, for the moment, to remain as a squire. He was eminently practical for he earned a fortune and he kept all that he earned. Michael, the youth we had rescued, would be the one who fetched and carried. He was the one who helped me to dress. Having two of them to watch my back was no bad thing. Michael could learn from Dai and when Dai moved on I had a ready replacement.

    My archers wore good sallet helmets and their padded jacks were studded with metal. Many of them had short mail hauberks beneath the jacks. Often my archers were forced to fight with hand weapons. The mail gave them a better chance of survival. Uniquely amongst the other mercenary companies, they were all mounted. It was not just a case of getting to a battle quickly. Although we had yet to lose, I knew that we could and the archers would be more likely to stay as long as the horsemen if they had their own means of escape. I had seen many routs where those on foot fled before they could be ridden down. The one arm in which we did not excel was the gunpowder soldiers. Many armies had not only handguns but also long tubes, often called cannons. From what I had seen they were noisy and inaccurate. Even more important was that they could be easily outranged by my longbows. We had a few of what many called the devil's weapons but we had fewer than most other companies.

    The land through which we passed had changed hands so many times over the years that the practical people who lived there had learned to smile at the ever mounted, mailed column that passed through. We had been paid well by the Marquis and so we paid for our food. William was not with us. He did not need to endure the rigours of campaign and battle. He had trained two clerks who accompanied us. They had the purses of coins to pay for our food and, where necessary, our board and when we collected treasure they kept the accounts. We were one company and we all shared both the dangers and the profits. The two men were there to ensure that all was seen as legal and above board. The land was, generally fertile. The looming mountains ahead were less so but it was where the rulers of this land had built their strongholds since the time of the Romans. Once we were within twenty miles of Saviliagno then we would be seen and I hoped that the sight of just fifteen hundred mounted men would encourage whoever commanded the town to come from behind their walls to attack us. They would not see my mounted archers for who mounted longbowmen? My archers were my secret weapon for none could stand against them. I had been an archer and I knew the power of their arms and their bows. I knew that if we used this trick too often then my enemies would get wise but for the moment it might just force a battle. I could not afford for the Savoyards to sit behind their walls and wait for them to surrender. My plan demanded a battle.

As we closed to within what I hoped would be battle distance I waved forward my senior captains. We would ride and talk. All of us were cloaked and that hid the shining armour beneath. Our banners and standards were furled. I was attempting to fool the Savoyards. There were many roaming companies in this part of the world. I did not want them to know it was me until they were committed to a fight.

"Robin and Martin, if they come forth then hold your men as a second line. I cannot be sure what formation they will adopt but as we know they have many Genoese crossbowmen with pavise then we can assume they will bring those. I just do not know if they will use them on their flanks or their whole line." The Genoese crossbowmen were mercenaries like us. They had pavesiers who carried their large shields for them and they were skilled men. Whenever we fought them then they were the first target for my archers.

Sir Eoin said, "It is more likely that they will use them on their flanks. If they do not then they negate somewhat, their efficacy."

"Perhaps." One part of this I did not like was that I did not know who commanded the enemy forces. I preferred knowing my enemy. The perfect leader for me was another captain of a company of condottiere as I knew most of them and how they fought. I was more arrogant in those days never having tasted defeat and believed that I had the beating of all of them. "My plan is to make the enemy think we attack with a double line of horsemen. We will not, of course. We will halt two hundred paces from the enemy line and that should give you two the time to dismount your archers and when we move then send ten flights at them."

Robin nodded, "And where will you move?"

"I will take half of our horsemen to the right and Sir Eoin the other half to the left. When your ten flights have been sent, we charge."

"And if the Genoese are on the flanks?"

I smiled at Sir Eoin's caution. It was a good trait. "I am expecting that our archers will hit not only their horsemen but the crossbowmen too. In any case, their attention will be upon the archers, albeit briefly. By the time they have loosed their bolts, we will be upon them. There may be casualties but that is acceptable."

The Genoese were the masters of the crossbow. Many of the Genoese crossbowmen had a youth to carry the large shield and to set it up. The crossbows were good but their major flaw was in the reloading. While a longbowman could send arrow after arrow in quick succession a crossbow necessitated the winding back of the cord and after the loading, it had to be aimed again. A longbowman could send missiles with unerring accuracy at the same target. I had watched Robin and his men at the marks they used. They could turn their head and not even look at the mark and yet keep arrow after arrow hitting it.

"We will be using lances and the pavise are there to stop arrows. A lance will puncture them as though they were made of parchment but I hope that a line of mounted and mailed horsemen will make them flee."

The skies had cleared of the clouds and we spied in the distance the towers and flags of Saviliagno fluttering in the icy winter wind. The walls could not be made out but we could work out where they were from the towers and fluttering banners. We were not riding hard. Our slower than normal approach might lead the Savoyards to believe that we were either nervous or tired. We moved ever west and when we were close enough to make out the walls, towers, gates and defenders, I saw the gates open and a host of soldiers emerged. There were foothills and the Savoyard commander would have to be a fool to ignore the defensive possibilities that they afforded. There were rocks and shallow gullies as well as shrubs and stunted trees. Everything favoured defenders and made it hard for attackers. His Genoese crossbowmen would use the rocks and gullies while the horsemen could wait before them. We kept our slow and steady approach as I watched the Savoyards descend from their town and array before us. My mind wondered why there was such a large force awaiting us. A town the size of Saviliagno could not muster the two thousand men I saw before me. Amadeus must have been planning an attack of his own. We had hurt him in two battles and perhaps he had hired mercenaries to bring the war to us. If that was true then my choice of targets had enjoyed a degree of luck. The question was, bad or good luck?

    I raised my lance and waved it. It was the signal for my men to form our three lines. There would be two of horsemen and one of archers. Our squires took our cloaks and as the sun glinted off the almost white metal it was a signal to the Savoyards and their mercenaries that they were fighting Sir John Hawkwood and his White Company. Dai took my cloak, however, unlike the other squires, he did not ride to the rear but draped it over the cantle of his saddle. He would ride close to the rump of the courser I rode. Michael was close behind with a spare lance in case I should need it.

    When the squires rode to the rear it was as though more than a third of our horsemen had left our battle lines and, as I had hoped, it encouraged the Savoyards to form their own lines. Knowing that they had Genoese crossbows to protect their rear and that their horsemen outnumbered ours, was the incentive for the Savoyard general to risk a counter charge. The slope to the foothills gave the advantage to our enemy. We halted just two hundred paces from their line of horses. We were outnumbered. I looked down our lines for I wanted them to think we were nervous. In reality, I was giving my archers time to dismount and hand their reins to a squire. They would be stringing their bows and putting their bodkin tipped arrows in the soil. The dirt on them might make the wounds they inflicted become infected. My archers took the long view. Better to eliminate an enemy than merely allow him to return to the field sooner rather than later.

I did not use a horn although Michael carried one for me. Instead, I waved my lance and my two lines of mailed men moved aside. Had I used a horn it would have alerted the Savoyards. As it was it took some moments for them to realise that we had moved position. Their plan was clear. They were going to react to whatever we did and that could only help us. It was like a game of chess and I was already two moves ahead of them. Archers can loose over horsemen and even as we began to move their first flight of goose feathered arrows was in the air. Many of the Savoyards had their visors up and as they looked up to see what made the noise above their heads then arrows plunged into unprotected faces. Even a war arrow would have been fatal. The bodkins that hit plate did not necessarily guarantee a mortal wound but the arrows drew blood more times than they did not. They also struck horses for the Savoyards did not use as much armour for their horses as we did. The animals were hurt. They reared and bucked as arrows tore into their bodies. By the time five flights had been sent, we were in position.

I turned to Michael, "As soon as the last flight has been sent then sound the charge."

"Aye, my lord."

In the time it took for me to give the command the last few arrows fell and I saw the devastation the missiles had caused. There were riderless horses milling around, their riders on the ground. Some other animals had been hit and were careering across the battlefield their riders unable to control them. There was no order to the enemy and as the Savoyard horn sounded for them to reform I spurred my horse and my lances headed for the disordered Savoyard horsemen. The Genoese crossbows had been untouched but they had no target for there was a mass of milling horses before them.

We covered the two hundred paces so quickly that we did not strike them at full pace. We did not need to. They were stock still and shocked. The first knight I hit had a yellow and blue chequered trapper upon his horse and the Imperial black eagle showed he was a Florentine with Ghibelline sympathies. He was a rich knight and I know many men would have attempted to take him a prisoner for ransom. I did not need ransom and I would not risk a wounded enemy hurting me. My lance drove into his side where his breastplate met his backplate. The knight's confusion allowed me to choose my target, his shoulder. The lancehead drove in and the knight tumbled from his horse, his falling body pulling it from the lance head.

I dug my heels in and rode to the next knight who had yellow and orange livery with a great helm. My bascinet had a bevor and afforded me a better view of my enemy. He had seen me kill his companion and he spurred his horse at me. Our lances punched at the same time but there the similarity of our blows ended. He tried to block my strike with a shield that was square on while I angled mine to allow his lance to slide along my polished shield. He tumbled over the back of his horse when my lance and archer's arm smacked into his shield. Dai would take his surrender and I galloped on.

We had broken the enemy horsemen and they were fleeing back to the town on the hill. The Genoese crossbows still awaited us but they could not release for fear of hitting their own horsemen. A bolt struck my shield and I headed for the Genoese. He had to reload. My horse was tiring as we rode up the rough slope to the first pavise but as I punched my lance through the shield, I struck the crossbowman who was rising to send a quickly reloaded bolt into my chest. The lance was blindly struck but I tore into his shoulder. He would never use a crossbow again. Not only my mailed horsemen were amongst the crossbowmen but also my archers who had mounted and followed us. They would show no mercy to the enemy they hated. The Genoese fled leaving crossbows and pavise where they lay.

"On, follow them into the town."

All the horses were weary but so were the Savoyards and enough of my men, especially the lighter archers, managed to follow the Savoyards through the gates. We had won! Some of those within the walls made an attempt to slow us down and close the gates but my archers quickly rode their horses at the men who realised the folly in fighting mercenaries and facing slashing swords they surrendered. Men who fight for a paymaster rarely fight when the standards that led them have fled and the Genoese and Florentine horsemen acknowledged defeat. I rode to the castle and quickly set myself up there in the largest hall in the castle. The first men who were brought to me were the leaders of the crossbowmen. They had not suffered as many casualties as they might have and their leader Ricceri Grimaldi accepted my offer to leave immediately. I did not demand reparations from him as who knew when the boot might, one day, be on the other foot. They left on the road south within the hour.

The Florentines were led by Enrico Montforte and they, too, were happy to return to Florence. Their journey would be a longer one than the Genoese. They returned across the battlefield which, even as they rode through it, was being stripped clean by my archers. That left the Savoyards of Saviliagno and they were a different matter. Lucci di Bracca was the lord who commanded the city. He had been wounded in the battle and I allowed his wounds to be healed while we ate. The delay allowed me to modify my plans and to work out the terms I would demand. The Lord of Saviliagno, along with his council, was brought before my captains and I. We were seated at the table with the remains of our food still littering it. I saw the looks of disdain the Savoyard nobles gave us. I knew that they were surprised that I led the White Company. The rumour was that Albert Sterz still commanded. I did not mind that misapprehension. We were still dressed in our war gear. Our blood-spattered armour, mail and tunics shocked the council. For most of them, war was something remote. It was what others did for you so that you could enjoy a fine lifestyle.

"My lord, we have your city and we have sent away your hired men. We can squat here and enjoy a warm Christmas."

Christmas was but days away and I saw the looks of horror on their faces. I had used the term city to flatter them and then the threat of staying for Christmas just to encourage them to agree to our terms. I had no intention of spending more than one night there. My men had reported a handful of horsemen riding north even as we galloped through the gates. Amadeus would know he had lost his city. I wanted to meet him as far north as we could manage.

"What I demand from you is every horse that you possess." I smiled when I saw the relief on their faces. They could buy new horses. For my part the taking of their horses was twofold. I would deny the Savoyards the ability to move quickly and I could mount more of my archers. My success in the little battle had shown me that this was the way forward. "I also want ten thousand gold florins. Have the money fetched now."

By making it a command rather than negotiating a price I had taken the initiative. I knew from William that their treasury contained fifteen thousand florins and I was not making them bankrupt. The wounded di Bracca nodded and gestured for his steward. By the time we were ready to retire the chests of coins had been brought and my men guarded them.

The surprise on the faces of the Savoyards as we headed not south, as they expected, but north almost made me laugh. By taking their horses we had denied them the opportunity to warn Amadeus and we headed north quickly. The snow on the mountains to the west had blocked those passes and roads. The only road to Lanzo and Milan was the one we rode. Now everything depended upon Giovanni marching along the Po to spring our trap.

Chapter 2

We had scouts out. We had amongst our men Savoyards and Milanese. We had hired them when we had been in France and knew their worth and now their knowledge came to help us. Riding ahead and in plain clothes, they were able to warn us of any garrisons that might slow us. There were but two and our archers captured them without loss to either side. There is something about English longbows aiming bodkin tipped arrows that makes most warriors think of their families rather than the glory of a bloody death. The most difficult part was skirting Torino and it was also the boldest move for there the garrison outnumbered us. The fact we rode horses and could move quickly but even more important was my decision to do so at night. The hamlets and villages through which we passed must have been terrified as our horses clattered by their homes and by the time they woke they might even send word to Torino but they would have no idea in which direction we went. Of course, as my men all knew, what we did was dangerous as we were now isolated in the heart of enemy lands. If Giovanni and the men he led, the bulk of my company, did not do as I had asked then we were in danger of losing all that we had so far won. I was gambling. Had Albert Sterz still led then we would not have even set out on this chevauchée. My victories had made me confident.

We were close to Rivarolo when the scouts reported the main army of Count Amadeus. To the south of us lay Torino and to the east of us Milan. The Green Count had moved faster than I had expected and he outnumbered us. I saw as they left the town and the Castle of Malgrà, that, like di Bracca, they had no intention of sitting behind their walls and allowing us to raid their lands. The Green Count must have thought that he could defeat us here. I saw signs that there were both men from Milan and from Torino amongst his army. There were no Genoese crossbowmen and that was a good thing. The river guarded by the town and castle was the Orco. It fed the Po. Count Amadeus was using the river to guard one flank while the other was protected by the rocks of the foothills of the mountains.

I had to change my plans. I still hoped that Giovanni would be heading along the Orco for his orders were to keep marching until he reached Lanzo. He would be on the north side of the river. Would he be able to reach us?

I whirled my sword above my head and my captains joined me. Their faces told me that they were not discomfited by the sight that greeted us. As yet the Count of Savoy showed no signs that he was about to charge. He had his lines of horsemen, spearmen, crossbowmen and the militia roughly arrayed but he was waiting to see what I would do first. That was a mistake.

"We fight on foot. Our horses have been roughly treated and I would not risk an uphill charge. There is no room for manoeuvre here. Archers, you will form two lines before us. The squires will guard the baggage and the horses. The heavy infantry will be on the flanks and the men at arms behind the archers. Had we time I would have us use stakes but I doubt that Count Amadeus will afford us that luxury. I hope that by dismounting we encourage the count to attack."

Sir Eoin asked, "And if he does not?"

I smiled, "We brought plenty of food from Saviliagno and if we begin to eat then I hope it will irritate the count into a foolish charge. I still hope that Giovanni will appear. With his men, we would outnumber the Savoyards by almost two to one. We shall see."

Michael took my horse to the rear. He and the squires found some fields that had been planted with winter barley and the animals munched away happily. William was not a warrior but he knew how to defend and he made a small fort of the wagons containing our food and the treasure we had taken. If the battle went against us then we had a refuge. Michael brought me back the poleaxe I had requested. I liked the versatility of the weapon. I had him stand close by Dai and me with his horn although I was not sure that we would need it. I never took my eyes from the Savoyards and I saw Count Amadeus as he reacted to our movements. He had his militia crossbowmen begin to move forward. Each of them had to carry their own pavise and I was happy for them to move forward and set them up in a line. They were within the range of our longbows and I was confident that, in a duel, they would emerge victoriously. He placed his militia and spearmen on his flanks and his horsemen, the nobles who made up his largest element were behind the crossbows. He intended to soften us up and then charge with his heavy horsemen. They were all armed with lances. We had faced such an enemy at Poitiers. Although we did not have the stakes that would have ensured victory, I still had enough confidence in my archers.

Robin was stringing his bow and he nodded towards the crossbowmen, "They are militia, Sir John. I wager that few of them have faced longbows before. They are in for a shock."

"Aye, make sure that the archers in the front rank are the ones who wear mail."

He shook his head, "And you will be teaching next, my grandmother how to suck eggs!"

It was a mild rebuke but I took it for I wanted no foolish error to bring defeat.

Robin looked down the line and, satisfied, returned to me, "We are ready."

"Then in your own time, Captain Robin."

He had placed our best archers in the centre. They were the ones who could hit a mark that was more than three hundred paces away. The crossbows were just two hundred and fifty paces away but the first horsemen were just behind them, their horses eagerly stamping, ready for a charge. The fifty arrows that soared made the crossbowmen hunker down behind their pavise. The arrows were not aimed at them. The fifty arrows fell not amongst the crossbows but the horsemen behind. Some hit plate and some hit horses. About half of the arrows struck and although only a couple of horsemen were felled it had an effect. I heard a horn and I knew that it commanded the crossbowmen to send their bolts at our archers.

Robin shouted, "Archers, loose!" and six hundred arrows rose into the sky. This time their targets were the crossbowmen who had to leave the shelter of their pavise to raise their heavy crossbows, take aim and release. The six hundred arrows struck before a single bolt had been released. The second six hundred fell as we heard the distinctive cracks of the crossbows being released. It should have been a cacophony but the arrows had thinned the crossbowmen. I saw that ten or so of my archers had been hit and one lay face down but there were forty bodies lying around the pavise and the crossbowmen had taken shelter behind their shields. They were reloading but I knew that they would be loath to step out. One or two braver souls did so but none lasted long enough to even raise their crossbows. Robin's archers did not even have to send a volley. The archers chose their targets.

The count's plan had failed and he sounded the horn. The crossbows apart, his whole line began to advance. Robin knew his business and he judged the moment to perfection. They loosed four more flights before he ordered them to fall back. We simply turned so that they passed between us and then nocked an arrow as they stood behind us. They managed one more ragged flight of arrows before the enemy struck us. The archers had done their work for the line that hit us were riven with holes where men and horses had been hit. I concentrated on the horses that were the closest to me. Holding my pole weapon in two hands I swung when the nearest horse was three paces from me. The axe head struck the horse in the side of the head. It had a trapper and a mail shaffron but the razor-sharp edge tore through both and the weight of the head smashed into the horse's skull. It was like the blow delivered in an abattoir and the horse veered to the right as it fell, and, dying, crashed into the next horse. The two men next to me anticipated the fall of the horse and simply stepped back. We were a well-trained company and the line behind acted as one. Two knights and horses were down and as my men stepped up again our line had regained its cohesion. The archers were now loosing better-timed flights and they were having an effect. On the flanks, our heavy infantry was holding its own against the Savoyard spearmen and militia.

It was at that moment that Giovanni d'Azzo arrived. He had the heart of an Englishman but the mind of an Italian. He had the north bank of the Orco lined with archers and he led the men at arms across the bridge as the archers showered the flanks of the Savoyard army. He and his lances had the backs of the Savoyard knights and the fleeing crossbowmen before them, and the militia all surrendered rather than face the wrath of my men at arms. His archers decimated the left flank of the Savoyard army which turned and tried to flee. It was impossible for in their way stood Giovanni and my men.

Raising my poleaxe I shouted, "Forward!" Michael sounded the horn but my stentorian tones had precipitated the attack in any case. The men I led seemed to be attuned to my thoughts.

The stunned horsemen before us did not know what hit them. One moment they had been charging forward and the next they had been badly handled by archers, then attacked by pole weapons and now attacked front and rear by men at arms. They surrendered there and then. They had gone from an army that outnumbered their enemies to one which became outnumbered and surrounded.

This time we did not have to charge the gates of the town, we simply marched in.

I had thought that Count Amadeus was with his army but he was not. We discovered, as we took the surrender of his army, that he was in Lanzo preparing to celebrate Christmas and the New Year. He had expected his army to stop us. He had been wrong. This time there were knights to be ransomed and after giving their parole their squires were allowed to return to their homes and fetch the money for their release. As with Saviliagno, I fined the city and its people ten thousand florins. William's spies knew the treasure to the last florin. My leaders and I met in the Great Hall of the castle to plan our next move. It was our servants who waited on us and I had our sentries guarding the doors so that none could overhear our plans.

"A timely arrival, Giovanni."

"We arrived last night and I was debating how best to force the bridge. Scouts told us of an approach by an army and we assumed it was yours. I thought it better to keep the surprise of our impending attack and it worked. I am not certain that we could have forced the bridge had not their attention been on you."

"Now that we have this place, we need to plan how to end this war. I had hoped that this battle would have seen the capture of Count Amadeus but the man is elusive."

Giovanni nodded, "It is Galeazzo Visconti and his brother, Bernabò, who control him. Milan is behind his continued resistance. I do not think that the Savoyards have any heart left for this war."

I did not say so but nor did I.

William spoke. He was a quiet man and always had been. When he did speak then he was worth listening to. "I have a spy in this town and he has told me that the count and his leading lords and nobles are at Lanzo." We had heard that and I waited patiently for him to continue. "As you know, Sir John, Lanzo was a fief of the Marquis of Montferrat. If we were to take it and return it, along with this town then the Marquis would be in a much stronger position to bargain for peace. We did not have to take this town's walls and even the men of Montferrat would be able to hold them."

"But how do we take the walls of Lanzo? It has a castle and strong walls."

He smiled, having the answer already, "If you were to attack at night using a ruse to gain entrance then you could take the town with just five hundred men at arms." He shrugged, "I am no warrior, as you well know, but I have the utmost faith in you and our men."

The idea, which sounded mad, had possibilities. There were conventions about fighting during holy days but they were not set in stone. We had risked the ire of the Pope before now and if we moved quickly then they would not be expecting us.

"How far away is Lanzo?"

"Seventeen miles but the roads are mountain roads."

Sir Eoin nodded, "And that suits a night-time attack. You know, Sir John, that if we left tomorrow at dusk, we could be there in just over an hour. We send in men to scale the walls and open the gates. Why we could have the town before midnight. I think William has hit upon a good solution to our problem."

"You are right. Giovanni, you could keep the army here to protect the road. If none pass here then we have free rein. We will do it. Sir Eoin, choose our best five hundred men. Let us see if this can be the blow that wins the war."

As I retired that night, I wondered if I was getting ahead of myself. My handful of victories had made me believe I was invincible. To take five hundred men and hope to take a Savoyard stronghold seemed madness yet I honestly believed I could do it. The years I had shared the leadership of my company with Albert Sterz had been an apprenticeship. I smiled. I had begun life as a tailor's apprentice; what would my life have been like had I stayed there. I fell asleep thinking about that path and the different man I might have become.

We had many good horses and I chose Ajax. He was a powerful horse but the main reason I chose him was for his colour. He was black and I wanted to be invisible. My polished armour would be hidden by the black cloak I would use and I chose not to wear a helmet. A mailed coif and arming cap would serve. If we had to battle then my plan would have failed and we would have lost. As I walked around the horse seeking any signs of weakness, I reflected that I was just gambling five hundred men. Admittedly they were the best that I had and I had the utmost confidence in them but their loss might mean that I was voted out of my position. I knew that I kept it because of my victories. The men who had chosen me over Albert Sterz were rich men thanks to my sharp mind. The Italians in my company had named me John the Sharp and it was because of tricks such as the one I was about to attempt.

It was an icy night as we headed along the mountain road to Lanzo. We had four Italians with us who knew the roads and they were the ones who rode just ahead of me. Sir Eoin was next to me and Dai and Michael rode behind. I had confidence in my two squires; one was almost a man at arms and the other quick-witted enough to react to any situation. They were the perfect combination for me and felt like part of my armour. As we headed towards the city we met few for most of the land was celebrating and indoors. We passed houses whence emanated the sound of laughter that stopped as our horses clattered past. In this part of the world, they were just grateful that the horses had not stopped. I dare say that within the houses they made the sign of the cross and drank even more to celebrate the fact that they had not been molested.

We heard the sounds of celebration even before our Italian scouts stopped and pointed at the walls. I nudged Ajax forward to view the walls of the town. Two brands burned in the sconces atop the gatehouse and I saw two sentries, their faces lit by the glow of a brazier. It was careless and told me that whoever commanded the night watch was a fool. A good cloak, gloves, hat and a fur would have kept the two watchers warm and not spoiled their night vision.

I turned to Sir Eoin and nodded. He and Dai, along with John of Ecclestone and William Hammer Hand walked their horses ahead of us. There were ropes on the four saddles. I watched their shadows get closer to the gate. They reached it unseen. Not only were the two sentries not keeping a good watch, but they also were not listening for they should have heard the sound of the four horses. While John and William held Sir Eoin's and Dai's horses, I waved forward the rest of the column but I did not take my eyes from the four men I had sent to gain us entry. Sir Eoin and Dai stood on the saddles of the two horses that stood patiently. The two men were tall and their fingers reached the crenulations and, using the walls themselves, began to climb up. We were within twenty feet of them and the sound of boots scraping on stone seemed to me inordinately loud but then I heard laughter from the gatehouse. The two sentries were oblivious to their duties.

Dai and Sir Eoin disappeared. Had there been danger they would have thrown down ropes for William and John to ascend. It was clearly unnecessary and I led my column to the gate. I did not hear the sound of the two guards being rendered unconscious but when I heard the bar on the gate as it was lifted and the two huge gates creak open, then I knew that I had won. Once the foxes were in the henhouse then there would be none to stop us. It mattered not how much noise we made and we galloped through the narrow streets. The Italian scouts now led again as they took me and twenty of my men to the hall where it was hoped I would find the Count of Savoy. Remarkably few men came out of doors to see what the commotion was and the ones who did so had their heads smacked by the sides of swords. We needed no deaths for there would be ransom aplenty. I rode Ajax up the steps of the stone hall and made him rear to kick open the doors. I ducked my head under the lintel and entered a brightly lit hall. There were two long tables and richly clothed lords and ladies enjoying their celebrations and a smaller one at the top, making a u shape.

Men stood and their hands went to their sides but none had brought weapons. Some women screamed but most of those within the hall just stared open-mouthed as more of my men rode into the hall. The horses stamped their hooves on the wooden floor and silenced the talk.

"I am Sir John Hawkwood, Captain of the White Company and this town and all those within are now my prisoners." I rode Ajax through the centre of the tables. I guessed that the important lords were at the top. I smiled, I had made the right decision not to wear a helmet, "Count Amadeus?"

A well-dressed man with pork fat still dripping from his beard nodded as he wiped his hands on the cloth that hung over his left shoulder.

"The Marquis of Montferrat has sent me. He wishes the towns you stole from him returned and the war against him ended. What say you?"

The count was beaten and he knew it. Milan and Pavia had encouraged his dreams of glory and I had shattered them. He nodded, "And I do not doubt Giovanni Acuto, that you and your men will want payment too."

"Of course."

We captured more than five hundred nobles. The ransom was worth more than the pay we had received from the Marquis. The count paid us twenty thousand florins for his release. In all, we stayed a month in the town before we returned, first to Rivarolo and thence to the marquis. The journey back was long and slow. That was partly due to the inclement weather, for the snows had come, but also because we had wagons laden with gold and coins. None of us minded the ride. We stopped first at Casale Montferrat where we delivered the news that Savoy was defeated and that Montferrat could reclaim her castles. The marquis should have realised that this meant the end of our association but he did not. On the way back we had decided to spend six months enjoying our victory before choosing our next employer.

Chapter 3

When we told him, the marquis was unhappy with our decision to leave his employ. It came to a head when he asked if we would supply the garrisons for the towns we had recaptured for him. William was with me when he came to visit us in the spring at the estate he had given us at Tornello.

"Sir John, if you and your men would supply the garrisons for the castles then I would pay you handsomely. You have had no more offers of work since you came here, I believe?"

I smiled, "And we have not sought any. You are not a warrior, my lord but we are and you need time to recover from campaigning. We spent the early part of winter fighting. There is another matter, William…"

When we had heard that the marquis was on the way we had spoken. When Albert had been with us then we had been forced to have three of us in agreement. It was much easier making a decision when there were just two of us.

William said, "My lord, you cannot afford to pay us. We have more than two thousand men. Had we not extracted ransom and gold from our enemies, not to mention what we took from the battlefields, then we would not have made a profit. I do no fighting and all that I am concerned with is profit and loss. If we serve you then we will be losing money."

I saw the disappointment on the nobleman's face and I sought to offer him some solace. "We have bought you time, my lord. The Visconti brothers are busy warring in Mantua and against the Pope. Their eyes should no longer be on you. We have almost bankrupted Savoy and I doubt that any will attack you for the remainder of this year. Use the money that you would have paid us and train men. If you wish to send them here to be trained then they can watch our men practise."

He nodded, "I beg you not to make the knowledge public. If my enemies thought that you were leaving me then all your good work would be undone."

"I promise, my lord, that to everyone who asks we still work for you."

It was a compromise but one which worked. Had he chosen to do so the marquis could have ordered us from his estates. I knew why he did not; he feared our army would simply take over his lands and, indeed, we could have done but Montferrat was not a rich country and my eyes were drawn eastwards. The fact that we stayed in Montferrat worked in our favour. A messenger arrived from the east and he wore the livery of the Visconti family.

"Sir John, I have been sent by Lord Galeazzo Visconti to invite you to meet with him."

I had with me, William, Sir Eoin, Robin, Giovanni and Dai. Before I could answer Robin snorted, "And if Sir John meets with your master, I doubt that he will leave, alive at least. Do you take us for fools?"

I shrugged for I agreed with Robin, "What assurances can you give that there will be no treachery?"

"My master invites you to meet with him in Pisa. As you know the city has no affiliation with either Pavia or Milan."

William had been looking at papers he had before him and, without looking up said, "And it is two hundred miles away. We have to pass close to Pavia and Mantua where the Lord of Milan wages war. Unless Sir John took his whole company then he would be at risk all the way."

Sir Eoin said, "And if we took the company then it might well be that the lands through which we had to pass might bar their borders. We do have a reputation."

The emissary looked nonplussed. While my men had been speaking, I had been listening. Why would the Lord of Pavia wish to speak with me? I was arrogant in those days but not so much as to think that the White Company would not be able to fight without me. Albert Sterz had proved that it was the men who won the victories. If Galeazzo wanted to speak to me then I wanted to know why. I knew that the Visconti brothers were ambitious and I was a pragmatic man. Perhaps they wanted to hire me and so long as it was not to attack Montferrat then I would consider their offer. They were too rich a family to dismiss out of hand.

The emissary said, "What would make you attend the meeting, my lord?"

I rubbed my chin as though thinking of a solution but I had already come up with one, "If the Archbishop of Pisa will guarantee my safety, then I will come."

When I agreed I saw the surprise on Sir Eoin's face. I gave the slightest shakes of my head. I would explain all in the fullness of time

The emissary beamed, "Then I will ride back immediately my lord. Expect me back here within the week."

I did not envy the rider his journey. He had come with a small escort of four men but the fractious nature of the cities and their constant wars meant that moving from one domain to another was dangerous.

When he had left, I asked William what he knew of Pisa. "More particularly what is the connection to the Visconti family?"

William smiled. He enjoyed the gathering of intelligence. Bookkeeping was his first love but he found the two went hand in hand. More money could be made with more intelligence. "As you know the glory days of Pisa are in the past. Since the Battle of Meloria, won almost eighty years ago by Genoa, the shift in sea power means that Pisa no longer dominates the seas. Their trade has declined and Florence seeks to take over Pisa. They have attacked their cities many times. The Visconti rule Verona as well as Milan and Pavia. The largest threat to them is Florence. I think that the Visconti may be plotting and planning." He looked at Sir Eoin, "Unlike you, Sir Eoin, I see only advantage in this. If the safe-conduct from the archbishop is forthcoming then it could be that the White Company could take advantage of the discord in the land of Tuscany."

Robin was more practical, "And who would go with you?"

"No more than ten men." I used my fingers to count them off, "William, of course, and his clerk to act as a servant. Dai and Michael, they go without saying. I would take Ned and Karl for they are useful men." I nodded to Giovanni, "You have an intimate knowledge of the politics of the land and you and your squire would be a help. That is eight. Any other suggestions?"

"I would suggest myself and Luke. It will be handy for us to see the land. The others can see the land from the viewpoint of a man on a horse. Luke and I are archers. We view things differently."

William said, "Ned is an archer."

Robin shrugged and his embarrassed smile told me that he had another reason for coming with us, "I confess that I would like to see this tower that leans. There are other wonders I should like to see but this one is close. Three archers are not too many is it Sir John?"

Laughing I said, "As I started my warrior life as an archer how can I argue? Do not worry, Robin, I am happy and Sir Eoin and Captain Martin can continue the training of our men. Did you wish to come, Sir Eoin?"

He laughed, "I am a warrior, Sir John. I will leave the politics to others. If you are happy then I am content."

William began folding his papers, "There is one thing you should consider, Sir John, the Great Company also serves in Italy and, who knows, Albert Sterz's new company may fight there too. How would you feel about fighting men alongside whom you have fought before?"

It was a good question and I had given it much thought already, "We are soldiers and swords for hire. We fight those who pay us." I pointed to Giovanni, "At Calais, Giovanni and I were on opposing sides. It should not matter."

William nodded, "And I have heard that von Landau and the Great Company are north of Milan. They are wintering there."

My eyes narrowed, "And why did you not tell me before?" I had a history with von Landau. He had robbed and murdered the Jew, Basil, who kept my treasure. I had wanted vengeance since that time.

"I only heard a short while ago and it was confirmed by a merchant who passed through three days since. There is little point in my giving you inaccurate information is there, Sir John?" William had grown from the mouse who had first come to me with his sister, Elizabeth. He was now willing to spar with me. And he was right. I did not want half-truths. "If you wish to find him and extract your gold, as you once said, then he is at Novara but he has his Great Company with him."

"You are right. I do not want information that is wrong. We will wait until we have returned from Pisa. Have your spies confirm his presence." It was not about the money for I had taken far more since the theft than I had lost; it was personal.

The Visconti emissary returned in six days and the weary horses of him and their men showed their exertions. "I am ready to take you back with us now, to Pisa." He flourished the safe-conduct from the archbishop.

I took it and handed it to William, "What is your name, my friend?"

"Rodolpho di Treviso, my lord."

"You are a knight?"

"Yes, my lord and I serve Lord Galeazzo."

"His lordship is lucky to have such a loyal servant who rides his horse to the point of exhaustion."

He smiled, "I hope I give my lord good service."

"You and your men, along with your horses, shall rest here for you need to recover."

He became anxious, "No, my lord, we must leave on the morrow at the latest. Lord Galeazzo is most anxious to meet with you."

"And meet me he shall for I will ride in the morning while you and your men shall remain guests here. You will be well fed and you can enjoy all that my home in Montferrat has to offer."

Realisation dawned; they were hostages. With the safe conduct in my possession, we did not need him.

As we headed, the next day, for the coast, Robin was still smiling about the look on the young knight's face, "He has learned a lesson there, Sir John, but if Lord Galeazzo is as ruthless as men say then he will not care if a young knight is sacrificed."

I nodded, "True but I have other reasons. I wish to scout out the town before we enter and I would take us directly to the archbishop. I know that the Milanese are Ghibellines and therefore oppose the Pope but the church is a different matter. No lord can afford to have an enemy of the church. We will speak to the archbishop and go directly to the Doge of Pisa. I want to keep the Lord of Milan off guard."

We rode hard on a slippery and treacherous road to Montaggio. We rode plainly dressed although, as all riders were, well-armed. The sumpter led by William's servant, Peter, carried spare clothes to be worn when I had to present myself to the putative paymasters of Pisa. The innkeeper, however, recognised, if not our names, then our profession for he fawned and fussed over us. No one upset a mercenary in this part of Italy. The land controlled by lords could change in an instant. There were few other visitors and part of his attention might have been the coins we brought him. When we dined, we spoke not of our destination but chatted as warriors do about past battles and men who had left us. We talked of other mercenaries for we knew them as rivals. Inevitably talk drifted to Konrad von Landau.

"You know, my lord, that since we have been in Italy, I have learned much about this knight."

"Do not give him the title knight, William, for that makes him seem noble and that he is not. He is a murderer."

William went on smoothly, "That he is but he has been fighting in Italy for a long time. Twenty odd years ago he fought for the Visconti family at the battle of Parabiago."

"If you are saying he may be a Visconti man then you are not telling me anything I have not already thought of."

William shook his head patiently, as though instructing a child. I did not like it. "No my lord, my point is that he has forgotten more about this part of Italy than we have yet learned. I am learning more each day but it is you who will be the one who needs to learn about the land. That is why I think this ride is a good idea. We are riding through a land that is, to us, new. But I urge caution when you plan your vengeance on your enemy."

William was right and I mentally forgave him for his comments. I would never do so aloud. I had to play the part of a strong leader. I trusted all my men, especially those close to me but as more men entered my company then so the odds on one who would seek to usurp me increased.

Once we reached the coast and headed along the road to Pisa then the journey became easier. The proximity of the sea meant that the roads were not subject to ice. The air was, as Robin said, fresh, but we could live with that. It was the Italian, Giovanni who found the conditions not to his liking. We skirted La Spezia for it was controlled by Genoa. They were not our enemies yet but I did not wish to risk incarceration by some lord who saw an advantage in it. We headed for Lucca. It had been an independent city but Emperor Charles had given it to Pisa. I did not think it was a happy relationship so we stayed one night to gauge the mood of the people towards their masters, the Pisans.

We learned, as we ate in an inn frequented not by travellers but by local men, that the city yearned for the days of Castruccio Castracani when the city had been independent. That he had been dead for thirty years, probably before most of them were born, led me to think he was a legend like Hereward the Wake or Robin Hood from England. They had given him qualities that he probably did not possess but what I found interesting was that he had been a condottiere and so successful that he had been made a duke. I stored that information. The people of Lucca did not mind a warlord and I could use that. William was not idle either and he spoke to merchants and travellers to gain insight into Pisa. As we headed towards the city, he told me what he had learned.

"They need a leader and an army, my lord. Florence is rich and powerful. More than that, the city is greedy and wants Pisa and its port to make itself more powerful. Pisa is rich and can afford to pay a great deal of money for our services. However, I heard that Florence was also willing to pay for mercenaries such as we. We might use that to our advantage."

"And Galeazzo Visconti, what did you learn of him?"

"Ah, he is a guest of the Pisans but the merchants of Lucca called him Florence's man. He has interests in Florence and owns one of the banks there."

Robin asked, "Then why is he so keen to have us serve Pisa? This stinks like last week's fish, Sir John. I smell a trap."

"As do I, Robin but not the one you think of. Trust me, I shall not be duped and I have my own thoughts but, until there is an offer presented to us, let us keep an open mind."

I had not said so but I thought I knew the plot. We had been a thorn in the Visconti side. He had a choice, defeat us in battle or eliminate us another way. By drawing me down to Pisa he was giving himself a free hand in Montferrat and as Florence had a larger army and more money, he hoped that they would defeat me if I agreed to defend Pisa. The Italians did not call me Giovanni Acuto for nothing. As in a battle with swords, I knew that sometimes you blocked, sometimes struck and, occasionally you simply moved away from the blow. I had choices and my company had choices. We timed our arrival for the early afternoon when people were ending their workday and heading for their homes. We watched, from the shelter of some trees, the main gate. We had spied the cathedral and the castle so we knew the direction we had to take once we reached the walls. Had we been with Rodolpho then entry would have been simplicity itself. The guards in the gate did not seem overly rigorous but I was taking no chances.

"Giovanni, take my archers into the town and watch the gate from within. I will come with the others."

He nodded and they headed towards the gate.

"William, you speak. You are a merchant and we three are your bodyguards."

William's Italian was far better than mine and he looked like a merchant. He was no longer the slim, almost undernourished young man I had first met. He had filled out and was becoming a little portly.

We had little need to worry and we entered easily. I was pleased as it meant that the Visconti would have no idea we were within Pisa's walls and if he planned treachery then it had been thwarted.

The archbishop was surprised at our arrival but I knew, from his effusive welcome that he was glad to see us. He found rooms for us and sent for the leader of the Pisan army and the chamberlain rather than the doge who, it appeared, was a sick man. The chamberlain was the paymaster. As we refreshed ourselves in the refectory, all of us guarded in our words, I reflected that the council had not been summoned nor Galeazzo Visconti. Our meeting was supposed to have been with Visconti at the archbishop's behest. What was going on?

The Chamberlain, Pellario Griffo, was as I came to know, a clever and cunning politician. He gushed when he greeted us but I saw, in his eyes, that we would be used if we chose to serve Pisa. "You are most welcome, gentlemen, but where is the emissary of the Lord of Pavia? Safe I hope."

"He is enjoying our estate in Montferrat my lord but I thought that we were to meet Galeazzo Visconti."

"You are but he is not staying in the city. He has a manor just outside. I have sent word to him. He may not arrive until the morrow, but we can speak before then. This is Manetti di Jesi and it is he commands the army since the unfortunate death of Ghisello Ubaldini."

I looked at the soldier. He was a hardened veteran and I took to him immediately. He had none of the sly looks of the chamberlain and he spoke honestly. He nodded at my unspoken question, "It was a fight in an inn and a knife was pulled. The man who did it fled but I believe that the assassin was a Florentine. Ghisello was a Florentine exile. Perhaps they hoped to weaken our resolve. It failed and now that you are here…"

I shook my head, "Our presence does not mean we will accept an offer to work for you. We come here out of interest. We are still paid by the Marquis of Montferrat but as there is no war at the present and we were curious we thought we would travel here." I nodded to Robin, "My captain of archers was keen to see your tower."

The chamberlain said, bluntly, "We can offer you forty thousand florins as a retainer Sir John and we can negotiate further payments. We would employ you for a year and, dependent upon the results, negotiate another price."

It was a good starting point but I had no need to rush my decision. I stretched, "We have travelled far and need refreshments and, as I said, we were invited by Galeazzo Visconti. It would be rude not to hear his words."

A liveried servant arrived and spoke in the archbishop's ear, "The food is ready to be served. Shall we continue this discussion while we eat?"

I nodded to my men as I answered, "Of course, Archbishop." My nod had been enough for my men to understand my meaning. William and Giovanni flanked the chamberlain while Robin and I sat close to the soldier. William could extract information about the treasury and I could assess the situation. Could Pisa be saved?

Manetti was more than happy to be honest with us and it endeared him even more to me, "We have soldiers, Sir John, but they are just warriors for the working day and the Florentines have the upper hand. I think that Ghisello had a plan but he died before it could be implanted. The Florentines have attacked our city many times. The towns of Barga and Montecalvoli are both under siege." He shrugged, "Our soldiers are not a standing army. They fight to defend our walls and then return to their work. When the Florentines attack then there is no work and we become poorer day by day." I noticed that he had lowered his voice so that Pellario Griffo would not overhear. "We need professionals, such as you."

I nodded and sipped the wine that came, I think from Chianti. It was delicious, "I can see that. Tell me about Visconti."

The look on his face told me that he did not understand the involvement of the Lord of Pavia. "He first came to speak to us four or five months since." I counted back and realised that was about the time that we had been at Saviliagno. Things began to make sense. "I did not command then and was with the army at Montecalvoli. From what I gathered the Lord of Pavia offered to help us hire mercenaries."

"Who brought up our name?"

He frowned and then said, "Why he did, I believe." I waited for there was more to come. "I was surprised for he has Florentine connections and all of Italy knows that you are a thorn in his side. I care not for politics, Sir John, and I am a warrior. I would like to fight under your banner for I know your reputation and your skill. This captain of archers you bring gives me hope for we have all heard of the prowess of English archers."

Robin nodded at the compliment, "But from what I have heard, and seen on my journey here, the land is mountainous and might not suit archers."

"The way the war goes here is through sieges that draw relief and then the Florentines try to bring us to battle. They have a good army and in any such battle, they will win. They have many horsemen. We have learned to withdraw when they bring such an army so that little by little they eat into our lands and Pisa becomes smaller month by month. If you cannot help us then Pisa will be no more."

We were given chambers in the archbishop's palace but we knew it not and had no idea if there were hidden orifices where they could overhear us. We each kept our counsel. There would be time for talk after we had seen Visconti.

We had barely breakfasted when he arrived. He had with him half a dozen nobles but they were not dressed for war. He swept into the hall the archbishop had provided like an emperor. He expected us to defer to him. We each gave a small half bow that did not please him but he covered his annoyance with a smile, "Sir John, I am pleased that you came but concerned that I do not see Rodolpho with you."

I smiled, "We thought he was tired after his rides and so we left him with my men to recover."

The smile left his face, "He is well?"

"Of course, and my men are showing him English hospitality. He will dine well for we have fine Savoyard wine and cattle for him to eat."

His eyes narrowed and then he laughed, "Aye, I heard that you have bloodied the nose of the Green Count. That is the reason I sent for you. I would like you to serve Pisa as you have Montferrat." I nodded, "I am happy to be the broker of this arrangement for Pisa is my friend." Pellario Griffo and Manetti kept straight faces.

"We are paid by Montferrat, my lord."

"Pisa will pay more."

It was Galeazzo who spoke and not Griffo. "How does Pisa know how much we are paid?" I looked at Griffo who turned to Visconti.

"Let us say, living at Pavia, close to Montferrat, I have friends who tell me such things. So what say you, forty thousand florins as a retainer and then one hundred and fifty thousand to be paid once the Florentine threat has gone?"

William apart, the others were unable to hide their surprise. Such an amount would make us the richest mercenaries in Italy. We could hire more men. I nodded, "Generous, my lord, and what is in it for you?"

His face suddenly became serious, "Let us say that I will feel more comfortable about my home if you are a hundred miles from it. I know that my brother, Bernabò, feels the same."

"And Montferrat?"

He shrugged, "The Marquis is safe for we would not wish him to hire you a second time."

I nodded, "Then, with your permission, my men and I will ride a little in the countryside while we debate the issue."

The archbishop swept an arm around his home, "You can have privacy in any of my rooms, Sir John."

"The fresh air will do us good." His words proved to me that there were places where they could overhear us.

We spoke not until we were a mile beyond the city walls. "Well?"

Robin said, "The money is a king's ransom."

I nodded and looked at William, who said, "Robin is right and I can see no reason not to sign the contract but…"

"Aye, there's the rub. Galeazzo Visconti wishes it and as much as I believe he would like us away from his lands I cannot help but think that there is an ulterior motive."

Giovanni said, "And I know what it is. He wishes for more influence in Florence. Our presence, even with the relatively small numbers we enjoy will weaken Florence. Your judgement in battle is the reason we will win and when Florence loses, she will turn, I do not doubt, to the Visconti family."

"And that means we can expect to be knifed in the back."

Giovanni beamed, "And that is why we wear a backplate. Knowing that we are going to be betrayed means that Master William here, can use his spies to give us a warning."

I reined in and surveyed the Tuscan hills to the east, "Is there any who would gainsay this? Are you all in agreement?"

They nodded and William said, "And Montferrat will be safe. It is too small a morsel for the Visconti. They want Italy, all of it."

Northern Italy 1363

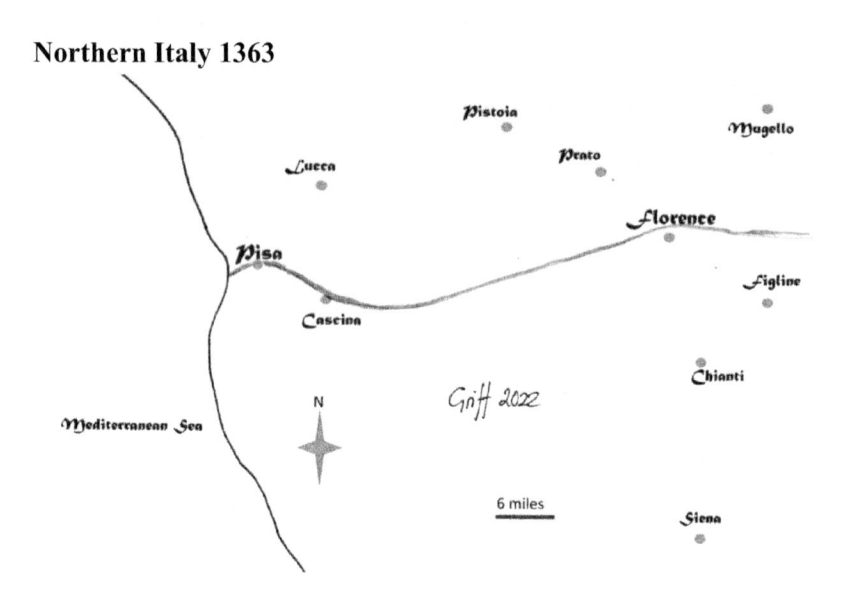

Chapter 4

The contract was agreed and we were given a house to use. I guessed it had belonged to the murdered Ghisello. The more I had spoken with Manetti the more certain I was that his death had been an assassination. The forty thousand florins were to be kept by the archbishop until our return. I spoke with Manetti before we left. I had plans I needed to be put in place. We would not return until the summer. Pellario Griffo was not happy about that as he feared a Florentine attack. It was Galeazzo who came up with a solution, "What say I visit Florence and tell them that Pisa is contemplating hiring the White Company? That should make them wary. Who knows they might even make a counteroffer, Sir John?"

I could not see what advantage he would gain from this but he was right. It would make the Florentines behave more cautiously. Galeazzo came to speak to us before we left. I felt in a mischievous mood as I asked him, "Tell me, Lord Galeazzo, do Albert Sterz and Konrad von Landau still work for you?"

He was quick thinking but not quick enough. He hesitated and the slight tic in his right eye told me that he was lying. "I have employed both men before now but as far as I know they are no longer in Italy."

Smiling I said, "I just wondered. Albert and I parted on relatively good terms but von Landau is another matter."

I left it at that. When we reached our home, wet and bedraggled thanks to a nasty rainstorm, I allowed Rodolph to leave my Montferrat home.

The young knight had been offended by his soft fetters, "I told you that there was no danger, Sir John."

"And I thought that you would be grateful for a few more days of rest." I waved an arm at the skies, "And as the rain is receding, I have saved you a soaking."

He gave us a rueful smile and left.

Although my men were keen to know the outcome of our visit, I chose to meet with just my senior captains. We were democratic but only in the sharing of the profits. The contracts were the responsibility of William and me. I left nothing out when I told them what we had learned. "We are being used but I do not see that as a problem. So long as we are aware of it then we are in control. Galeazzo Visconti will betray us but not until we have enjoyed some victories against him." I paused and looked around. The ones who had been with me in Pisa knew my mind but Sir Eoin, Martin and the others did not. "To that end, I intend to take our men at arms north to Novara."

"Novara?"

"Yes, Sir Eoin, there the Great Company under von Landau are wintering, or so they say. I do not think they are and I think they plan something against us. It is a feeling I cannot shake. I may be wrong but... I have a mind to ride there and beard von Landau about the money he took from Basil of Tarsus."

Martin said, "I can see the reasoning behind this but why not take archers too?"

"If there is to be violence then it will be in the town of Novara. Archers would not help us that day. I want von Landau lulled into believing that we go there to talk."

Sir Eoin said, "But you do not."

"No, I hope that this will just be a duel between the German and me but I fear it will not be. For that reason, I want volunteers only. If men come with me then they must know that we go not on company business but personal."

Giovanni nodded, "There is much bad blood already between the two companies. This is the best way to settle it, I for one, do not wish to be looking over my shoulder while we serve Pisa. That is a treacherous enough nest of vipers as it is."

I looked at him, "Then you do not think we should take the contract?"

"Far from it. The nest of vipers means that we can shift alliances easily enough. This is my world, Sir John. What I mean is I am happy to have Italians trying to slit my throat but another band of mercenaries? No thank you."

Sir Eoin said, "And Albert Sterz?"

William said, without looking up from the lists he was scanning, "He has hired on to serve with Annechin Baumgarten and his company as its joint captain. We may have to cross swords with him at some time in the future but for now, he is too far away to be a threat and as Sir John told the Pisans, we parted on good terms. I made sure that he was given enough money by us. The fact that he has spent it all is his problem."

I addressed all the company the next day and told them of our new contract and the pay. It took some time to quieten them down. "And I will take some volunteers, northwest to Novara. Know that I ask no man to come with me but I will happily share any profits that we make with you all."

In the end, five hundred and fifty men, mainly Englishmen and Hungarians chose to come with me. The new Englishman, Andrew, also came and I think it was because he was keen to impress me. Lazlo also came and I wondered at that. His countrymen served with von Landau. We all rode and while we did not wear helmets, we were well armed and armoured. For the first time since I had been an apprentice and living in London, I was doing something personal. I knew that my company would benefit if we eliminated our most serious opposition but I cared not. Von Landau had hurt me and I would hurt him. Novara lay to the west of Milan and was just twenty miles from our lands. We reached it during the late afternoon.

His company was a mixture of Germans and Hungarians. Any English soldiers had left him to join my company. His Great Company had shrunk since our success. Lacking archers they were largely made up of men at arms and knights. As we rode into the small town, we could hear them for they were gathered in the town square and it sounded like they were drinking. We did not gallop in but rode quietly through its narrow streets. Giovanni knew the town and he led us through back streets so that when we entered the square, we had complete surprise and our arrival silenced the hubbub. I dismounted and Michael led my horse away. As my other leading warriors dismounted their horses were taken by squires and they formed a protective wall of steel around my back. None of us had weapons drawn but we were all ready. I saw a man dash into a large inn and when four men emerged then I knew that the best armed had to be Konrad von Landau. As he strode towards us, I estimated that our numbers were about equal. A third of his men looked to be Hungarian. Their garb, like those who fought for me, was distinctive.

It was soon clear who he was for he was the oldest of the four. He had good mail and plate while a long sword hung from his baldric. I pointed a mailed hand at him, "Konrad von Landau you are a thief and a murderer. You took my treasure from Basil of Tarsus and I would have it back but first, you and I will exchange blows for Basil was my friend." I drew my sword.

I saw the German's eyes flicker to the men around me. I admired his bravado for he waved a hand and said, "I do not fight with apprentices. Rolf, kill him, I have wine to finish."

Everything happened at once. I think he thought I was hot-blooded and reckless when I was the very opposite. I slipped my dagger from my belt as the warrior named Rolf came at me with a poleaxe. I heard the hiss of swords being drawn behind me and saw that Konrad von Landau had donned a helmet. It was an old fashioned one with a nasal. As Rolf's poleaxe came down to strike at my unprotected head, I held up my sword and it struck the langet, the metal protection for the head of his weapon. Sparks flew and my sword deflected the axe head so that it slid down my mail. I rammed my dagger into the cheek and skull of the German. When the tip entered the brain, the warrior fell dead.

I might have died then had not my new Englishman, Andrew de Belmonte lunged and skewered the second German who had stabbed at my side with his spear. Giovanni, Sir Eoin and my other warriors formed a protective phalanx and we began to drive the Great Company back. We held the advantage, not in numbers, but in sobriety. A drunken warrior is fearless and can be a daunting enemy but if you keep your head and watch for the wild swing that opens the body then you will win. Even as I ripped open the stomach of a mailed German with my sword, I noticed that the Hungarian contingent was not fighting. They looked to have withdrawn and I wondered at that. A wild swing at my head with a war axe made me drop to my knee and drive my dagger up into the groin of a Swabian. As he fell, I saw that von Landau had felled James Duggan, one of my Irishmen. Before I could get to him, I heard a roar and saw the German I had felled in Montferrat race at me. It was Karl von Sturmz and he raced at me with a war hammer in his hand. Rising, I took two steps forward and ran at him with my sword and dagger held like a cross above my head. It was a powerful blow he struck but the two well-made weapons held and as our faces came together I brought my mailed knee up into his groin. His eyes told me I had hurt him. If I had worn my helmet I might have headbutted him but I wore just a coif and arming cap. Instead, I punched at his face with the hilt of my sword and gouged a hole in his cheek. He roared in pain. His war hammer was the wrong weapon for such close-in fighting and I rammed my dagger into his eye socket. He fell dead at my feet.

I turned and saw von Landau moving menacingly towards me. I swung my sword across his helmet before he could even think about a swing. My sword was a good one and the blow well struck; the nasal broke. The dent in the side told me that another blow would render the helmet useless.

Von Landau drew his own dagger and laughed, as he spat out a tooth, "You have spirit, Englishman, but there is no money. It is all spent. Your visit here is a waste of time."

I was watching his eyes and saw that he was using the words to put me off my guard. When he lunged with his dagger at my eye, I easily deflected it. "Old man, the money means nothing to me. I will take the retribution from your tired body and there I will have satisfaction." I feinted with my dagger and when he brought his sword and dagger up to block them, I swung my sword at his thigh. I hurt him and drew blood.

He stepped back, "Visconti was wrong, eh? He said your greedy little mind would take you and your men directly to Pisa. I knew he was wrong. Still, when you die, I might take the contract."

He swung at me but I had seen it coming in his eyes and I pirouetted around to slash my sword into his side. The blow, on top of the one to his thigh, really hurt him and he staggered back. Now was the time to finish it and I launched a flurry of blows with sword and dagger. He blocked most of the blows and that was to be expected. He was a veteran who had been fighting for thirty years and his body reacted almost without thinking. I was in my prime, in those days, and I connected enough times for him to fall back and lie prostrate on the ground. I could have ended his life there but I had no need. He was finished.

I raised my sword and shouted, "Von Landau is down! End the bloodshed!" The command was intended for my men. We were winning but I did not want to lose any of these brave men who had volunteered to help me.

My men stepped back and I saw defeat on the faces of the Germans of the Great Company. Everyone sheathed their weapons and a woman and a priest ran from the inn to kneel next to the clearly dying mercenary.

The woman was French and, after taking the helmet from von Landau she kissed his head, "Why did you fight? Did not the fortune teller warn you to fear the white knight?"

The priest shook his head and made the sign of the cross, "My child that is blasphemy! Let me hear the count's confession." He leaned in and whispered to von Landau who whispered his own words into the priest's ear.

The woman, who was in her late twenties, looked up and said, "And what of me? Am I to be a spoil of war?"

I admired her courage for she spoke fearlessly and I shook my head, "The White Company does not make war on women."

Von Landau's voice was weak but we all heard it, "Let her go with my men, Hawkwood. She is right I should never have…" Konrad von Landau died.

I waved over the men who were now clearly the leaders of the Great Company, "He is dead and I have had my vengeance. Take him and this lady, as well as your dead. Leave and you can depart unmolested. For our part, this is now over. If the time should come when we fight alongside each other then all will be forgotten but if you ever face us again then expect no mercy."

One of the Germans nodded, "And what of von Landau's treasure?"

"I will give you enough to care for the lady and to feed you through to summer but the rest is ours. It is the spoils of war, what is it the Vikings called it, weregeld?" I cocked my head to the side and put my hand on my sword. My meaning was clear. If they wished to fight for it then men would die.

He nodded, "Aye, you have given us our lives and I do not doubt that your archers are even now watching us. We will go." He turned, "Come, let us bury our dead and return to Milan. We have pay waiting for us."

It was a throwaway comment but it told me all I needed to know. Allied to von Landau's words I now saw the complicated plan of Galeazzo Visconti. Had we left immediately for Pisa then the Great Company would have fallen upon Casale Monferrato and the Marquis would have lost all that we had won for him. We were leaving Montferrat but, if the Marquis did as I had advised him then he would be safe from the greedy Visconti family.

We had lost a dozen men either wounded or dead and that was sad. The Great Company had lost twenty men and that showed me the quality of my company. We stayed in Novara and buried our handful of dead in the cemetery there and I had the treasure we had taken guarded. It was a shadow of the money he had taken from me, even before I gave the small chest to the woman and the slightly larger chest to his lieutenants, but it had not been about the money. The forty thousand florins we had been promised by Pisa and Galeazzo Visconti more than made up any shortfall. The fight had been about vengeance and it laid down a clear marker. We were not the only company for hire but we were the best. The Great Company had ruled Italy for years but with the death of von Landau, they were a spent force. They would fade into obscurity. As was the convention of such things the men slain by my warriors had their belongings taken by the victors. All understood that and the Great Company carried their own dead off to bury. Their leaders saluted us with their swords as they led their horses south-east towards Milan.

I knew that the presence of my Hungarian contingent had helped with the victory. The Hungarians in the Great Company refused to fight their countrymen. Less than twenty Hungarians chose to join my company but the ones who did, proved to be the finest of warriors and they would be the greatest treasure that we took from Novara.

That night I rewarded Andrew with von Landau's sword, "I owe you a life, Andrew, and I shall not forget it."

He shook his head, "I now have a home and I feel like the White Company warriors are brothers, brothers in arms."

There had been food prepared for von Landau and his men. The people of Novara had no intention of upsetting the White

Company and we ate and drank well. While we did so and with our squires guarding the doors, I discussed our next move.

"Visconti and, I do not doubt, the Florentines, know that we will be heading, sometime, to Pisa. Their army that waits around Pisa will be waiting for us. The last thing I want is a battle there. My plan is to take the war to the Florentines. We use the speed of our horsemen and mounted archers to strike where they do not expect us."

Sir Eoin wiped his hands on his cloth and, after drinking some of the wine said, "Easier said than done. How will we achieve that?"

I smiled, "They expect tricks but they do not know the manner of them. We will send a column of fifty men into Pisa. It will be led by Giovanni and Captain Martin. They will arrive before the date we agreed and announce to all who will hear that the rest of the army is following. I will have the rest of the company and we will head to Lucca. Then we can choose our targets."

That pleased them.

"Sir Eoin, you will lead the men back to our home and I will ride with Giovanni to tell the Marquis of our plans. We owe him that much."

While the bulk of the men headed back to our home, we rode to Casale Monferrato. I think that the Marquis must have heard about the new contract we had signed for his face was as dark as thunder when we were admitted to his hall.

"I am disappointed, Sir John. I thought we had an agreement."

"We have fulfilled the contract, Marquis. Not only have we defeated the Savoyards and ensured that they will not attack but also we have eliminated the threat of the Great Company."

He frowned, "I did not know that they were a threat, Sir John."

"They were and my men and I have sent them hence. They will not attack you but you should know that the Visconti family still harbour thoughts of taking over your land. We warned you when we first defeated them that our presence was temporary. You need to protect yourself."

"I can pay more Sir John." His voice was pleading.

"Marquis, if you paid us the same as other cities, richer than yours, then you would be bankrupt. As I told you once before, use the money you would pay us to hire garrisons to guard the castles we recovered for you. They are well made. Put your defence in your walls and men to guard them. Men on horses might look grand and impressive but they are expensive. Make your towns hard to take and you will not be bullied by Milan and Savoy."

He could see that he was defeated, "You will, of course, vacate the home I loaned to you."

As I recalled it had been a gift but I would not argue. I already had plans to buy somewhere. I smiled, "When we are ready to move then we will leave Marquis."

He nodded and waved a hand, "Have a safe journey." We were dismissed.

I did not mind the abrupt dismissal. I was a mercenary and while we had been overly loyal to him, I could not expect the same in return. We rode hard and reached our home well after dark. I would miss the home we had enjoyed for the last couple of years.

Chapter 5

William had an efficient team of clerks and servants. All that we needed was packed up quickly into the wagons we had brought from Savoy. We would leave in three groups. William and a handful of my lances would ride to Pisa and negotiate a home for us. It would not be for the company but the servants, clerks and William. The company would spend at least six months warring. The second group would be Giovanni and his distractors. The largest group would be led by me and we would not travel the coastal route but, instead, take the harder, less well-frequented roads through the mountains.

As I rode at the head of the column, flanked by Sir Eoin and Robin, and with archers and Italians scouting ahead of us, I felt excited. This was like going to war for the first time. The complicated plan relied on Giovanni causing enough of a distraction to make the Florentines watch him and also on William finding a place for us to use. As we had found in Montferrat having a secure base was vital. This time we would not rely on the apparent generosity of our hosts. We would use the money we had made to buy something that would be ours.

I was happy with my part in the plan for I always felt more confident when I led. We were heading for Lunigiana, high in the Tuscan hills. We were gambling but Giovanni had assured me that the Malaspina family had issues defending their land against not only fellow Lombards but also the French. They had no standing army and no military reputation. I hoped that they would let us pass peacefully through their lands hoping we would not ravage it as we passed. I had no intention of doing so unless provoked. The advantage of this route was that it would take us beyond Lucca so that we could attack Pistoia. The town had been captured by the Florentines almost ten years earlier and the Pistoians were less than happy about the Florentine rulers. We hoped for support from within. I had no intention of either taking or holding the city. We would ravage the rich lands around the city and when we had done enough harm to Florentine interests then we would retire to Pisa. If our plan worked then Giovanni would join us with the Pisan army. I wanted the Pisans to become more confident. The adventure in Montferrat had shown me the folly of doing all the fighting. The Pisans would have to be a real ally. Our aim was to make the Florentines withdraw from Pisan land as they tried to anticipate our next move.

The army moved slower than I would have liked and so I rode ahead to the city with a handful of men. My name afforded me entry but when we crossed over the drawbridge the gates closed, ominously. I was not fearful. Had I been the lord of this land I would have been cautious.

Antonio Malaspina was lord of the land. He was young and only recently inherited the title. This part of Italy was rife with other families trying to take land and when he spoke, he almost deferred to me, "Sir John, to what do we owe this honour?"

"I have ridden ahead of my company to assure you that we are just passing through this land. This is not a chevauchée."

I almost smiled at the relief on his face.

"I am pleased. And where do you go?"

He was young and had not yet learned how to ask indirect questions. "We have recently finished our work in Montferrat and seek another employer." I knew that it might not yet be common knowledge that we had accepted Pisan gold.

"The Florentines?"

"My lord, we work for any who will employ us. Perhaps you might…"

He shook his head vigorously, "Oh, no, Sir John, we have neither the need nor the finance for the White Company. You and your retainers are more than welcome to spend the night in my castle but I fear we cannot accommodate your company."

I smiled for I had not expected to be housed. No one invites a pack of wolves into their sheep pen, "My men are hardy and will camp without. Michael…"

My youngest squire nodded, "I will deliver the message." He looked at Lord Antonio, "And do I have permission to return here and serve Sir John?"

"Of course." When he had gone the young lord said, "What a pleasant youth."

I nodded, "As are all my men and now is there somewhere we can wash for we are soiled from the journey."

"Of course, and this night you will be feted for I am a keen historian and wish to know about those battles where you defeated the French."

"I played but a small part however I am happy to play the troubadour for they were great victories."

That evening I felt shabby for the Malaspina family had set out to impress me. Antonio had unmarried sisters and, as I discovered each time I stayed with an Italian noble family, one was paraded before me in the hope that I might take a fancy to her. I was flattered but Antiochia was still a raw memory and Elizabeth had borne me sons. Azzolino Malaspina was young, no more than seventeen or eighteen, and she was pretty. She flirted with me all the way through the meal. Dai and Michael, who served me at the table, were mightily impressed by her. It made me smile. I remembered when I had been a young man whose loins itched. I spent more of the meal speaking with Antonio. I discovered much about the politics of this land. It was riven with castles but unlike those in England, the purpose was not to control lands where there was danger, such as the Welsh Marches or Scottish borders, but were places where the noble families could safely wait out any incursion into their land. It would be the ordinary people who suffered. I decided, after speaking to him, that it would be folly to risk an attack on Pistoia's walls. There was nothing to be gained. The city was less than twenty miles from Florence and our presence would, I hoped, encourage the Florentines to draw all their men closer to their city. It was a way to impress the Pisans without much danger to us.

When we left, the next day, I knew that Lord Malaspina would waste no time in letting his neighbours know that there were mercenaries loose but as we only had thirty miles to go and we were on the main road to Pistoia then I was confident that the Pistoians would be blissfully unaware of the plague about to descend upon them. My messenger would have reached Giovanni in Pisa so that my full force and Pisan soldiers would all gather at one place, Pistoia.

Our timing was perfect; we reached Pistoia at dusk and I sent my men to make camps around the city. The first that the city knew of danger was when the fires flared in a circle. The bells in the city sounded but by then it was too late for we held them in a vice-like grip. All now depended upon Giovanni and the Pisans arriving.

As dawn broke, I sent out four groups of riders. Twenty archers and ten men at arms made up each group and I sent them to round up as many animals and collect as much food as they could. They knew without being told that they would only need to use violence if there was resistance. The people of this land had learned to endure raids such as this. We were like locusts; we would devastate the land but pass on and they could get on with their lives. Giovanni and Manetti di Jesi arrived with three thousand Pisans. The bells sounded once more. The Pisan general was in a good mood.

"Your plan was a good one, Sir John. When your men reached the city, we rang our bells and the Florentine spies, anticipating the rest of your army, fled the city to spread the news of your arrival. Such is your reputation that the Florentines abandoned their siege of Montecalvoli! Now we can reduce the walls of this town."

I poured water on his plan, "No, my lord. We threaten to do so but my aim is to spend a fortnight taking all that this land has to offer and then, when the Florentines assemble an army, return to Pisa. We will then choose another target. This war will not be won overnight. I want the Florentines wondering where we will strike next. Eventually, they will be forced to bring a large army and then we can defeat them. You may, if you wish, ride to the walls and demand its surrender."

The idea appealed to the Pisan. I did not accompany them for while they knew I was present, my banners told them that, I wanted to remain an elusive shadow. The fear of something you had never seen was greater than the reality of the man. Giovanni rode with the general under a flag of truce. He demanded the surrender of the city which, of course, they refused. Giovanni was laughing when he told me what the Pisan did next. He had his handful of archers send arrows into the city, not to kill or wound but with messages written on them like, 'Pisa sends you this.' They burned effigies of the symbol of Florence, the lion, and then when crossbowmen came to the walls they fell back.

I shook my head, "And this is how they make war? It is no wonder that they have had no victories."

He nodded, "Aye, Sir John, it is the way of war in these parts."

"Then it is good that we are here and we can all make our fortunes."

We stayed for a fortnight and plundered the land around Pistoia. To the great disappointment of the Pisans, when fourteen days had passed I ordered our army to lumber back to Pisa. When my men had been raiding, they had not simply taken. They had questioned the farmers and travellers. We also sent riders close to Florence who saw that they were gathering an army there. I knew that it was only a matter of time before they came to fight us and we were not yet ready. When we fought the Florentines, I wanted a victory. My company was ready but not the Pisans.

Unlike his general, Pellario Griffo was more than happy with the result of our small scale raid. He invited Giovanni, William and myself to dine with him. He was a clever man and he wanted to know what we had planned. "Your first attack has proved more than successful. With the siege at Montecalvoli raised trade has increased and our people feel safer. The animals you have brought will feed Pisa and there will be famine in Florence. All is good, Sir John, but what next?"

The food we were eating was superb. While the Pisan fleet of traders was diminished they still had enough warships to protect their fishing fleet and the fish we ate was delicious. I waited until I had swallowed the last piece before I answered. "Chianti seems to be a good place to raid. The Val d'Arno is a rich part of the Florentine's domain and any disruption there would draw their eye thence." I sipped some of the wine. It was a rich, full-bodied red, "And as Florence is also fighting Siena, to the south of Chianti, then any soldiers they have in the region will be already engaged with the Sienese.

He smiled, "Clever. You have hurt them in the north of their land and their army will be moving in that direction. Chianti is to the south and will be vulnerable. If you can strike quickly then they will not be able to move their army to counter you." He drank some wine and then frowned, "But can an army on foot move that quickly? You are a soldier and know such things."

"No, Chamberlain Griffo, and for that reason, when we go, I shall take just the White Company. We are well mounted and my men feel more confident about the enemy we face. William will continue to hire men while we are away in case we have any losses."

Our numbers had been swollen by the Hungarians who had joined us from the Great Company and a trickle of soldiers, drawn by the lure of our success, had begun to arrive in Pisa. William was more than able to hire them.

"Good."

Lazlo Kaepernick had proved to be an invaluable addition to my army. Giovanni knew of him from his time as a wandering sword for hire and his commanding presence at Pistoia had impressed me. I involved him in our planning. Having spoken to the Hungarians who had defected to us he had intelligence that aided us.

"Ranuccio Farnese commands the army to the east of Chianti. He has with him some two thousand German mercenaries." He saw my look of surprise, "They are not the best. If they were then they would either serve with you, Albert Sterz in Perugia or the Great Company. I tell you this not to fill you with fear but as a warning. I have fought the Lombards more often than you. Their horsemen are a threat but they have few of them. Their heavy infantry lack backbone but the Germans, dull though they are, can stiffen the defence. I tell you so that you can plan."

"You seem to know them well."

He nodded and rubbed the scar that ran from his eye to his chin, "Aye, one of them, Heinrich von Spetz served with the Great Company. He did this to me when we fought in an inn." He shrugged, "I was drunk, else it would have ended differently. When he fled, he joined Farnese and is one of his captains. When we face them, I would like the chance to face him. He thinks he is a champion but a champion would not have run."

An idea began to form in my mind when he told me that.

It was more than forty miles to Chianti and so I waited until the horses had enjoyed plenty of rest before we left. We departed at night. There were Florentine spies who watched the city but there would be fewer of them at night and we slipped out, unseen, disappearing into the dark. Robin and Martin had not been idle and they had already scouted out the roads we would use with the Italians who had joined our company. They had done so under the pretext of hunting but it meant that we made good time as we rode through the night. There were no strongholds until Chianti itself and the villages and small towns through which we passed kept closed their doors.

We reached the small town of Figline at dawn and we had complete surprise. There was no castle and no real defences. We breached the town gates without any trouble and, unlike Pistoia, we had a secure base from which to raid. The convent, abbey and monastery that lay close to the town were terrified that we might raid and take from them. I confess the idea had crossed my mind but it proved unnecessary. In return for leaving them unviolated, we were fed. The loss of the gold from their religious houses was a small price to pay. The townsfolk of Figline were a different matter and we taxed them heavily. For a week we raided the local area and then we were joined by Manetti di Jesi and the Pisan army. I did not mind that they had joined us but I knew that had they marched with us then there would have been no surprise and Florence, which lay less than fifteen miles to the north would have sent men to defend Figline's walls. Although we had more men at our disposal there were drawbacks to the presence of the Pisans. They had suffered at the hands of the Florentines and whenever they captured a noble or one of their soldiers, they treated them badly. After two nobles and their four men were hanged and their bodies burned by Pisans, I put a handful of my lances with each party of Pisans. Di Jesi understood my motives but the ordinary soldiers of Pisa were not happy. Blows were exchanged before my men could exercise their iron grip.

Inevitably, and before we had completed our plunder, the Florentines were advised by Malatesta Malatesta who was on the Florentine Council of war, to send Ranuccio Farnese to rid the land of us. Our scouts spotted the army as it headed towards us. They camped more than two miles away. Our scouts had been unable to ascertain the exact numbers we faced and so I devised a plan that would not only give us that information but if it succeeded, weaken the resolve of the German contingent. I saw that they camped far enough away so that we would have to attack and shift them from their position. Malatesta was worried that we might attack Florence and they guarded the road north. That I had no intention yet of attacking that city was irrelevant. It was what they believed.

I took Lazlo Kaepernick to one side, "Would you like to have the chance to have your vengeance on this Heinrich von Spetz?"

"I would give anything."

"Then I will dress as your squire and bring Dai, Michael and Giovanni, similarly attired with us and we will ride to the enemy so that you can challenge him to a duel. While you fight and hopefully defeat him, we four can observe their men more accurately."

He laughed, "A good plan and trust me, he will be defeated."

We chose poor horses and wore no mail. We carried just daggers and we were all hooded. It was the end of September and even in this part of Italy, there was a chilly feel to the air. To the English, it was nothing but the Italians were all wrapped up against the cold. Leaving Sir Eoin in command and with the Pisans and our company stood to in case of a surprise attack we rode to the enemy camp. They were wary and we faced a barrier of spears and lances.

Lazlo Kaepernick, his helmet held by me, spread his arms, "I come here to challenge that foul backstabber, Heinrich von Spetz, to single combat. This has nothing to do with this war and is personal. I bring only my unarmed squires." He raised his voice, "Are you ready to face me, coward, or will you run away once more?"

The huge German pushed his way forward, "I will fight you, spawn of the Slavs and on the morrow, we will defeat the scum with whom you now fight."

"What is it to be, on a horse with lance or on foot with a sword?"

I had not noticed a large horse herd and when he shook his head and said, "We fight on foot." then I knew they had a weakness in cavalry. The German retired to his tent to dress for war.

Giovanni took Lazlo's horse and I handed him his helmet. He took his two-handed sword from his scabbard. "The man is cunning. I beg you, Sir John, watch for tricks. I can beat him in a fair fight but if any interfere…"

I was unsure what we could do with just daggers but I nodded, "We will keep watch."

When the German emerged, I saw that he had the same weapon as Lazlo. I scanned the enemy and saw no sign that any would interfere. Indeed, they all seemed intrigued as to the outcome. As is inevitable amongst soldiers money was already being wagered on the outcome. I guessed that many of the Germans knew of the feud and also of Lazlo and his skill. While the two men knelt and a priest heard their confessions, I watched the Florentine leader. He was dressed in fine armour and seemed almost disinterested in the combat. That told me that he was not as good a leader as he thought. A victory would put heart into his men whilst a defeat would be a disaster. I saw that his horsemen had tethered their horses to the west of the main camp. That could have been to keep the smell and the pollution of the water to a minimum but I also saw that there was a wood and a valley there. I wondered if they were the reason he had placed them there. The rest of his men were camped in what looked like groups of men linked by nationality. I saw the Florentine standards flanking those of the Germans. The two thousand Germans would be the backbone of the enemy. They had crossbows and a couple of handguns but I dismissed those. Most importantly they had no ditch.

The two combatants stood and faced each other. This would, I knew, be brutal. It was personal and there would be no quarter given. The two men walked quickly up to each other and swung their swords almost simultaneously. Both weapons hit the plate of the other. I winced when I heard the ring. The two plates were dented. I wondered at Lazlo for I had thought him cleverer than that. I would have blocked the sword's strike. I hoped he knew what he was doing. They circled each other and the German swung first. I now saw why Lazlo had done what he had. The German swung his sword at the undented side of Lazlo. This time Lazlo anticipated the swing and his own sword struck the German's. Sparks flew and the German's sword was knocked in the air. Lazlo had fast hands and he backhanded his sword into the German's middle. It was not delivered with all of Lazlo's power but it was enough to make the German reel and Lazlo took the offensive. He swung his sword at the dented side of the German's plate and forced the German back. Lazlo swung again and this time his sword went beneath the breastplate and tore through the mail. There was a wail from the German's supporters as blood flowed. The German raised his sword but the wound had weakened him and when Lazlo brought his sword down it knocked aside the sword and split first the German's helmet and then his skull. It was over and had taken just a handful of blows.

The enemy warriors were stunned. I walked over to Lazlo to take his helmet from him and Giovanni led his horse. We had seen enough. Lazlo was sweating when I took his helmet. He shouted, "I have my vengeance." He turned to Giovanni and me, "Take his armour and weapons!" As we started to strip the body Lazlo sheathed his sword, mounted his horse and rode down the enemy line, "Is there any other who would challenge me?" It was a clever move for none would dare face him and it put fear into the whole of the Florentine army.

We loaded the armour, mail and sword on our horses and rode back to our lines. We had the information I needed and I began to plan the attack. The moment we reached our camp and while Lazlo went to have his armour repaired, I gathered my leaders. I had a plan.

Manetti asked, "Do we attack now?"

I shook my head, "Have the men pretend to celebrate the victory. I want the Florentines to be overconfident thinking we have spent the night drinking and carousing. We will attack at dawn." I waved my leaders around me and using a stick in the soil mapped out the attack. It was simple but with the knowledge of the enemy's likely formation and what we had learned of the elements, we would be facing I hoped that our surprise would win the day. I wanted the Pisans to enjoy a victory in the field. Thus far they had just raided and not faced a Florentine army. I needed a victory so that I could use them again.

I was using a tent and the three of us went there to prepare my armour and weapons for the next day. Michael asked, "Will I get to fight tomorrow, Sir John?"

I looked at Dai. He had been about the same age as Michael when he had first begged for the chance to fight. I shook my head, "You are almost ready but you still have growing to do. Your body needs to be stronger and you do not have the skills," I saw his face fall. I knew that my brutal honesty had not been kind but that was my way. I was being thoughtful for if he fought there was a good chance that he would fall. I softened the blow, "Dai will fight alongside me tomorrow and you can carry spare lances for the two of us. The Germans are mailed men and lances break. You will be close to the action and you will see that skill is needed and those skills are, at the moment lacking in you. If you work hard and build up your body then you will become as Dai. When Dai is knighted then you shall begin training to join him."

His face brightened as he polished the white metal, "And you, my lord, when did you make the change from squire to knight?"

I laughed, "I did not follow that route for I began life as an archer. My body was already filled out and I had great strength. I did not have the skills with either a sword or a lance at first but I was so strong that I won despite my lack of skill. I was lucky and I know it."

Dai was quite skilled with his hands and he had just finished repairing his mail hauberk. As he laid it down, he said, "Sir John's experience as an archer helps the company, Michael, for he knows how to use archers well. He understands what they can do and what they cannot. The other leaders of men, Sterz and von Landau, only understand how to use men at arms. They misuse crossbows and I have no doubt that they will misuse the handguns we now see appearing. Sir John is the master of the bow, lance and sword."

I had not realised just how perceptive Dai was. I knew that I should have given him spurs before now but part of me was selfish. My squire gave my right-side better protection than most of my knights. There was just Sir Eoin with whom I felt safer. I suspected my new Englishman, Andrew, might prove as reliable. He had shown great skill the last time I had fought with him and

I would watch his progress. Sir Eoin, Robin, Giovanni and Martin were all natural leaders of men. Dai and Andrew had the potential to join them. The key to my success was my ability to use every arm to the best. Dai was right in that but it was more than using just archers well. I knew that you had to have leaders who knew what they were doing and, more importantly, would follow every order well.

The Florentines would know we were preparing for an early attack. It is hard to move horses around silently but I hoped that they would not expect us to be as efficient as I knew we were. Most armies had some bands that were tardy and did not arrive on time. There were also some rituals that armies uses such as a priest blessing them or the parading of some religious artefact. Those of my men who needed to be shriven would have done so the night before. Once dawn broke then we would be ready. The key to this battle would be arrows. I had three blocks of horsemen who would ride in an arrow formation. I would lead the centre one, Giovanni the right block and Sir Eoin the left. Those horsemen would be interspersed with four groups of archers protected by heavy infantrymen. The newly arrived billmen would be given a stern test. Unlike most armies, we did not use banners. We did not need them. It seemed to me that you wasted a mounted man if he had to carry a flag. I knew that it confused enemies who liked to focus their attack on a banner. As Michael was carrying four spare lances it would be Dai who sounded the charge.

It was still dark as we walked our horses to the mark I had placed in the ground the night before. It was less than three hundred paces from the Florentine camp. As we neared the mark, I heard the Florentine horns as they called their men to arms. I knew that the veterans, especially the Germans, would have slept with arms close to hand and would be dressed and ready for war quickly. Some might even have eaten. We mounted and I waited for the sun to rise from the east. Our horses snorted and stamped for they were eager to get into battle. I looked up at the first lance I would use. This one had a gonfanon dangling from it. It was not for vanity; it would be a visual signal to augment the horn. When I lowered it then the arrows of mailed men would know we charged to battle. Andrew de Belmonte was to my left and he grinned at me. He was keen to make his fortune and our fight against the Great Company had already brought him more money than he had expected to earn in a month.

The sun peered over the horizon but I waited to give the command. I wanted the field bathed in light to reflect from our armour. We were called the White Company for good reason. It was not just my livery but the shining armour we used. The light that reflected from it aided us in battle and any distraction helped us to win. Robin and Martin's archers flanked us and as the golden orb rose to send sparkling beams of light from the east I said, "Now, Dai," and I lowered my lance.

As we walked forward the archers ran so that they were ahead of us. They had strung bows and when they had run forty paces they stopped and I heard the creak as they drew back on their war bows. The release was not completely instantaneous but close enough. By the time I had reached their now static line, their first flight was in the air. They would send five flights each. By that time we would be almost at full speed and nearly at their line. When I rested my lance with the fluttering gonfanon on the mailed hood of my horse I saw the first arrows strike. Martin and Robin's men had used bodkins for we faced the Germans. On the flanks, the two blocks of archers had used war arrows. I saw mercenaries fall as the arrows plunged down. Some had shields and the crack as arrows hit them rippled along the line. The Germans were dividing their attention between the plunging arrows and the charging lances. We had no such distractions and I had chosen the German I would strike with my first lance. He wielded a halberd and had been lucky enough to avoid serious injury from the arrows. I suppose some might have hit his helmet and made his ears ring but he was ready with the weapon that would take my horse's legs. Unlike when we face horsemen, they had not embedded stakes before them. They would rue their error.

I pricked my spurs into my horse's side and he leapt forward to cover the last twenty feet. It was enough to unnerve the German who swung too early. It mattered not for my lance was longer than his halberd. I pulled back my arm when I was fifteen feet from him and my lance struck his mailed chest, avoiding the sharp blade that swung across it. The steel head drove into his chest breaking his breastbone. His body began to fall as the halberd dropped from his fingers and his hand tried to drag the lance away. I bowed to the inevitable and let the lance go. I held my right hand out and I felt the wooden shaft of the next one proffered by Michael. I pulled it and let the shaft slide through my mailed hand. We had practised this many times and as I gripped the haft where we had smoothed it down, I lunged at a surprised German who had thought I would reach him without a weapon. His shield was still above his head to protect him from the arrows he expected. His sword flailed across his body as my lance rammed into his screaming mouth and drove through his skull. This time his body fell from the lance.

Our arrow formation meant that we had driven deep into their lines at three points. I now faced the last line of Germans. They either had poor mail or no mail. That is not to say they were without skill or that they were inferior. In fact, these were the most dangerous as they wanted my plate and my mail but they had no support behind them. I skewered one German whose shield and sword were not close enough to each other and my lance drove through his mail and leather. I pushed hard and in his dying, he grabbed my lance. I had my sword drawn in a heartbeat. Ahead of me, I saw the baggage and the servants who looked up in terror as I led my horsemen towards them. Our archers were more than capable of taking prisoner the Germans and Florentines through which we had ridden. We had broken their lines and now I had to take advantage of the situation.

I saw the Florentine leaders and I shouted, "Take them!"

Some of the men I led still had lances but it did not matter that some of us only had swords. The knot of leaders and their bodyguards held neither lance nor spear and as we rode towards them showed their indecision. Did they stay and fight or flee? Their hesitation cost them. I recognised the livery of Ranuccio Farnese and I headed for him. Not all were as ready as their leader to fight and some fled back towards Florence. It was the moment I knew that we had won. With their leaders broken the rest took to their heels. The only ones who might have stood against us were the Germans and my men had broken them.

Ranuccio Farnese had courage but not as much skill as I. I easily blocked his first strike at me with my shield and I used my heels to move my horse around, forcing his, inferior mount back. It is harder to fight when you are going backwards. There is always the fear of tripping on something and even before I had struck a blow, he turned his head. It was a momentary distraction but it was enough and I swung at his upper arm. He wore mail and he had padding beneath it but I hurt him and, as it was his sword arm, he yelled, "I yield."

I shouted, "Michael!"

"I have him, my lord." My youngest squire leaned from his saddle and picked up the fallen sword, "Come with me, my lord, I will make sure you survive the wrath of the Pisans."

His thoughtful words must have been a comfort for I saw some Florentines dragged from their saddles to be assaulted by Pisans who had endured insults and injury from their hated enemies for many years.

I saw that I had my men with me and I shouted, "On to Florence."

Andrew de Belmonte had a good horse and he began to race ahead of me. I did not mind for it showed that he had courage. He began to draw closer to another noble who turned with terror etched on his face as we drew closer. Many of the Florentines had enjoyed victories won by others and they had forgotten how to fight. I saw Andrew gallop up behind him and, at the last moment, he switched from the Florentine's left to his right. He swung his sword and used the flat of it to smash into the Florentine's side. The noble fell. Andrew's squire was not close to hand and so my new English warrior was forced to rein in to take his man prisoner. More of my men were forced to do the same. Only Dai and Michael had been close to us when we had attacked. I reached Florence and saw the gates slammed with just one hundred men remaining with me. My horse was lathered and I let him rest. Sir Eoin and Dai were close to me and Sir Eoin had a look of joy upon his face. "Had the rest of our men been with us then we could have taken Florence!"

I shook my head, "No, we could not. See, the walls are manned. They have not only crossbows but also machines of war. This victory was easier than I expected but the greatest result is that they will now fear us. We attacked them to the northwest and now the southeast. They will be bewildered and have no idea where we will attack next. Their horns will be drawn in and, I hope, the Pisans will be more confident."

Dai said, "They are a vindictive people, Sir John. They mistreated our prisoners badly."

"I know and while I do not condone it, I understand it. So long as we do not then all will be well." I lowered my voice, "Who knows, one day we may fight for Florence. It would not do to soil our bed before we have even slept in it."

We waited until another two hundred of my men had joined me and then we rode around part of their walls in a sort of victory parade. We stayed beyond crossbow and onager range but it was a good feeling. As the afternoon threatened night, we headed back to Incisa and Figline. Now that the Florentines were shut within their walls, we would have free rein to plunder the land that had thought, being so close to Florence, that it was safe. We had shown them that it was not. We could raid wherever we chose.

Chapter 6

I sent a rider to fetch half of our army. I wanted our camp close to the gates of Florence. While I had no intention of assaulting the walls it would do no harm to let the Florentines think we would. The rest I ordered to occupy Figline. When Giovanni arrived, I was able to form my plans using his local knowledge.

"What is this gate before us?"

"The Porto San Niccolò, Sir John."

"Then we will hold here and have men ride each day around the other gates to ensure none leave. I would have this camp begin to make preparations for an assault. We use the night to raid. I will alternate men staying here and at Figline. I want none bored and I want the enemy to think we watch them with more men than we have."

Having established a camp, Dai and I rode back to Figline where the treasure we had taken was being gathered and the prisoners sorted. The mercenaries, once we had taken their weapons and mail would be allowed to go. It was a convention amongst warriors such as we. I made certain that they headed south. The Sienese would be more than glad to hire them and, at the moment, we had not been asked to fight Siena. The prisoners who would be ransomed were watched over by my archers. The two most senior were Ranuccio Farnese and the knight unhorsed by Andrew, Luca di Totti de'Firidolfi da Panzano.

Andrew was like an excited child, "My lord, I have made my fortune already from this one knight. Why, the armour, gold, rings and his horse alone would buy me a small manor in England."

I smiled at his enthusiasm, "And there will be more. Did you learn anything when you brought him back?"

He nodded, "Aye, their leader sent five hundred horsemen to flank us but they must have become lost for they did not materialise where he had hoped."

I realised that we had been lucky. Ranuccio Farnese was a better leader than I gave him credit for. A flanking attack or, even worse, an attack in the rear might have made the Pisans panic. "Rest tonight. Tomorrow we begin to take all that there is in this part of Florence."

Before I spoke with Manetti I went to Michael and Ranuccio Farnese. The Florentine stood and gave a small bow, "I must compliment you, Sir John. Not only did you devise a good plan but I can see that you know the qualities of your men. Michael here is a polite and courteous squire. I would happily have him serve me."

"And I thank you. I compliment you on your plan. Had your five hundred men reached us then I might have lost."

His face fell. He had not known that his attack had never happened, "I should have sent a better leader with them." He shook his head, "They will be back in Florence by now."

"And there they will stay for we have siege lines around the city."

He sank down to sit on the chair Michael had fetched for him. "Then I have failed my city. We should have hired you." He looked up at me and his face brightened. "Is it too late? We will double the fee the Pisans are paying. We are a far richer city."

"And while the offer is tempting I must refuse for I have given my word and a company that changes sides is one that will lose all hope of future contracts. While your other knights will be ransomed, you, my lord, will remain as my guest until… let us just say that you may be with us for some time."

I kept to myself the offer. It would do no one any good if that news was to leak out. I needed both the Pisans and the White Company committed to what we did. I sought out Manetti di Jesi who was with his commanders. The laughter that came from their camp told me about their mood before Dai and I reached them.

"Sir John, a great victory! The Florentines must now sue for peace. We have their leaders and their mercenaries are routed."

I shook my head, "They have both more men and more gold to hire mercenaries. Come, my lord, walk with me and I will tell you what I plan." The last thing I was going to do was to allow any decisions to be made by the Pisans. They had suffered so much that their judgement would be coloured by the need for vengeance. "I want half of your men. Tonight they will go to

Florence and join my men who are besieging the city. I will return here and we shall spend our time raiding."

"And why cannot we do the raiding and you do the watching?"

"Are your men mounted?"

"Some are."

"Do your men have the experience of riding and raiding at night?" He shook his head. "It is horses for courses, my lord. My men are masters of this sort of warfare. More importantly, I have leaders whom I can trust to obey orders."

He bridled at that, "And I do not?"

It was time for honesty. "My lord, your men are blinded by hatred and the need to have revenge. We have prisoners to ransom, you have corpses."

He could not help but glance beyond me where the despoiled corpses of the men taken by the Pisans lay. They were awaiting cremation. "We have been much abused by the Florentines."

"And if you continue to butcher them and treat them badly then we will have the local population rise up. I will raid and take from them but I will leave them enough so that they do not starve. Your chamberlain hired me to win this war. It will not be over by winter. We will return to Pisa and spend it there. The Florentines will starve and, in the spring, we will return to the offensive with fattened horses and warriors who are eager to fight."

"And we will be at Florence's walls?"

"Of course." What he did not know was that I would be leaving Robin with him to ensure he obeyed my commands. Robin was not intimidated by titles. I did not mind if the Pisans taunted and insulted the Florentines but I could not afford to lose any warriors in fruitless attacks on the city walls.

By the next day, we had switched all my horsemen from Florence and replaced them with the Pisan infantry and three hundred archers under the command of Robin. For the next three weeks, we raided the land around Figline. We took over a thousand head of cattle and captured half a dozen small castles, taking prisoner more of their lords. Even had we not been paid by the Pisans it would have been worth our while to stay in the area. Every one of the White Company made money.

The one castle we left alone was Figline and there were a number of reasons for that. Firstly, we used it as our base but, more importantly, Andrew de Belmonte had fallen in love with the lady of the castle, Monna Tancia. Her husband Guido had abandoned her and fled to Florence when we had arrived. Andrew behaved as a courtly knight and treated the lady with respect but Giovanni and I recognised that she would have welcomed him to her bed had he made more amorous advances.

It was November when I decided that we had enough. The ransoms had all been paid and the last castle we had tried to take, Tre Vigne, had proved too hard a nut to crack and we lost six men. Even that number was too many and so we left the fortress alone. It was the single Florentine success of the campaign. Sir Eoin led the cattle and prisoners back to Pisa while I went with the bulk of the army to Florence. It must have terrified the city for the Pisans who besieged it were suddenly reinforced. Church bells rang and the walls were manned. We slipped away back to Pisa in the night.

As we headed back to the city that paid us, I smiled as Andrew gained a stiff neck from looking back to the east and Figline. He was too much of a gentleman to ask Monna Tancia to return with us but I knew she was in his heart. The rest of the company might be looking back but their thoughts would be more mercenary. They would be thinking of the plunder we might have had if I had let them assault Florence. The city was famous for its banks making it the most desirable city in Italy.

I allowed Manetti di Jesi and his Pisans to enter the city first and they rode in like conquering heroes. None of us minded and if it meant they would fight well the next time we went to war then so much the better. The chamberlain held a feast for us, the second night after we had returned. All the leaders were invited. Robin, Martin and my other captains were bemused by the spectacle for we had won just one battle and then raided. We had done far more in Montferrat. I was seated at the high table with the great and the good. Pellario Griffo had me seated on one side and Manetti on the other. William sat on the other side of the chamberlain. He would listen more than he spoke. The doge was still unwell. It was rumoured he was close to death. I had never met the man. I allowed the Pisan warrior to regale the chamberlain with the embellished tale of our victory. The Pisans had not had much to do but he enlarged their role. The breakthrough of the German lines was now credited to him and his Pisan warriors. Michael was serving food at the feast and I saw him roll his eyes as di Jesi spoke of Pisan swords slaying mighty German warriors. He knew, as I did, that all the Pisans had been required to do was chase their fleeing foes from the field. When the stories were exhausted and di Jesi had inflated the Pisan egos with tales of taunting the Florentines in their own city the chamberlain asked me my plans.

"My plans, my lord? It is winter and warriors need to rest. When spring comes, we will fulfil the rest of our contract."

My words came like a thunderbolt. The top table went silent and the other Pisan nobles looked at us in surprise. Griffo said, "But I thought you would be here for some time, Sir John."

I smiled, "We took the contract for one year and you told us that we could renegotiate a new contract. We will serve Pisa until summer and then we will review the choices we might make."

Back in England young men kick an inflated pig's bladder around the village greens. Sometimes they kick too hard and the bladder bursts, the air knocked out of it, it deflates. The feast was like that. In their hour of celebration, they were told that we might abandon them.

"What will it take for you to remain here and serve us?"

I took the goblet of wine proffered by Michael and drank deeply before answering, "We have yet to spend a year here. As General di Jesi will attest, fighting for more than three months, as we have done, weakens warriors. We need to be sharp when we do raid."

"So you will do nothing in the winter except live off Pisan hospitality?" There was an edge to the chamberlain's words and I shook my head, "If we inconvenience you then we will simply take our one thousand cattle and make a camp. We would not wish to impose upon Pisa."

"I did not mean that, I meant will you not sally forth? Barga is besieged by the Florentines. Perhaps you could remove that threat."

I shook my head, "Those of my men who choose to will raid Florentine land but Barga is, I believe, in land held by Pisa. If General Manetti wishes to build upon the success he enjoyed at Figline then he could take the Pisan warriors and remove the blockade from around Barga."

Di Jesi's face was a picture. The thought of attempting to dislodge the army around Barga was beyond his and his men's abilities and he knew it. "My men have families and they will want to return to their hearths for the winter."

"Just so and my men and I will raid when we choose so that come the spring we can return to the field and make Florence sue for peace."

The chamberlain snorted, "Peace? I want Florence to bow their knee to Pisa as they did in the time of my great grandfather!"

"Those days are gone, chamberlain. Florence is now stronger and richer. They can buy ten companies the size of mine." I knew that there were other companies to be hired and while, thanks to my archers, they were not as good as my men, if they bought enough of them then they would make our success unlikely to be continued. "Chamberlain, let us not detract from our great victory. After Christmas, there will be time for negotiation. We will convene again in January."

They were not happy but they had no choice. We were the most important army in northern Italy.

Despite my words to the Pisans, we did not stop work but we met each day to plan our strategy. William was the master of the finances, "Sir John, I like not having so much money here with us. I think we should send it back to Bordeaux, or even England."

"Sir John?"

Sir John Braynford was my father-in-law. He had given me a fine home there and now cared for Antiochia, my daughter, named after my dead wife. Even more important was the fact that he was a rich merchant with strong rooms that could guard my treasure. He was no Basil of Tarsus who had just a couple of hired men to guard my chests.

"Aye, and while in London I could seek more men to join us." He looked apologetically at Giovanni d'Azzo, "No offence

Giovanni, but from where I stand English soldiers are better than Italians."

Giovanni grinned, "Aye, you are right and I am the only one who is the equal of an Englishman."

We all laughed.

"You would need men to protect you on the way home."

Dai volunteered, "There are some of the older warriors who have been with us since we fought in Burgundy. They are ready to return home. It is better, is it not, Sir John, to keep men here who wish to fight rather than have those who might hold back in a fight?"

It was then that I realised I had lost touch with some of the men. Time was I knew them all personally but now there were some whose faces I recognised but could not put a name to. "Then do so. Dai, you and William can select the men. Ask the chamberlain for a ship to take us home." William nodded. "And buy something nice in London for Elizabeth and the boys. Call at my home on your return and ask Roger when my boys will be ready to join me as squires. I would not have them tied to their mother's apron strings."

Roger had been one of my closest friends until he and Elizabeth had fallen in love with each other. We had resolved our differences but we could never be close friends again and I did not want him to influence my sons too much.

William and our treasure sailed at the start of December. I knew that I would miss his sharp mind but it was more important to save what we had. Sir Eoin, Robin, Martin and some of the other leaders also sent treasure back. Andrew did not and I knew why. His future lay with Monna Tancia. He would keep his treasure and use it to win the lady.

Christmas was a time for celebration but not for the White Company. We were warriors. Indeed, on Christmas Day, I rode with Sir Eoin, Giovanni, Robin and Martin, along with my squires to scout out the road to Barga. I had no intention of trying to relieve the blockade but if there was a chance to take plunder from the Florentine blockaders we would do so. Already some of my men, mainly the Hungarians and Germans, had raided Florentine land towards Pistoia. I did not mind for it would keep the Florentines wondering where we would attack next. That they lined their own purses was immaterial. I took the lion's share of the florins in any case. There was irony in that for the symbol of Florence was the lion.

We spied the barricades across the roads to Barga. The Florentines had cleverly used the rocky passes to prevent any from resupplying the beleaguered city. We could have winkled them from their perches but it would have cost men and more would have replaced the blockaders. They could stay there. Manetti di Jesi must have realised the difficulty of the task. We would war on the Florentines in spring but it would be in a manner which rewarded us.

We arrived back to a city celebrating the birth of Christ. We had enjoyed Christmas in Gascony, France, Burgundy and Italy. The celebrations and the food were different to England. We celebrated simply. My archers had hunted and we had some venison and wild pig. Our men had begun roasting the animals on Christmas Eve so that when we returned, in the afternoon of Christmas day, the meat was falling from the bone and the cooks were pleasantly inebriated. We ate outside. Italian winters were like autumn in England and it was good to eat outside. Of course, there were fights as drunken men quarrelled over the most innocuous of things. It was mainly between nationalities but we had enough clear heads so that no weapons were used. There might be broken noses, even gouged eyes but no deaths. The next day all would be friends. We had a rule about that and if two men could not settle their differences amicably then they were ejected from the company. None had yet to suffer that punishment. We were too profitable.

In January, before William had returned, the chamberlain invited us to meet with him. He had an offer for us. "Sir John, Pisa is more than grateful for your services thus far and I have been authorised to extend your contract for this whole year."

I nodded but remained silent.

"We will pay you one hundred and fifty thousand florins. How you distribute it is your concern."

He did not know my company. He thought I would take the lion's share and this was an attempted bribe. We had strict rules about such things. I did not determine the pay. William had negotiated with every man and the king's ransom we were being paid would be allocated with scrupulous fairness.

"A fine offer and we shall discuss it amongst ourselves. I take it that so long as we did not attack Pisa or its allies there would be no problem with our raiding further afield?"

As most of the cities around Pisa were her enemies the Pisans would not object and the chamberlain said, quickly, "So long as the Florentines are held then attack whomsoever you wish and you should know that we are quite happy for you to keep whatever treasure you take."

I said, "Thank you," but we both knew that we would have done so in any case.

As I expected, when we put the offer to the company, they were unanimous. It was the first time we had agreed on a contract without the advice of William but I was sure that he would agree with our decisions.

It was only a few days later that Andrew came to me, "My lord, have I given you good service thus far?"

I nodded and wondered what was coming. Was he trying to negotiate a larger fee for his services? I replied, cautiously, "Of course, in the short time you have served with the White Company none have impressed me more but why do you ask?"

"My lord, I would court the Lady Monna. Now that I not only have money but also the guarantee for more for the next year, I would court her."

I laughed, "Then do so for I am not your father."

He looked embarrassed, "I would be a knight."

Of course, he would. I had been remiss with Dai and I now saw a perfect opportunity to knight those who had served me well. "I shall do so." While I had the right to knight, I wanted it in a public setting. My mind was already working out how to take advantage of this. If I knighted Andrew, Dai, Martin and Robin it would show all those who served in the White Company that such advancement was possible. A man at arms, a squire and two archers would demonstrate the democratic nature of our company. After leaving him I sought first the archbishop and then Pellario Griffo. They were more than happy for the ceremony to take place in the cathedral. I could have used a civic building or the fortress but I want it seen to be sanctioned by the church and by God. The other three were surprised at my suggestion.

Robin was the most unimpressed, "It will not change me as a man or an archer, will it, my lord?"

"Of course not. You will all still be the same men. Your fees will not increase. You can say no, Robin. I will not make any man change his title if he does not wish to do so."

"I am happy enough, my lord, for it means that when my shoulders and back cannot help my arms to draw a bow I can return to England and I will take the respect for my title. Returning as an archer would mean that lords could look down on me. This way they cannot."

"You will have money aplenty when you hang up your bow, Robin."

"I know but now I think about it, a title cannot hurt."

William arrived back before the knighting of the four and he brought with him twenty men. There were six men at arms, six heavy infantrymen and eight archers. The ceremony in the cathedral seemed an opportune time to welcome them into the company. We celebrated afterwards although Sir Andrew drank sparingly and asked permission to ride to Figline to see his lady. He took with him his men and I wondered if he would return. If he did not, I would be sad for he had proved himself not only brave but also clever. On the other hand, his fees and those of his men would come to me.

He did return, just ten days after he left. He had made his advances and Lady Monna was happy about his proposal. It now depended upon her husband. He had not been seen since he had fled and abandoned her. Sir Andrew had too much honour to take advantage of the obvious love she felt for him and told me he would be happy to wait.

I should have waited but I made my first mistake. Many of my men had now tired of inactivity and were keen to raid. We left Pisa in four columns to plunder and raid. Perhaps God did not smile on us for we had travelled barely five miles when the snows came. They were not unknown but the weather had been so benign that I thought we could take a chance. It was not just the weather but the peasants and lords of the land. They fought us and I quickly realised that while we could defeat them it would cost us men and there was little to be gained. We returned to Pisa where an air of gloom descended upon the company.

Chapter 7

Annechin Baumgarten arrived in Pisa with Galeazzo Visconti and three thousand Germans. That I was surprised at their arrival was an understatement. The Pisans were delighted that they had more mercenaries to fight for them especially when it became clear that Galeazzo Visconti would be paying their stipend.

He was gracious when he spoke to di Jesi, Griffo and me, "Captain Baumgarten has served me well in Lombardy and I no longer need his services there. I thought he could see the rest of his contract out here, serving Pisa."

I knew he wanted something and when he and the chamberlain disappeared for a private conference then I had confirmation. I did not like Annechin but that may have been because he was German and I feared we would lose our contract. However that he was a good warrior was clear when he, di Jesi and I spoke of war. He had been a mercenary almost as long as I had but this was the first time that we had met each other. I took heart from the fact that the reputation of my company was greater than his. I made it quite clear to the other two that I would be leading the army when, in spring, we took the war to the Florentines. They both concurred but I could not rid myself of a nagging feeling that this might not turn out to be for the best.

When Visconti and the chamberlain returned it was clear they had made an agreement. I did not trust Visconti for the man had a serpentine mind and I envisaged his slippery coils strangling us. I knew he had been instrumental in our leaving Montferrat and that he had placed us in Pisa. I could still not determine his true reason. Was he plotting to grasp Florence too? I put that thought from my mind as I had more pressing matters. We had a war to win. The five of us sat to devise a strategy. It was obvious that we had to put pressure on Florence. Prato had been against Florence and allied itself to Naples. When the Queen of Naples sold the city to Florence there was some resentment. We decided to make a move on Prato. The city lay to the northwest of Florence. As Figline lay to the south-east we hoped to cause confusion. We now had more than six thousand horsemen and with my archers and the infantrymen who marched on foot we could muster an army of almost ten thousand. If we needed to, we could attack Florence's walls. I still hoped we would not need to but we could.

We left in April. William stayed in Pisa where he was negotiating for the purchase of an estate such as the one we had in Montferrat. We had a house already but we needed an estate outside of the city. This time we would buy one so that we could not be evicted. Manetti di Jesi and his men had gained in confidence and they asked if they could lead the army. I preferred local men stiffened by my archers but the victory at Figline had encouraged the Pisans and I concurred. Julio di Navaccio led a hundred men. As we approached the fortress city of Prato, they boldly rode up to the city gates and banged on them. It was pointless bravado and even worse, they returned to us in such a manner that one would have thought they had defeated the whole Florentine army. We pushed on towards Mugello.

We were now heading into mountainous country but my plan was to threaten those parts of the Florentine Empire that were far from Pisa and felt safe from attack. I planned on attacking Florence at some time in the future but I wanted the time to be right. I was with Annechin, Manetti and my leaders. Baumgarten was the sole leader of his company and, apart from his squire, Rolf was alone with us. He seemed happy to be so and genuinely at ease with us.

Sir Robin shook his head, "I like not, Sir John, the eagerness of these scouts. They are too far ahead of us."

Manetti did not like his men being criticised. Di Navaccio had been his choice, "You, archer, rode ahead when you scouted and this, remember, is our country."

Robin had thick skin and he ignored the barbed comment, "Aye, my lord, but, if you remember I had archers who kept both us and the head of the column in sight so that if danger manifested itself we could summon help."

"Julio has one hundred men and they are the best that Pisa has. They can handle whatever comes."

It was an hour later, as we neared Mugello that we heard the clash of steel, the neigh of horses and the cries of stricken men. I spurred my horse and Sir Robin and my other leaders followed me at the gallop. The others emulated us but their reactions were slower and there was a gap behind us. The rest of my company moved as quickly as we did and I was not afraid for us. As we rounded a bend, we saw the remains of the bloody encounter. I saw forty Germans on their horses and they were slaying and unhorsing Pisans seemingly at will. More than twenty horses wandered around and I saw eight of the Pisans heading back to us. The Germans looked unwilling to move and so I drew my sword. With Sir Eoin, Sir Andrew, Sir Dai and Annechin, not to mention my two archer captains I was not fearful. We had enough men coming behind us if we got into trouble but I wanted the Germans to know whom they fought. The leader deliberately slew a wounded Pisan knight who tumbled from his horse. It annoyed me and I spurred my horse to follow him. He insolently turned and led his almost untouched band away.

I could have halted then for we had saved the majority of the Pisans but professional pride took over. I did not like being bested. It had been the snow and outraged peasants that had held us in February. I did not want another setback. The five of us hurtled after the Germans. Although they did not speed up for we were travelling up a slope, I knew that most of them would escape my anger but a few at the back, probably still celebrating their victory heard our hooves and turned to fight us. It was their mistake for we were not Pisans who had just fought in tourneys and learned beautiful strokes. All of us were killers who fought to win.

My shield still hung from my cantle and so I drew my sword and rode at the German who tried to charge me with his lance. His comrades next to him made the blow more difficult and as the long wooden lance swung around, I simply hacked through the haft. The German, wearing an open sallet, was surprised and when I swung my sword at his chest he simply tumbled from his horse. Two of those who had thought to face us realised their error and, hurling their lances at us turned to gallop up the road. The others were slain. There was no point in hurting our horses. We had a prisoner and I waved Michael forward to take secure him. "Guard him, Michael!" Turning to Manetti who was lumbering up the road towards us I shouted, "Have the wounded dealt with. We will question this prisoner and I will decide what we do next. Sir Robin, send your archers to form a skirmish line. I would not be disturbed by the Germans while we speak with this man."

Sheathing my sword I dismounted. I allowed my horse to wander to the grassy verge and graze. He would not move while there was food. I spoke German and I said, "Get up!" The man rose to his feet. A fall from a horse, even wearing mail usually meant an injury and I saw him holding his shoulder. A doctor had once told me that there was a bone there called a clavicle and I guessed he had broken it. He would not be a threat. "Take off your helmet." The man had to use his good arm to unfasten the leather ties and I saw that the effort hurt his other arm. I pointed up the road, "Who was the warrior that led you?"

I think that if he had not been hurt he would have shrugged but he just rolled his eyes and said, "I know not."

I used a mailed forefinger to poke him in his injured shoulder. It was not hard but, patently, hard enough. He cried in pain and for a mercenary that was a rare thing. "He led you and paid you. Either tell me or I will hand you over to the Pisans you attacked and you know what they will do to you."

He nodded, "Our leader is Henrich Paer and we serve Malatesta Malatesta and Count Henri de Montfort. Our company waits for you at Mugello."

I smiled, "There that was easy enough. Michael, the man has a broken bone in his shoulder. Take his weapons and armour, fashion him a sling, give him some food and a skin."

The German looked at me as Michael first took the weapons and then, as gently as he could, took the mail from him. He obviously thought he was going to be killed. I had spoken to Michael in English and I guess he did not speak it. "I am letting you go. We will take your horse. You may return to Mugello or leave, I care not. You will not fight again this campaign season."

When Michael had finished the injured German turned and headed up the hill. Cupping my hands I shouted, "Let him pass." I turned to Annechin and Manetti who had watched it all. Baumgarten looked bemused. "There is little point in heading towards Mugello. This is not the country that will suit us." I turned and pointed southeast, "Florence lies that way. Let us turn and divide into columns to disappear into the forests. We will convene again on the slopes of Mount Morello."

Manetti, clearly disturbed by the encounter pointed up the hill, "What about the Germans?"

"We will be the rearguard. The White Company will ensure that we are not followed. Take whatever you can from the Florentines. By using our columns like the tentacles of an octopus we keep the Florentines guessing as to our plan."

"And what is your plan, Sir John?"

"Why, Captain Annechin, to attack Florence."

I had not planned on doing it quite so early but the disastrous performance of the Pisans had forced my hand. While the other two parts of the army filtered through the forests I waited with my men. "Sir Robin, Sir Martin, have your archers dismount and string their bows. Have the squires act as horse holders. When Malatesta sends his scouts we will wait until they are close and then discourage them."

"Aye, Sir John."

"And I will be with you for I would like to see the mettle of these men."

Michael took my horse and I went with Robin, Martin, and the archers. There were four hundred of them and ambushes such as this one were what they were made for. I wished I had a bow in my hands although as I had not practised every day, I would embarrass myself if I tried to loose one but there was no greater feeling than pulling back the string of a war bow and feeling your muscles burning. The thrum as it was released was like a paean, a song of death. Robin and Martin did not need to use their bows but they did and I watched them, one on either side of the road, as they selected the best arrow and checked that it had a bodkin head. Gone were the days when we had to worry about using such a valuable head. William paid a local blacksmith and he churned out four hundred a week. We would have enough for a major battle such as Poitiers and still enough to spare.

The trees along the very edge of the road had been cleared but it helped rather than hindered us. The horsemen would be less than forty feet from my archers when we would release. At that range, it was impossible to miss and any arrow that struck, if not mortal would incapacitate a warrior so that he would be out of action for many days.

We heard the galloping and the rattle of hooves on stones long before the riders appeared. We knew from the sound that there were many of them. Robin, Martin, and I had placed ourselves at the end furthest from the first archer. It would be Robin and Martin who would release first and rather than a horn or a cry it would be the sound of the bow that initiated the attack. The warrior, Heinrich Paer, who had, by all accounts unhorsed twelve Pisans and killed two, led the column. He wore a good breastplate and had a full-face helm. His arms and his legs were covered in mail as was his horse. He must have felt impregnable, especially after sending the Pisans packing with such consummate ease. The first arrow slammed into his shoulder and drove through both the plate and the mail as though they were parchment. The knight fell backwards over the back of his horse which continued to run down the road. The fine animal would be secured by my men at arms waiting beyond the bend for any who survived our attack.

The other Germans looked first at their leader as he fell and then at the trees. In that time more than three hundred and fifty arrows flew from the trees. Many men were struck by multiple arrows and some fell from their horses but a horn that sounded as the third flight was sent made the survivors of the ambush gallop up the road. The next time they would be more cautious in their approach and having lost the leader of the Germans there would be less heart in them.

"Well done, archers. Take what you will but do not be tardy. I would quit this road and disappear before they send skirmishers into the woods."

By the time it was night we had travelled more than fifteen miles and descended upon the village of La Catese. There were less than a dozen houses but they had food, animals and we were able to make a makeshift camp with their wagons so that we could light fires and eat well. This was Florentine land and we dug up the treasure that they had beneath their floors. We left the next morning and I dare say that they rued the attack by the Germans. Had we not been attacked we would not have been forced to head through the forest and they would have been left alone. In the next two days, we raided another four farms and villages. It fed us and we did not have to use the salt pork we had brought with us.

We met the others and discovered that with the exception of the castle at Petraia, every settlement had been raided and taken. As we had headed south, I had used my Italian scouts, selected by Giovanni, to scout out the suburbs of Florence. I knew that we could use the forests to get very close to their walls and I had a plan. We met at a nameless village pillaged by the Pisans. Whilst we and the Germans had not harmed any villagers, the Pisans had hanged the menfolk. It was a mistake but unless I kept an impossibly tight rein on the Pisan steed then it would happen again.

We ate in the headman's house that just accommodated half a dozen of us. My men knew the plan and so I told the Germans and the Pisans what it entailed.

"We ride to Fiesole. It is close to the Porta San Gallo. I intend to draw them into battle. The trees there will aid our archers and enable them to loose over the heads of our men. We fight on foot. This is not the place to risk our horses and I will rely on our men at arms."

I saw Manetti's face fall. His nobles preferred to ride to battle on horses but as the skirmish had shown even that was not a skill they had in abundance. The ordinary citizens would be better suited to this type of war. They could use pole weapons and could fight in serried ranks. I would not risk them in a vulnerable part of the battle but they would be useful.

"We will press as hard as we can and try to take a gate but I will not risk the whole army. We have already diminished the ability of the Florentines to supply their people and in our journey to the city we will continue to do so." I looked at Manetti, "The White Company was hired to defeat the Florentines, not destroy them. Whilst I know that many Pisans wish that it will not happen." I allowed silence to fill the room. I wanted my meaning to be unequivocally clear. "My aim is to bring the Florentines to a point where they demand peace. Our presence," I gestured to the German, "will guarantee the safety of Pisa."

Eventually, the Pisan general nodded, "You are right but after so many years of abuses being heaped upon us it is hard to bear."

"I know. We leave on the morrow and those who are mounted will race to get to Fiesole before the Florentines even know what we are about. I do not want their defences bolstered."

After they had their instructions, I went to speak to my archers. When I had said we would leave the following day I was being economic with the truth. Robin and Martin would ride with their men and occupy the slopes overlooking the Florentine suburbs. I did not care if I offended the Pisans, they had shown me that they were not even warriors for the working day. I was unsurprised now that they had been trounced at every turn by the Florentines. They had lost the art of war and it was a lesson for me. Pisa had been the most powerful of the mainland Italian states and it had lost that power. The White Company was the most powerful company. I would not allow us to slide into decline.

Chapter 8

When we reached Fiesole word of my archers had spread and all along our route Florentines fled to the safety of their city. That could only help us for there would be more mouths to feed and the garrison would hardly be bolstered by farmers and winemakers. Robin had taken some prisoners and discovered that our rampage through Tuscany had resulted in the retirement of their general. Malatesta was hanging up his sword and Count Henri Montfort would lead the defenders. I was glad for despite our success I knew that Malatesta was a good general. Montfort was younger and less experienced. If he could defeat me then he might become an adversary to fear. I had to make sure that we won. Even as we arrived, on the last day of April, he had men making barricades in the suburbs. I went with Robin to inspect them and saw that they were crude but effective. They had put carts and wagons between the houses. The longer we delayed in attacking then the stronger they would make them. I told di Jesi and Baumgarten what I required of them and on the next day, when the Florentines would have been celebrating May Day, I launched the attack.

My men were hidden in the woods behind my archers. My archers sent ten flights of arrows at the barricades. They used war arrows as we were uncertain how many mailed men were there. Even as the last flight was in the air the rest of our men attacked. The White Company attacked as one. Most of us had a long weapon, either a sword or a spear but I had thirty of my men at arms with axes. This time I allowed Michael a weapon of his own. This would be the day he fought alongside the White Company. On the ride to Fiesole Dai had pointed out that both he and I had already fought in battles when we were his age. I warned him to stay behind me, "You are the guardian of my back!"

Wearing an open-faced bascinet I led my men down the slope towards the barricades. I saw Grimaldi's Genoese crossbowmen on the walls of Florence but they could not yet unleash their bolts for fear of striking the defenders of the barricade. We had devasted the defenders with our arrows and bodies lay spread-eagled over the wooden barriers that had failed to stop the rain of death that fell from the skies. There were survivors but most were just trying to save themselves. As we reached the wooden barricades my axe men began to hack at some while some of the younger men at arms clambered over them. I waited for a gap to be hacked through them and saw men pouring from the Porto San Gallo. These wore mail and armour. I guessed they had saved their best men for just such an eventuality. The men on the barricades had been sacrificed.

The axes made short work of the carts and wagons and we poured through the streets. Robin and Martin were leading my archers to give us close support from the rooves and buildings of the suburbs. Flanked by Sir Dai and Sir Andrew, with Sir Eoin and Giovanni in close attendance I ran at the most heavily armoured of the men at arms. I knew my skill and I had not seen any whom I feared. I trusted the men I led and knew that they would guard my flanks. John of Ecclestone and William Hammer Hand were close by and they were two of the veterans in my company. The enemy would know who I was from my armour and the fact that I led from the front. They hurtled towards me; it was a death race for I had no intention of risking a wound in an attempt to take a prisoner.

The warrior I faced had a visored bascinet and carried not only a shield but also a sword. In theory that gave him a slight advantage over my poleaxe. I heard Giovanni shout, from my left, "Sir John, that is Henri Montfort!" He shouted in English. I was fighting the Florentine leader. I admired the man's courage.

My pole axe was held vertically above my right shoulder. It gave me a number of ways to strike. Henri de Montfort saw my unprotected front and he took the bait. He swung his sword to hack across my chest. Had it struck it would have been a wounding blow but I had already pivoted and brought the axe head of my weapon to smash into the backplate he wore. It cracked it in two and I heard the grunt of pain. One of his guards ran at me with a spear and a shield. I flicked away the spear with the langet of my poleaxe and then brought the axe head into his side. It sliced through his wrist on the way and from the blood I knew I had rendered him ineffective. I turned quickly as the Florentine general brought his sword around to hit my neck. I barely managed to block it but one advantage of a poleaxe is that you can use two hands to block it. The blade hit my langet. I would have to be careful for the rest of the battle. I had taken two hits on the metal that protected the head of my poleaxe and sturdy as it was it could be broken. The blow deflected and as he raised his sword for a blow to my head, I changed my grip and lunged at him with the spike on the end. He did not expect it and although he managed to swing his shield around, he did not manage to completely block the blow and the spike ran along his breastplate to pierce his right shoulder. It was his sword hand and eventually would cost him dear.

When I had begun the battle, I had been determined not to take a prisoner but this was the leader of the Florentines. I went back on my decision and said, "Count, you are hurt. Surrender." I knew that if he did then his men would lose heart.

He must have known it too for he shook his head, "No, I will fight on. The hurt is but a little one."

The poleaxe had a second spike at the bottom of the haft and I lifted the poleaxe. He thought I would swing the axe at his head but, as he raised his shield, I rammed the bottom spike through his foot. He wore sabatons but they were segmented to facilitate movement and I found a gap. This time it was not a grunt but a scream and he reeled. The men around him looked at the cry and my knights took advantage. The cry cost five good Florentine warriors their lives. I lifted the head and brought the axe head down diagonally. I hit the side of his helmet and I saw his legs give way. He crumbled in a bloody heap at my feet. I did not know if he was dead or alive but it mattered not. He and his five best men lay dead and as I roared, "White Company!" The other defenders fled back through the gate.

It slammed shut leaving more than fifty men stranded outside. Giovanni shouted, "Throw down your weapons and come towards us if you want to live. If not, then our archers will end your lives." The drawn bows of Robin, Martin, and their archers left them in no doubt that Giovanni meant what he said and throwing their weapons down they raced towards us with their hands in the air. They must have thought that we had reneged when our archers loosed. Many threw themselves to the ground in fear but the arrows were sent at the walls and many of the defenders, including the Genoese crossbowmen, were plucked from the walls. When two of my billmen were struck with bolts I turned to Michael, "Order a withdrawal."

The horn sounded and my men at arms and infantrymen began to withdraw. The Germans also withdrew but not all the Pisans obeyed and more of them were slain than I cared for. Our archers now began to win the duel of the missiles. The cracks of the crossbows sounded more ominous but they found little flesh. More of the crossbowmen were struck. In fact, barely half a dozen of my archers were hit and their wounds were minor. The Genoese found easier targets amongst the Pisans who were slow to find cover. My archers were able to ascertain their target and then step out to loose an arrow before a crossbow could be sighted. Darkness brought an end to the attack and we withdrew back to Fiesole to enjoy plundered food and wine.

Both Annechin and Manetti were in good humour. Manetti, in particular, seemed to think that we had all but won the city. I shook my head and disillusioned him, "We won today but if we assaulted the walls we would lose. It is one thing to hack at improvised barricades made of wagons and carts but the walls of Florence are a different prospect. Our archers won this day because they could keep up a great rate of missiles. Attacking the walls with men means that they would have to cease when our men neared the walls and then the crossbows would have free rein." I waved a hand around the town using the drumstick of a fowl to do so, "We raid this part of Florence. Pistoia was raided and her granaries emptied. Chianti and the land to the south has been devastated. We have barely begun to take from this part of Florence. Let us raid for a week or so. The hills of Arcretri and Bellosguardo will provide rich pickings. We destroy their orange groves and let our horses eat the new wheat. It will either bring them to talk or to fight and either one suits us."

Manetti was not convinced, "And what if they sally forth?"

"I hope that they do for we will defeat them but I fear they will not."

"How do you know?" The Pisan general showed his lack of experience. Annechin and my leaders knew the answer.

"Today I killed their leader, Count Henri. It will take time to appoint another and as Malatesta has already resigned a position I cannot see any obvious takers."

Giovanni said, "There is his brother, Sir John. Galeotto Malatesta. I know not if he is in Florence. He has estates in Rimini and he may be there but he is as good as his brother was."

I smiled, "His brother who decided he could not defeat us and left?"

He laughed, "Aye, he is the one."

"Then I will worry about him when the time comes."

Lazlo Kaepernick now commanded my Germans and Hungarians. Since his single combat more of his countrymen and Germans had joined us. He was a good ally and very popular with those who were not English, "Your plan is a sound one, Sir John. We raid and we wait. The Germans your archers defeated were the only real threat to us. If Florence wishes to defeat us then she must get more mercenaries and there are few to be had. We are the best and all know that."

It was true but Galeazzo Visconti's involvement still gave me sleepless nights. I could play chess well but Galeazzo appeared to be thinking many moves ahead of me and I could not see the trap he must be laying. I put it from my mind and we sent men out for the next three days to raid, seemingly at will. Manetti even sent his drummer boys and those with trumpets at night to the Port alia Croce where they made such a racket that the citizens thought they were being attacked and they assembled men on their walls. The only other attempt to terrify the city was at the instigation of Robin and Martin. They came up with a plan to close with the walls at night and, using the cover of darkness loose arrows blindly into the city. We had nothing to lose but arrows and I agreed. The plan seemed to work until nature or, perhaps, God, interfered and a sudden and vicious rain shower made their bowstrings ineffective.

Everything was going well and we raided at will. My men's purses bulged and I allowed myself the thought that the war would be over and we could return to Pisa as victors. The Greeks, so I had been told, believed that such arrogance was punished by their gods. It was not a Christian concept but events, a month after I slew Count Henri made me believe that, perhaps it was true. I had thought we had won but I reckoned without the treachery of Annechin Baumgarten and some of my own men. I learned all of this after the event. While I was with my archers and half of my men at arms raiding to the south representatives from Florence arrived in the camp and a bribe was paid. By the time I arrived back, it was all over. Indeed, so complete was the treachery that Annechin Baumgarten and his men had already departed for the north. A shamefaced knight, Sir Andrew de Belmonte and a smug Lazlo Kaepernick greeted me with false words, "We have won, my lord. The Florentines have paid Annechin Baumgarten and his men thirty thousand florins to leave Florence and we have been paid seventy thousand to do the same. We all agreed on a truce of five months."

Sir Andrew spoke the words but I saw, behind them, others whom I had thought loyal. The Germans and the Hungarians had followed Lazlo Kaepernick and that I had expected but for the man I had knighted to betray me made my hand go to my sword. Five months would give the Florentines the time to hire another army and build up the finances needed to continue the war.

Dai ghosted up next to me and said, in my ear, "Is this the time for us to draw swords with one another, my lord? The Florentines would destroy the victor. Use your mind. Let us work a way out of this."

He was right and I deeply regretted that William was not here. Had he been then he would have found a way to stop this betrayal. Forcing myself to keep my voice calm and even I said, "And Manetti and his Pisans?"

Lazlo Kaepernick pointed south, "They were raiding to the south." He shrugged, "They are still there."

I nodded, "I do not agree with this decision." I kept my hand from my sword but I knew that this was a momentous event.

Lazlo said, "Although William is not here our terms allow for a vote on such a matter. Let us put it to the White Company." He stared at me, "This will save bloodshed and you know, Sir John, that if you try to overrule us then blood will be shed. Seventy thousand florins is a king's ransom and we would have it."

I had been outwitted but I was confident that the men would vote to support me. Of course, without the three thousand

Germans of Baumgarten, we could not hope to continue to ring Florence. Visconti had won although I still could not divine what was in it for him.

There was no room large enough to hold us all and so we met in an open area. It was good that there was a truce for the only men we had as sentries were the Pisan servants left at their camp. What Manetti would make of all this I had no idea but first I had to thwart the attempt to take control of my company.

As had been the case when we had ousted Sterz, men stood with like-minded fellows and worryingly, as Sir Eoin and Giovanni flanked me on the wagon, I saw that I appeared to have fewer supporters than I would have liked. Robin hauled himself up behind me and said, "Do not worry, Sir John, your words will sway them."

I nodded and began to speak before either Lazlo or Andrew seized the initiative. "I come here to speak to you on a matter that is the heart of what we do. These two men have told me that you wish to renege on our contract with Pisa and sell our soul to the devil. Think about this. If we cannot be trusted then who will hire us? Is this not like Judas and his thirty pieces of silver?" I darted looks of pure venom at the two men. Lazlo seemed unconcerned but, to his credit, Andrew still looked shamefaced. "You know that we have defeated the Florentines. They will pay us off and we will not have to lose our honour. The White Company has a good reputation. Let us not sully it."

I heard my leaders on the wagon murmur, "Aye, Sir John."

An English voice came from the throng. I did not recognise it save that it was a northern voice and that meant a Cheshire archer, "The Pisans are piss poor soldiers, Sir John, and not worth fighting for. I for one would take the gold in hand. Let us fight for Florence. They pay better."

The murmurs of agreement were like a dull roar. I was losing my company. "Have I not led you well? Do we not win under my leadership? Would you divide the company for a few pieces of gold?"

A different voice, a London one shouted, "The twenty-five florins I receive, Captain, means I can return home and buy an inn. It might be a few pieces of gold to a rich man like you but to me, it is a fortune and if we stay to fight for Florence, we are promised double that."

There was more to this than a mere bribe. There had been a tacit agreement to fight for Florence. I looked at Lazlo whose face was impassive. He was trying to take over the company. He had agreed to fight for Florence and I saw that now I had lost.

"Know that I will keep my word. Choose now. Those who wish to take the devil's gold and follow men with no honour then stand on their side."

Lazlo reacted to my barb, "Go carefully, Sir John, for I will not be insulted."

I turned to face him, "No matter what the result of this vote is when it is done then you and I will take our swords and only one of us will live."

He nodded, "So be it."

As the men began to move to the two sides it became clear that all the Hungarians and Germans sided with Lazlo and Andrew. That only a third of the English did so was immaterial. The vote was clear and I had lost.

I nodded and waved a hand at those who had deserted me, "You are no longer the White Company. Any monies you left with William will now be forfeit and I have done with you." I turned to Michael, "Fetch my shield." He nodded and hurried off. "Giovanni, prepare the men. We ride for Pisa. I will not stay another moment and I trust them not."

Sir Eoin said, "You will fight Lazlo?"

"I will for it is personal."

"He is a good fighter, Sir John."

I gave him a wry smile, "And I am not?"

"No, but there is no need for this."

"There is for if he commands the ones who are left, he will seek to destroy the original company, I can see that now. Andrew is thinking with what dangles between his legs. He does this to win his lady. I know not what he was promised but he was promised something. Dai, discover what it is."

"Why, my lord? Do we want him?"

"He saved my life and I owe him that but if we can get more Englishmen to defect then I will be happier."

The crowd did not disperse for they knew what was coming. Both Lazlo and I were armoured and needed just our helmets shields and weapons. Men began to form a circle in which we could fight. I saw that Lazlo chose his two-handed sword. It would give him a greater reach. I did not think that the outcome would change the decision of the majority of men who had deserted me. Some might come with me but enough had voted against me to make it clear they had chosen Florence. I might end up having to fight my own men, I was just happy that less than forty archers had left me.

Michael fitted my open sallet and fastened the leather thongs. I slipped my shield onto my left arm. He said, "Your sword should be sharp enough Sir John for you have not used it since I put an edge on it. Know that I saw Lazlo's squire smearing dung on his blade." I looked at Michael and he nodded confirmation. It was a trick used by men who wanted to ensure that their enemy died if not in the combat, then of a poisoned wound.

"Thank you, Michael. I will ensure that he does not get close to me."

As I passed Robin my archer said, "I have an arrow nocked in case of treachery."

"There would be a bloodbath."

He grinned, "And what better way for the White Company to end than in such a battle. If you are not here to lead us, Sir John, then I will kill as many of our enemies as I can and return home."

Lazlo had an open bascinet on his head and he was making practice swings with the long sword over his head. He would have a greater reach than me. He was relying on the fact that I now had a few grey hairs sprouting on my head and that I might be too slow. He would learn that the work I did with Michael and Dai each day ensured that I was still fit.

We said nothing to each other. The time for words had passed. My insults had ensured that. Andrew recognised his own treachery but his carnal needs had overridden his sense of honour. His head still hung low. He was a conflicted man for he believed in honour and had behaved dishonourably but he wanted his lady. I put his troubles from my head; the Hungarian would take some beating.

As we warily approached each other I did as I would have done surveying a battlefield. I used the ground to my advantage. I made sure the sun was at my back and I looked for the flattest piece of ground. I sought out the dangers he, in his overconfidence, might have missed. And he was overconfident. Everything about his movements oozed the belief that he would win. He was bigger than I was and he was younger. He had just won the battle for the hearts and minds of more than half the company. The fact that the majority were his countrymen or Germans was immaterial. However, I had seen him fight in single combat and he had not seen me fight. That was my advantage. I also had far more experience than he did.

When he raised the sword, I knew what he intended to do. I had watched him do the same thing to von Spetz. He would swing the sword at my side knowing that all I could do was to block the blow with my sword. His weapon was far heavier than mine and if we blunted our edges, he could simply batter me to death. I would not let that happen. I had already ascertained that the ground was flat when I walked towards him and as he began his swing I simply stepped back. The tip of the edge might have torn a jupon had I worn one but I did not. The swing took the sword in a circle and as it passed, I stepped forward quickly and punched at his arm with my shield. The move did little harm save to unbalance him and he stepped back but I had not finished. Even as he steadied himself, ready for another swing, backhand this time, I stabbed at his knee with my sword's tip. He wore a poleyn to protect it but there was always a gap and I found it. Having inveigled my way through the plate and touched flesh I stabbed, twisted and then pulled my blade back as the mighty sword swung around once more. I was lucky. The wound slowed the swing and made his hands twist a little. Even so when the flat of the sword hit my shielded left arm, it hurt. I would be bruised but if a blackened piece of skin was to be the worst of my wounds, then I would be a happy man. He was now regretting his choice of weapon. He had counted on a lack of mobility and I was highly mobile.

I saw blood trickle from his knee and knew that he was wounded. It would slow him and he was too good a warrior not to realise that he had to end this combat quickly. He swung and rushed at me but I simply scampered away from the flurry of blows that struck the air. I made sure that I kept to the flat ground and avoided the one patch of mud I had spotted. My moves brought catcalls and jeers from the Germans and the Hungarians. I ignored them. I could see his face and the sweat that poured down it. His next move was to bring his sword over his head and advance towards me quickly. He did not strike but he gave himself the option of three possible blows and so I would not be able to dance out of the way. I did the unexpected. I ran at him with my sword held just above my shield. He tried to bring down the sword quickly but I covered the length of his blade before he could do so. He was a big man but my shield hit his chest while my sword hit the mail below his shoulder. The tip tore through the mail links and sliced across his gambeson. Blood spurted and, more importantly, although his hilt hit my helmet, my arming cap took the blow. I also knew that my right leg was between his and so, hooking my foot behind his I pushed and his spur caught the ground making him fall. This was no time for mercy and, if I am to be honest, none was in my head. I swung my sword at his falling body and hit him in the side. As he landed, I lifted my sword and stabbed it at his middle. He was not yet willing to die and his sword deflected my strike. Instead of killing him I merely drove my sword deep into his left side, below the rib cage. It was a bad wound but, as he lay there, he managed to swing a leg and knock me from my feet. Had he been able to rise quickly then he could have skewered me like a stranded fish but his leg, side and shoulder made him rise like an old man in the middle of the night. I was on my feet at the same time as him.

"You are a trickster, Hawkwood, and that tells me that you are a poor warrior and I shall win."

He was buying time and trying to get his breath, I saved mine for I now knew how I was going to end this. I moved around so that the sun was, once more, in his face and I stepped a little nervously back. I wanted him to think my fall had hurt me when it had not. He had to end it before his blood loss weakened him and he ran at me. I stepped back and to the side. The sunlight blinded him long enough for him to miss the patch of slippery mud and his foot slid along it. He was unbalanced. I stepped in and hit him with my shield so that he fell. This time I was in a better position and I brought my sword down and hit the side of his helmet. I dented the helmet badly and I raised my sword to use every ounce of strength I had left and hack through his coif and his neck. The widening pool of blood told me and the rest of the company that he was dead. The English cheered while the angry Germans and Hungarians muttered threats.

Robin's voice rang out, "Archers!"

My captain of archers had been ready for just such an eventuality and the bodkin arrows were aimed at the angry Germans and Hungarians.

"If I give the command then you all die and, to be honest, that may not be a bad thing but we signed a contract with each other and we have shed blood together. Today, I will be merciful. If you still wish to leave my company, the White Company, then depart now and, with your tails between your legs slink like the vermin you are into Florence's walls."

One Hungarian, obviously a friend of Lazlo's drew his sword and ran at me. He made just four feet and then six arrows slammed into him.

I smiled, "Does anyone else think they can outrun a war bow?" They were silent, "Leave!"

The Hungarians and the Germans obeyed. A hundred or so English men at arms, led by Andrew followed. The man I had knighted gave me an embarrassed shrug as he passed.

Sheathing my sword I said, "Have the body stripped of his armour. Find his horse and, before his squire takes it, his treasure also. If he objects then kill him." Dai and Giovanni hurried off. Turning to Michael I said, "Take three archers as an escort and find the Pisans. Tell them what has happened and that we will join them in Pisa. We have been betrayed and our Florentine foray is at an end."

Robin and Martin joined me, "Thank you both. Before they realise what they have left have all the food, animals and weapons loaded on our wagons. We will leave for Pisa before someone can send their army after us. We are now seriously outnumbered."

Robin nodded, "It is not necessarily a bad thing, my lord. If a bow has a weakness better for it to break before it is needed. We have time to get to Pisa and we are better off without men who have now proved unreliable."

I was downcast and my voice betrayed that, "Did you think we would be abandoned?"

Robin said, "No, but think about it, Sir John. If Baumgarten had not taken the bribe and left then would the others? He was the carefully placed rock that ensured failure."

It came to me, "Visconti!"

"Exactly. We had noticed riders arriving at the German camp from Visconti but we put it down to the fact that Baumgarten served him. Perhaps he was being passed instructions."

"But Sir Andrew and the others?"

Martin's face darkened, "We were all taken in, my lord. Everyone likes Sir Andrew. He seemed like an honest young man. I think so many went with him because of that. It was the woman."

"What do you mean?"

"Lady Monna's husband, Count Guido is a member of the Florentine council. One of those archers who left us told us that he has agreed to a divorce. He has sold his wife to be rid of us. Sir Andrew can now marry the lady and he has enough money to buy land although I think the Florentines will give him some. They could not defeat us in battle but they found other means."

Michael returned and, after we had loaded the wagons and, with archers protecting us we headed back to Pisa. There were less than one thousand of us and at one time there had been more than three thousand. Sterz and this latest desertion had cost us dear. When I had killed Count Henri I thought I was at the pinnacle of my career. I was about to defeat Florence and now I had lost everything. I had been outwitted. Riding through the night I decided that I had not been ruthless enough. From now on I would rule the company with a mailed glove. I would speak to William and we would tighten up the contract and the pay. I would not be betrayed again.

Chapter 9

We reached Pisa at the same time as Manetti di Jesi. Like me, he was angry that we had been outwitted. Hindsight is always perfect but the two of us, when we sat with Pellario Griffo and William, saw all the signs that should have alerted us. Surprisingly the chamberlain did not seem as put out as we were. I had not seen this solicitous side of the Pisan.

"It is not a disaster. You, Sir John, still have your archers and they are a potent force. We lost no Pisan warriors and we hurt the Florentines. Our granaries are full and theirs are not." He turned to William, "And you can hire more men, can you not, Master William?"

"I can but it takes time."

"Let us make time. Sir John, will the Florentines attack us?"

"Of course, but not for six months or more."

"Then you have that time and, who knows, some of those who took the Florentine's gold may well decide to return to serve with you, Sir John. Your reputation is still intact."

I became angry and banged the table, "They can rot in hell before I will take them back! They betrayed me."

William had, as usual, been quiet up to this point but now he spoke, "Sir John, let us be practical. We both know that the Englishmen you hired are the best warriors in Italy."

"Anywhere!"

William smiled and nodded, "And are they now worse soldiers for this betrayal?"

He was right. The skills of Sir Andrew were still there but he had betrayed me. "No, they are not but can they be trusted?"

"You know that I am just a bookkeeper and know not how war works, save that it brings in coins but I believe that the vanguard is often the place of most danger."

"It is."

"Then if any return to join us, we make them sign a new contract that benefits us more than them and when you go to war you have soldiers you can use for the most dangerous of tasks."

It was cynical but it was also brilliant. "You are right." I turned to Manetti, "And while your men did well, they must be better trained. I know that they are militia and have other jobs but on the days you have them you must make them fight as my men do, to obey orders."

"We will do so for, and I mean no offence by these words, Sir John, the sooner we can do without your mercenaries the better."

"I am not offended and you are right."

As we rose to leave, Pellario held out his hand, "Sir John, I have a particularly fine wine that you may enjoy."

There was something in the way he spoke that made me nod, "Of course, Chamberlain. I will catch up with you, William. We have much to talk about."

The chamberlain poured the wine. It was excellent and I nodded, "You are right, Chamberlain, it is excellent but why not tell me the real reason you have kept me here."

"You are sharp, Sir John. As you know the Doge is not a well man." I nodded. I had never met the man and if I tripped over his body, I would still not know him at all. "He is not long for this world. How would you view his successor?"

"Pellario," I deliberately used his first name for I knew he was plotting, "as I have only met you in my dealings with the rulers of Pisa you will excuse me if I regard you as the power here."

"You are kind to say so. In my own small way, I try to look after the best interests of Pisa and I will continue to do so. What do you look for in a doge?" He smiled, "A new one who might take more of an interest in war, perhaps?"

I shook my head, "As far as I am concerned, I would prefer a doge who knew nothing about war but continued to pay me."

His eyes had a triumphant look on them, like a lion that has taken its prey, "And suppose you were paid thirty thousand florins to make sure that such a man became doge, what then?"

Thirty thousand florins was the amount given to Baumgarten and his Germans to betray Pisa. Who was I betraying? "And who is this man? Is he in the pay of Pisa's enemies? I have just turned down a greater bribe to be loyal to the commune of Pisa and I will not betray her to a foreigner."

"You have my word that the man in question is a Pisan and a patriot who believes that Pisa should be great again."

I did not necessarily trust his word but the thought of such a sum of money had my interest. "Then, on those terms, I might be happy to support such a claim so long as there would be no conflict as a result."

"Sir John, if you back this man then no one in Pisa will oppose you. We will talk again when I am able. For the present know that you and your company will still be paid." He paused, "By the way, is it still the White Company? The name matters not to me but I am interested."

I shook my head. We had spoken of this on the way back to Pisa, "For the moment we are the Company of St George. We are now made up entirely of Englishmen and the name of that saint will draw the type of men we need but one day we will be the White Company once more."

"Good. It is your company and I still have faith in you."

A few days after the meeting and when I had reflected on the chamberlain's words and made my decision, I held a meeting. William had bought a fine house that we could use and which was now occupied by my senior leaders and those we called vintenars and centenars, captains of twenty and a hundred respectively. I had rewarded those who were loyal to me and had served me well, men like John of Ecclestone, William Hammer Hand, Ned, Karl, and Luke. The others had been curious about the meeting but, until that moment, I had kept my counsel.

We dined at a large table in the smaller dining hall. William, Giovanni, Robin, Sir Eoin and Dai were the only ones present and Michael our sole servant. I wanted privacy. With the door secure I spoke. All were attentive and as usual, William could not help scribbling as I spoke. He liked to keep a record of what was said.

"We have fallen far since the heady days of Montferrat and I blame myself. I believed I could do no wrong. The Greeks have a word for it, hubris, and the company has paid the price for that arrogance. I wanted to speak to you because we, that is to say, I, have been asked to support a Pisan who wants to become doge. There will be a great deal of money involved. I am not concerned with the morality of it but after the mistakes in judgement I have made I would value you, your advice."

I could see that my archers were unconcerned. To them every Italian was untrustworthy and it mattered not which one ruled. Giovanni shrugged, "Take the money, Sir John. The Pisans owe you that much for your loyalty."

I looked at Dai and Eoin, "And you?"

Sir Eoin shook his head, "Politics baffles me. I prefer the simplicity of combat. There you know your enemy. He faces you and you kill him, just as you did with Lazlo. They are my politics."

Dai said, "Whatever you decide is fine with me. You think you have made mistakes, my lord, but I do not see them. I was surprised when so many chose to take the Florentine gold but that was nothing to do with your leadership and I believe that most will return to the company for we have yet to be defeated and that is rare is it not?"

His words underscored what Griffo had said. I would have to accept back any who had left me. It took young Dai, however, to convince me.

I looked at William who simply nodded and then said, "They are right, Sir John. The company, in spite of the desertions, is still successful. As the men who left us had pay due, we are all richer and I will arrange a bonus payment to those who remained loyal. Refusing to employ those who signed a contract would be like cutting off our own nose and we are not that foolish. As for supporting the new doge; why not? We have never seen the old one and the man who has been our conduit is Griffo. If he wants this new man to rule Pisa what difference will it make to us? I say that you agree to support him."

I nodded, "Thank you all but I feel that your confidence in me is misplaced. Now, what of the future?"

Giovanni said, "We ensure that the Pisans are ready to go to war when the Florentines organise themselves and attack and attack they will."

I looked at Robin, "We have plenty of arrows and it was not the archers who left you. The problem is that while the archers can turn a battle in our favour what we cannot do is what the men of arms manage. They can force walls. We can hold up an enemy, we can discourage an enemy but at the end of the day, it will be you and the knights who win the day. Have we enough?"

He was right and I was unsure. "William, how are the finances and what are the chances of hiring more men?"

"We have a steady trickle of men arriving in Pisa to join you. I can send word to Sir Roger in Bordeaux to advertise for more men. He is more likely to find us archers." William added, "And you should know, Sir John, that while in London with your father-in-law, we bought two more large manors close to London. At the rate the city is growing their value will rise and John is happy to watch over them for you. You have a steady income and if you should choose to give up war then you can. He sends his regards and your daughter is growing into a beautiful young girl. She is delightful and you can sleep well for she is well-loved by her doting grandparents. As for your sons, they are too young yet for war."

His words made me silent. I doubted that I would ever see my daughter and if I did, she would not know me. I had two sons and saw little of them. What was I doing all this for? William seemed to read my thoughts and he said, quietly, "You are a rich man Sir John. You have three manors in England as well as one in Bordeaux and now one here in Pisa. Your children will have cause to thank you for they will never need to work."

I nodded, "But they will. Being idle produces men of weak character like Sir Andrew. Had he done as I did and been forced to live alone he might have had more backbone."

Robin laughed, "It is not his backbone that was the trouble, my lord, more like his front bone!"

The laughter put us all at our ease and I resigned myself to building up the company.

Over the first weeks, after we returned, we heard that Baumgarten had now named his company the Flower Company and that there was a new company led by Bernabò Visconti's son, Ambrogio. Dai said it was a sign of our success that others were emulating us. William and I were summoned by the chamberlain, a month or so after my meeting with my leaders. We did not go to his home but the huge mansion of Giovanni Agnello. He was one of the richest merchants in Pisa. When Pisa had lost its sea power, he had hired Genoese sea captains to ferry his goods and while his competitors lost money he continued to grow his empire. As we headed towards the house William said,

"This will be the new doge. He buys Pisa and quite rightly too for he is the richest man here." William admired those who could make money more than those who could win battles. I think he understood that you needed soldiers to hang on to your money but the money makers, to William, were the most important.

Pisa was hot, even in the early summer but the house was well designed with much marble and was remarkably cool. As entered servants brought us damp cloths to wipe our faces and our hands. We were given iced wine to drink and then led to the opulent and tastefully furnished drawing-room where the merchant and chamberlain awaited us.

Agnello was smooth. He reminded me of my father-in-law, John. His voice was cultured but you saw in his eyes the shark that would devour any competitors. I wondered why he needed me. "Welcome Sir John and can I, on behalf of all the merchants of Pisa, thank you for your service up to this point. I appreciate your loyalty and I will ensure when I become doge that you are recompensed for that loyalty."

"I gave my word and what is a man if his word cannot be relied upon?"

"Quite. I believe that you are a man of your word and for that reason, I will speak bluntly. I wish to be doge. The city needs a man who can steer Pisa back to greatness. With the chamberlain here I believe I can do this but there are those who might oppose me. For that reason, I need your company to guarantee my election. I would have your knights accompany me when I address the deputies tomorrow."

"Just accompany you?" He nodded, "And for that, you will pay me thirty thousand florins?"

"And for your continued support."

There was, as my men had said, little to be lost in my agreement, "Then I agree."

Pellario Griffo added, "And we need to extend your contract by six months for my spies tell me that Galeotto Malatesta is assembling an army to attack down the Arno Valley. We will have to be ready to face them. William, come with me and we will word the contracts." He smiled, "There must be no ambiguity, eh?"

When we were alone the merchant said, "And you have not taken a wife, eh, Sir John?" He shook his head, "A man needs a wife and children."

I said, quietly, "I had a wife, my lord, and she died. I have a daughter and two sons. They live in England and France."

"I am sorry for your loss, but take another." He leaned forward, "I have four daughters and three of them are of an age to be married."

I laughed, "I am flattered, my lord, but I am content with my state."

He wagged a finger at me, "When we dine with my daughters we shall see. They are beautiful and they will turn your head."

We spent the next hour speaking of the politics of Pisa and Italy in general. I learned much about the Visconti family, not least that Bernabò Visconti was a close friend of the merchant. I guessed that was a good thing in that Bernabò might be willing to leave alone Pisa especially while there was a chance of winning Florence for that was the prize jewel. Her banks had made her an attractive prospect for a predator. Griffo and William returned not long before we were summoned to dine. The merchant had running water in his home and we availed ourselves of the opportunity to clean up. The water had been there since the time of the Romans.

As I expected in such a fabulous home, everything was done to perfection. His wife, Sophia, was beautiful as were the daughters and their fluttering eyelashes told me that they had set their sights on me. There might have been a time when I would have been interested but Antiochia and Elizabeth had both been beautiful flowers just coming into bud. I was older now and I appreciated flowers that were not quite so innocent. I smiled at the young women who, so far as I could see, were not yet twenty. However, while we ate, I spent more time speaking with the merchant and the chamberlain.

William, on the other hand, seemed besotted, already, with Bianca, the middle daughter. With her jet-black hair and piercing green eyes, she was stunning. Fortunately for William, the young woman appeared to reciprocate the mooning eyes and faltering words. I suppose there is such a thing as love at first sight although I had never experienced it. The three women in my life had all been attractive, each in their own way but none of them made my heart ache. The normally business-like William was lost to us while we ate. The master and the mistress of the house seemed to approve and I do not wonder at that. William was part of my company and any dalliance cemented the bond bought by gold.

The meal and the meeting ended well. Giovanni Agnello was pleased with the outcome. True he had not managed to persuade me to take a daughter off his hands but he had seen that one of them would soon fly the nest and William was a reasonable second choice. He had two more daughters and there were many more alliances he could make.

As we headed back to our home William confided in me. He positively gushed, "Is she not beautiful Sir John? Do you think that Signior Agnello would consent for me to court her?"

I laughed, "I do not think that there will be any impediment placed in your path. Is it what you want?"

"I think so. When I went to England and saw the joy that Antiochia brought her grandparents I envied them and I am now an uncle to John and to Thomas. I have seen how close Elizabeth and Roger are and… I am sorry, my lord. That was thoughtless of me."

I shook my head, "That was in the past and she is a good mother for the boys. Roger will only be part of their lives for a short time. Perhaps if you do marry then I might be able to bring the boys here sooner."

"How so, my lord?"

"I cannot be a wet nurse to two boys and dab their eyes when they mewl but if you were to wed Bianca then there would be a feminine presence that would soften my harder side." From his face, I saw that he did not see it that way but a man cannot change his nature and I knew that I was a cold fish. It was a good thing that John and his wife were raising my daughter. If I had the responsibility then she would be less loved and that would not be the child's fault.

Over the next week, neither William nor I had much time to think about Bianca or my sons. Men did begin to return to the fold. All of them came sheepishly and their stories were all different but by the end of the week, even more men had come back, including all the archers. Robert Duggan had been a soldier, like Sir Andrew, in whom I had thought I had a future leader. His elder brother, James, had fallen in battle and Robert was keen to show that he was a better soldier than his dead brother. He was both brave and clever. More importantly, men followed him. He was desperate to allow me to take him back. "John Onslow and myself were duped, my lord. We were led to believe that we would be captains in the new White Company but Sir Andrew chose others to lead."

"And you think that after what you did, I will let you lead?"

His face was resolute, "If you just give me the chance then neither John nor I will let you down."

I nodded, "We shall see. For the moment you are a member of the company and soon we shall see if you are as good as your word."

I had similar conversations with all the returning deserters.

I let Robin and Martin either accept or reject the archers and they told me that the reason they had returned was a lack of respect amongst the companies that tried to hire them. Robin shook his head, "These foreigners see English archers as mindless machines with broad backs and thick skulls. You know better than that. They have realised the error of their ways, my lord and will not stray again."

It was Giovanni, Dai, and I who interviewed the men at arms. Some had let the new money they had received go to their heads and in a variety of ways had lost it. Some gambled too heavily, others had spent it on false friends while some were simply robbed. The old White Company had given them a structure. Men like Sir Eoin and Robin had made rules for them to live by. I confess that I knew I would still view them all with suspicion but we needed the numbers for reports came to us of an army heading down the Arno. We still had time to prepare but I was less than happy with the lack of progress amongst the Pisans. Far from heeding my words, Manetti di Jesi seemed happy for his men to play at training. My men knew that when you finished training there should be sweat, bruises and even blood. If you were not out of breath then you had not trained hard enough. The ones who had returned to us showed that the short time they had been away from us had weakened them.

William and I went to speak to the chamberlain. I was keen to know how many men we would be taking to war. He promised me five thousand. As the army that was approaching had eleven thousand foot soldiers and four thousand horses we did not have enough men to defeat the enemy in any kind of traditional way. I realised that I would have to scout out the enemy and seek weaknesses in either their army or the terrain. I was not hopeful.

I returned to our home, we now called it the headquarters and I summoned my inner council. I confess that I regarded the company as mine. I no longer had to share it and so I used it as my own private army. "I intend to scout out the enemy. Dai, you, Giovanni and Robin will come with me. We will travel incognito. While I am away, Eoin, I want the men honed to battle readiness."

He was sceptical, "Sir John, if we are outnumbered almost three to one do you really think that we can win?"

"There are many kinds of victories and one would be that we halted the Florentines before they could get to Pisa. Do I think we can defeat them in open battle? Of course not. The bribes effectively ended all chance to that." I leaned forward, "I would have you impress on all the men, especially those lost sheep who returned to the fold, that it is highly likely that we will be fighting old comrades and they should be prepared for that."

None tried to dissuade me from this potentially dangerous act for they knew that doing it made me the leader I was. I would not risk heading into a place I did not know. I thought back to the battles in which I had fought where luck played a large part. I wanted luck to be the tiniest element.

Chapter 10

I found myself getting excited as we prepared for the reconnoitre. I chose one of my plainer horses and a dull though well-made cloak. This was no time to risk Ajax, my warhorse. The mail I wore also lacked polish. I wanted no one to recognise us. Robin was the biggest sign of who we were for he had his bow but in its case, it might be mistaken for a pole weapon. We wore coifs covering our arming caps and we did not bother with a sumpter to carry our supplies. We each had a hessian bag containing the food we would need. I donned an old and serviceable pair of buskins and I made sure that I had my leather sap as well as four daggers. One would be in my boot, two in my belt and one in a scabbard on my saddle. Shields would not be needed and I took my favourite sword. It was well balanced and with a good fuller, not as heavy as some. I also took my bow, in its case, and a handful of arrows. It was for a disguise. I did not want to be recognised as Sir John Hawkwood.

We left before dawn with hooded cloaks. The increasingly hot weather would mean that we would have to discard the cloaks soon but this way we managed to get ten miles up the Arno valley before anyone knew we had left. The Florentines had spies in Pisa and our absence over the next day or two would be noted. They might even guess which direction we had taken but they would not know for certain and that was the key. It was good to be free of the army I normally led. We rode at our speed and as we were all good riders with sound horses then that was a faster speed than even a company of cavalry for we were not mailed. We made good time and when we needed a rest, about an hour before noon, we found a small hamlet that, miraculously, had not been raided. As we paid for the food and the use of the water trough we were welcomed. Men such as we were not uncommon in this part of Italy. The truce had released men and the roads often had small groups of warriors heading home, seeking new masters or returning, as many of my men had done, to their former companies. What we all had in common was the need to be invisible. It was only my handful of men that had sinister purposes.

After establishing that no riders had come west, we ate the food we had bought beneath the shade of some walnut trees. "We could find the Florentines just a few miles down the road, Sir John."

"No, Dai, for their scouts will be well ahead of the main army. There are fifteen thousand men coming down the road and the only way to keep that number hidden is to have a handful of scouts several miles ahead of the mainward and a good company of horsemen half a mile or so close to the scouts. The handful of scouts would ride back if there was danger and bring up the horsemen. It is what I would do."

"But are their leaders as good as you, Sir John?"

I smiled at the compliment, "Giovanni, many of the men who left us, like Sir Andrew and the others, were competent leaders. Both men rode with us for some months. I think that, if they were with the Florentines, they would offer advice. If you pay a fortune to men then only a fool ignores their advice. We have to be far cleverer than we were. The enemy has an insight into our methods and they outnumber us. To escape this next encounter with our lives will be a good result."

Only Robin nodded. The other two looked shocked at this apparent lack of confidence. "But why do we even scout if you think that we will lose? Let us squat behind Pisa's walls."

"Because, Giovanni, that would mean the Florentines had won. They would rampage through Pisa and plunder where they would. I want them to know that this dog still has teeth and while we might be hurt, we will not always be."

We pushed on after the sun had dipped a little. The noonday heat was unbearable. I stored that nugget of information. We rode on into the night and camped in a clearing in the forests to the south of the river. We lit a fire for I could smell the woodsmoke from those who lived in this part of Italy. Rising before dawn we headed for Empoli. It was as we neared the city, before the noonday sun, that we saw the Florentines still camped there.

"They are moving more slowly than I expected, Captain."

I nodded, "Aye, Robin. I am guessing that whoever commands wishes to keep them together. They fear that we may ambush them. That helps us as it slows their approach and we will have time to meet them." We dismounted and headed up into the trees. I did not wish to be seen and the extra elevation would give us a clearer picture of what we faced. I leaned against a tree and drank from the ale skin. Giovanni could never understand why I drank ale instead of wine. I found ale more refreshing and it was what I had grown up with. I spied their scouts, both the ones who ranged ahead and the light horsemen. They were close to the river beneath a stand of trees, their horses grazing on the grass. I had been right. There were about a hundred horsemen all told and they would, I did not doubt, leave the noonday halt first. They were mounted and it was clear that with the bulk of their men on foot it would take some time to march the thirty odd miles to Pisa. What I saw troubled me. I spied the mercenaries we had last faced in Montferrat. I recognised the pavise of Grimaldi's Genoese crossbowmen. We had beaten them then but we had enjoyed more than a fair degree of luck. When we had fought them at Florence, we had enjoyed a superiority we no longer had. I also saw the horsemen of Enrico Monforte. Again they had been defeated by us but I had used the terrain to do so. The bulk of the army appeared to be Florentine militia but I recognised the Germans of Baumgarten. He had not taken long to return to the paymasters. What was Galeazzo Visconti playing at? He seemed to me like a puppeteer who was moving marionettes around at will.

What I did not see were my Englishmen. I could not see the men at arms who had followed Sir Andrew. There would be former comrades with Baumgarten but the one good part was that we would not have to fight fellow countrymen.

I had seen enough, "Come, let us walk our horses through the trees. I would get beyond San Miniato Basso before their scouts."

Robin said, "You have a plan?"

I nodded and spoke over my shoulder. We were in the forest which was cooler than the road and none could hear us, "I would ambush their scouts. I want their light horsemen cautious and nervous. We need to slow them up. I had hoped to stop the Florentines at Pontedera where the river is close to the city but they will reach there before we can muster the army and return. Cascina is the next best site to halt them and even that is perilously close to Pisa but I can see no alternative. I think they will reach Pontedera at about noon tomorrow. The scouts will ride beyond the town and ensure that the road ahead is clear."

Robin said, "No offence, gentlemen, but Sir John should have brought archers instead of men at arms."

"You forget, Robin, that I brought my bow."

"And without offending you, Sir John, may I ask how many years is it since you drew your warbow? Five? Ten?"

"I know what you are saying and you are right, I have less than my full strength now but I still have skill. I was at the mark last year with Martin and while I could not hit the long mark the shorter ones were no problem. You and I will halt them in the road and Dai and Giovanni can cut off their escape. I want no prisoners. We take their horses so that their horsemen waste time looking for their scouts."

"You assume we can take them, Sir John, and yet you do not know the exact numbers."

"I counted six men who were apart from the bulk of the horseman, Dai. They carried neither shields nor helmets. I can hit one man and Captain Robin here should be able to deal with two. That leaves three men for you two and Robin and I can help. I believe we can succeed. When that is done, we ride for Pisa and the army."

The road out of Pontedera twisted and rose around some ancient, tumbled rocks and when we reached it at noon, our horses were exhausted. Trees had sprouted along the side of the old road and it was a place of shade. Normally such trees would have been cut down but here the need for shelter from the sun allowed them to live and although they were not as green as they would have been in England, there was enough cover to disguise Robin and me on either side of the road. We tethered our horses where they would not be seen and Giovanni and Dai rode back towards Pontedera to find a place they could stay hidden with their horses. I did not need to check on them for they knew their business.

When they had gone Robin said, "Sir John, you are no longer an archer. You are a knight who can use a bow and that is good but here I command." I nodded. "Do not draw until you see me draw and you release when my arrow is in the air. You take the one on the right and I will eliminate the one on the left. You may try a second but if we manage to hit two then I think they will flee. I am confident of hitting a third but you…"

I nodded but growled irritably, "You are right to speak to me thus, Robin, but do not make a habit of it. Believe me, I know my own limitations. Besides it is good that I get to loose an arrow here in Italy for I have not sent one in anger since France."

I only had five arrows and all were war arrows. The barbed end would cause a nasty wound. I chose the straightest shaft and the fletch that took my fancy. It was what all archers did. Choosing what you thought was the best arrow gave you confidence. I nocked the arrow and held the bow and arrow lightly in my left hand. An archer wanted all his strength for the pull.

We heard the horses in the distance but we stayed hidden. The art of ambush was to hold your nerve until the moment you struck. By making the distance between the scouts and us as short as possible we maximised our chances of success. We heard the horses draw closer. It was tempting to peer out but the flash of a white face would alert them. The sun would be in their eyes and I hoped, blind them just a little. I knew that the men would be about ready to turn around and join the army that would be resting at Pontedera to avoid the noonday heat. That would be when they would be at their least alert and that was why the ambush site was a godsend.

I kept my eye on Robin for archers have a sixth sense that I had lost over the years. I saw him nod to me and draw. Stepping out I began to draw and even before I was half way my shoulders were hurting. I saw the horsemen as Robin's arrow flew. Three riders were before us and less than forty feet away. It was even shorter than the shortest mark archers used on Sunday morning and I pulled back and released. It was not a full draw but it was enough and it slammed into the chest of the rider on my right. Even as I pulled a second arrow the third rider was wheeling his horse around but it was too late for him as Robin's arrow knocked him from the saddle. The other three had turned and the range was longer but my old instincts had returned and I pulled back and released. Taking a third arrow I kept my eyes on the three men as I watched Giovanni and Dai emerge from cover.

My second arrow hit one of the scouts but it was in the shoulder. Robin's was a mortal strike and the arms in the crucifix position told me that a fourth scout had died. The two scouts had barely drawn their swords before my two knights slew them.

"Get the horses."

Robin was unstringing his bow as he said, "Not bad, my lord. If you were to practise every day, we might find a use for you."

I laughed, "My burning shoulders tell me that it is easier to be a man at arms than an archer. We need to dispose of the bodies in the river. The current will take them from view and the horsemen will have a longer search.

The disposal of the bodies allowed all the horses a longer rest than they might have expected but time was pressing. When the scouts failed to return, then men would be sent to seek them and I wanted to be well down the road before that happened. As I mounted and took the reins of the horse I would be leading I saw the patches of blood on the ground. We had no time to clear it and it would tell the Florentines where the ambush had taken place. We headed down the road and soon reached Cascina. It was where I planned to halt the Florentines and although time was pressing, I took the opportunity to inspect the town. It had narrow streets and there was rough ground. It was close enough to Pisa so that when they raided the land around the attack would draw an army to them. That was my hope. I needed a day more and if they stayed in Cascina then we had a chance. It was a slim one but a desperate man who is drowning clings to any branch no matter how flimsy. Four miles from Cascina we passed the abbey of San Savino. It had good walls and I determined to make that my headquarters. We hurried the last miles to Pisa and while my men went to rouse the company and prepare them for a morning march, I sought out the doge, chamberlain and Manetti. I told them of the danger and my plans.

"We will need every man from Pisa who can wield a weapon. The narrow valley means it is unlikely that we will need horsemen and I will bolster your militia with my company."

Pellario Griffo asked, "Can we win?"

"Honestly?" He nodded. "No, but not winning does not mean we might be defeated. We need to stop them and that is the best we can hope."

The doge nodded, "Thank you for your honesty."

When I reached my hall Robin said, "I have sent ten archers to watch for the enemy. Ned and Karl lead them. We will have notice of their arrival."

"Good and now we eat!"

A good soldier always ate when he could and the rigours of the last few days had meant I was starving.

In the end, we were granted two days of grace. My company had occupied the abbey, despite the complaints of the abbot and di Jesi's men had begun to arrive when my archers reported that the Florentines were fortifying the town of Cascina and digging ditches. They were plundering the land. Sad though that was for the Pisans who lived there, it would allow me to bring as many men as I could to the battle and I began to plan.

I had a limited number of men with me. There were less than nine hundred who came from the White Company. We had yet to call ourselves the Company of St George. We were just seven miles from Pisa and if we did not hold them here then the Florentines would have won. I spoke with the abbot of the monastery and warned him that we might end up defending San Savino if my plan failed. The man was no fool and he and his friars began to take all that was of value into Pisa. The cathedral would be the place where they could secure their gold. It meant that, as darkness approached, we had the monastery to ourselves. I gathered my leaders and we ate the food the friars had prepared for their own evening meal.

"My plan is a simple one and has been forced on me by circumstances." Manetti had come with us and I nodded to him as we devoured the simple meal, "General, I intend to make three feint attacks before noon. I want them fatigued and I need to have the sun in their eyes. The real attack will be after the sun has reached its zenith. The defenders will be tired. I will send in one hundred of my men with a third of yours to assault the ditches. My two archer captains will direct arrows into their camp. Our only hope is a quick victory and to drive them from Cascina despite our lack of numbers. They will believe that their ditches will hold us but they will not."

Manetti nodded, "And who will lead this assault?"

"I have two men in mind, Robert Duggan and John Onslow. They are popular amongst the men and both good fighters."

"You do not need one of the Pisan knights to lead?"

"General, we will not be using horses. The ground does not suit and we must assault trenches. I will keep the bulk of my men and the archers to exploit the breach our men will make."

Manetti returned to his men to decide who would be in the vanguard. I sent for Robert and John and, as I had expected they were delighted with the promotion. Being mercenary men, as we all were, they asked what the payment would be for their service.

"Carry the ditches and you will both become captains. Your pay will double as leaders. Is that enough?"

"Aye." They were both eager. I gave them the list of men they would be leading and they seemed satisfied. They left to prepare the men they would lead.

My inner circle remained and we drank the monastery's wine and spoke of how we would exploit a victory. Sir Eoin said, "Of course, Sir John, they may realise that all the men that they lead were the ones who deserted and returned."

I wondered if any other would notice. I shrugged, "And should they not be given the chance to redeem themselves? Why should those who remained loyal be the ones to take the risks?"

I could see that I had not convinced them but I did not need to. I was now the single leader of the company or at least the half that had remained loyal. As far as I knew Andrew de Belmonte now led the rest of our men and he and my former compatriots were raiding around Perugia, trying to take the Neapolitan lands.

Robin spat into the fire, "They are warriors and warriors fight. If they do not then they should find a farm and raise children and beans. If you were to send me to lead, I would not be unhappy, Sir John. I am a good archer and I know how to survive."

"You and Martin will have to use your skills to judge the rate of arrows. I shall be with the mainward and the battle will be determined by Duggan and your archers." I looked at each of them in the eye. "I cannot afford to lose the rest of my company. If I did lose them then I doubt I would gain such a fine company again."

Giovanni shook his head, "You are allowing the desertions to be a greater betrayal than it really was. We are all mercenaries. Are you really surprised that they took the offer of gold?"

"None of you did."

He laughed, "And that is because we know there will be more treasure with you. None of the other leaders of the mercenary bands has your skill, Sir John. Trust in that skill."

Chapter 11

The Battle of Cascina 28th of July 1364

We left the monastery before first light so that when the Florentine night sentries were relieved the new sentries suddenly found, as the sun rose, a Pisan host before them. I went with my leaders and captains of archers to the vanguard. All were eager and ready to fight. Robert Duggan had managed to make both the Pisans and the English he led, keen to get to grips with the Florentines. He was a good leader. The Florentines prepared their battle lines and I waited until they had arrayed most of the crossbows, handguns and archers before I gave the order. Our horns sounded and then Robert and John led their men in a wild charge. The Florentines sent volleys from crossbows and handguns at them and the smoke from the handguns obscured the attack. By the time it cleared our feint attack had returned. We had lost not a single man. I smiled as Malatesta reorganised his men.

An hour later we repeated the attack and once more the guns blasted and the crossbows cracked. The horsemen mounted their horses. All this time the bulk of our men were resting, out of sight. It was just this one part of our army that was engaging the Florentines. The third attack was launched an hour before noon and I noticed that fewer guns fired and only a third of the crossbows.

I nodded, "It is almost time. I will go and rouse the rest of our command and fetch forward the archers. Have your men rest." I shaded my hand against the sun whose heat was making even me feel tired and I had not stood to, like the Florentines. The mail and plate we all wore was good protection but, in this heat, it also sapped energy. My archers had all been resting, their bows yet to be strung. So far all was going well and my plan seemed to me to have a one in three chance of success.

Michael had my ale skin waiting for me, "Do I fight with you, this day, Sir John?"

"No, Michael, but stay close. You are the one messenger that all know comes from me. When I give my orders then you will be the one to deliver it." He nodded. "Captains Robin and Martin, now is the time.

"Are all their crossbows on the front line, Sir John?"

"No Robin, but I put that down to the heat. I counted about half of Grimaldi's company."

I did not don my helmet, Michael carried it as we headed back to the front line. I waited until the churches in Cascina sounded noon before I nodded to my archers. The Florentines were, generally, lying down and taking what shade they could. I could not see them but I guessed that many would be asleep in the shade afforded by the bottom of the trenches. The echo of the last bell had drifted away before I said to my two archer captains and to Robert, "Now is your time. Remember no cheers and shouts, Robert. Let them slumber before you grant them the gift of eternal sleep."

Robin said, "Archers, draw." Our front line had drawn up closer to the enemy lines than in the three false attacks. We had five hundred archers and their arrows would tear huge holes in the enemy lines. Robert and John stood and waved their swords in the air. The whole line rose and even before they had taken two steps a flight of arrows soared into the air. Our attackers moved quite quickly but the archers still managed to send another four flights before a hundred paces had been covered. The cries from the Florentines told us that they knew they were being attacked but their horses had been withdrawn into the shade and the handguns and crossbows were not loaded.

By the time the arrow shower had ceased our men had taken the first of the ditches and I shouted, "Forward!"

We did not run for it was hot but our solid lines moved as one and we followed the triumphant Duggan and Onslow as they now screamed and cheered as they ran into the centre of Cascina. I did not allow myself to get carried away. We had hurt them but victory was far from in our grasp. The Florentine front line was broken and I saw men fleeing. By the time the main part of our army reached the ditches I saw that we had slain more than three hundred men with arrows, swords and, it must be said, surprise. The attack had been underway for less than an hour when I saw the character of the Florentines.

Grimaldi's Genoese had cut loopholes in the buildings along which Duggan and Onslow led our men. Our most advanced men were now in the Florentine camp and the baggage. I think they might have endured the bolts if they had not been attacked on the other flank by Enrico Montforte and his German and Florentine horsemen.

I saw that the main part of our army, the one I led, was in danger of being cut off from the abbey. It was time for a dramatic decision. "Michael, sound the retreat. Archers, cover us!"

The enemy horsemen had managed to outflank us by heading south out of sight and their advance was close to our camp. I donned my helmet and drew my sword. With my best knights, I ran at the horsemen. The ground did not suit cavalry and that was why I had not used them. Their lances, however, allowed them to pick us off at will.

"Michael, find men to get the wounded back to the abbey." Already men who had been struck by bolts were struggling to get back to our lines. I was not concerned about the Pisans but my men were valuable. I needed all of them, including those with wounds.

"Aye, my lord. You four fellows come with me. You heard Sir John's orders!" Michael was growing day by day.

Dai and Sir Eoin flanked me and we ran fearlessly at the charging horsemen. I saw that John of Ecclestone and William Hammer Hand were with me. They were both good warriors. I wore mailed gauntlets and when the German mercenary pulled back his lance to skewer me I stepped to the other side of the German's horse and punched it on the side of the head. It wore a mail shaffron but I hurt it and as it veered away, I hacked my sword at the mercenary's leg. It was unprotected and I sliced through to the bone. Falling from his horse he kept hold of the reins and the already shaken animal fell to the ground. The horses who were following also had to veer away and the German line was unable to maintain its cohesion. Dai and Sir Eoin hacked at the legs of the horses and those at the rear saw what was happening and chose to head away from us. there were easier targets, notably the Pisans. The Pisans, even the nobles were intimidated by the horses. We were not for we had fought mounted and knew how to hurt a horse and rider.

"Fall back but face your front!" The worst thing you could do when chased by a lancer was to turn your back. You would be a dead man running.

We glanced back to see that the ground was clear and then marched back steadily to the abbey which was now three miles away. I think, that despite our courage we might have all perished but for our archers. They sent flight after flight at the German and Florentine horsemen who were the greatest threat. Our attack had failed but we had delayed their men on foot and it would take them time to recover and to follow us. The arrows did not kill a great many but they wounded both men and horses. The heat of the day began to get to me but we kept a steady, albeit slow pace back and that enabled more wounded to be recovered than we might have hoped. It was our archers who reached the abbey first and then manned the walls. We entered and I stood at the gate with Dai, Eoin and Giovanni to guard it while the rest of the army arrived. The Pisans who had survived did not enter the abbey. They kept running for Pisa and many paid with their lives as the lancers chased them down. When the last survivors of the attack, led by a badly wounded John Onslow reached the abbey, we slammed shut the gates. The sun was setting and no one fought at night. We had lost but it had not been a disaster.

Manetti di Jesi had reached us and we had some of his Pisan doctors. Leaving Sir Eoin to watch the gates and the enemy I went with John Onslow to the doctors. His shoulder and leg had been laid open to the bone and the Pisan doctor shook his head and said, quietly, "I could remove the leg if that was his only wound but the shoulder." He nodded towards the hammer that was kept to end the lives of those too wounded to be saved.

I shook my head, "He is my man and I will stay with him."

His eyes opened and he said, "We almost made it, Sir John. Robert died well and he took three of those Germans before they slew him. We have regained some of our honour." He winced.

"You are dying, John."

He opened his eyes again, "I know, my lord."

"Do you want me to end the pain?" I took out my dagger.

"No, my lord. I am soon to have the long sleep of death and warriors bear pain, do they not? If you would, my lord, I would have you stay with me until I pass."

"Of course. What would you have me do with your money? I will honour our agreement."

"I have a sister in Wigan, my lord. it is a small mean village and she and her husband struggle to raise pigs. Whatever I have left from my pay and when the others sell my war gear will make them the richest in that village. Perhaps she will think better of me."

"Forget your sister, John, we shall remember you."

"I know I let you down and that this was my last chance at redemption. I am content. I made a mistake and I paid with my life. I am tired. I pray you to hold my hand to help me in the darkness."

I took his hand and when he could grip no longer then I knew he was dead.

Michael was next to me. I turned and said, "Take his war gear and his coins. We shall do as he asked and send them to his sister."

"Aye, my lord. And the others?"

"Take their war gear. Find a wagon. When we have buried our dead then we head back to Pisa. We live and we shall fight another day."

Like thieves in the night, we crept back into Pisa. The journey, short though it was seemed to take forever. The carts we had taken to carry our wounded were laden and we greased the wheels before we left. Our horses walked slowly so as to make as little noise as possible and to make the journey as jolt free as we could. The fleeing Pisans had warned the city and doctors were ready as we filed through the gates. I did not report to either the doge or the chamberlain. I had walls to man and my wounded to see to. The warriors who remained unhurt I put on the walls and spread them around so that the shaken Pisans had a steel band of my company to firm them up. Our archers were similarly spread out.

I found Manetti at the main gate. He shook his head, "It was a brave and bold attempt, Sir John, but we failed."

I agreed with him but I had to show confidence. They say that a defeat makes a good leader great for he learns from his mistakes. This was my first major defeat and I did not like it. "We hurt them, my lord, and I do not think that we have given them free rein to raid. My company is still horsed and we can sally forth if they try to make this into a chevauchée. I will not allow them to make the lives of the Pisans a misery as we did with the Florentines. They shall not take the animals and crops that will feed us through the winter."

He smiled, "You are a professional and I can see that your pride has been damaged but do you really think that your men, how many are there now? Less than six hundred? Can such a small band hurt the mighty war machine of the Florentines?"

"You forget one thing, General, my archers emerged intact. It is they who can control enemy raiders. We can strike from distance and, being well mounted, ride away again. Hit and run. I will get William to hire more men. They will come."

That was one thing my leaders had said to me on the ride back to Pisa. My bold plan, although it had failed would draw men to me. I now knew that the men who had deserted me still had heart. John and Robert had died well. I had been wrong to dismiss them for one mistake. My trouble had been that I had taken it all too personally. We were a business and my men had received a better offer. Was I that different? I had resolved, as the night had passed, to lead in a different way. If Andrew and any of the other men who had fought for me tried to return then I would welcome them with open arms. John's deathbed confession had touched me. He had known that he and the others had been sacrificed and yet he had still been proud to serve.

It was almost noon when the Florentine army arrived. It was clear that they came to gloat rather than to fight. They made a point of doing as the Pisans had done at Florence and rode around the walls insulting Pisa and offering single combat. I noticed that they did so beyond the range of my archers although I could if I had chosen have ordered my best archers to send a few barbs of our own in reply to their words. I chose not to. I wanted the Florentines to think that we had lost good archers when, in fact, the best warriors were still intact. This was the time to let them think that we had been beaten. They stayed for one night and then headed back to Florence.

I rode with some of my men back to the scene of the battle. Bodies still lay where they had fallen although they were stripped and naked. After ensuring that the Florentines had gone, we buried them. We buried Robert with his friend John. Their graves were together in the abbey of San Savino. We would remember them. I, certainly, would never forget them for they had changed me and my view of my world of war.

The Florentines had taken two thousand Pisans prisoners. The members of my company who had been captured were set free and thirty of them rejoined us a week after the battle. Giovanni Agnello was now secure as doge and he was true to his word. He paid me the money he had promised and William banked it for me. There was an irony to the fact that while we had been defeated my company was now better off financially than it had ever been. The defeat had not diminished my reputation and I began to plan.

William, however, was distracted as he was now courting Bianca Agnello. I did not need him for what I planned next. I took Robin, Dai, Michael, and Giovanni with me when we rode, in late August, to Lucca. We had word that the White Company, as they now called themselves, commanded by Sir Andrew, and the Flower Company were raiding around Lucca. I wanted to get close to them for I still harboured the thought that I might win back the ones who had deserted me. Even as we rode north to Lucca, it struck me that my task was impossible. Why should they leave the financially rewarding camp of the Florentines to join me? I suppose pride made me go and as we had successfully proved the last time my little band was more than capable of hiding in plain sight.

We learned as we headed into the mountains that, as autumn approached, it could be cold in the Tuscan hills and I was pleased that Giovanni had been the one to advise us to take with us furs and good well-oiled cloaks to keep out the wind and the cold. Unlike the last time we had scouted we wore mail. As we neared the area controlled by the two companies, we saw evidence of the devastation caused by them. There were burnt out farms and unburied corpses. That was the difference between the English and German companies. The Germans and Hungarians were quite happy to use terror but the English, perhaps prompted by my philosophy, just took their goods and not their lives.

Robin waved a hand as we passed through another empty farm, "This is the work of the Germans."

"How do you know?"

In answer, he pointed to the buildings, "Those are quarrels, crossbow bolts, Sir John, and not arrows. Sir Andrew employs archers. We will know when we reach the land that is controlled by our former comrades for there will be fewer bodies and no bolts."

My wise old archer was right and when we reached the area that was being raided by the White Company, we began to look for their camp. As we had headed further away from Pisa an idea had begun to form. I would seek a reconciliation with the rest of my company. It was, in terms of numbers, the greater half. We found their camp to the northeast of Lucca. We rode into their camp on a desperately cold night in the first week of September. I knew it was a risk as we did so but sometimes you have to take such a chance and I believed, perhaps arrogantly, that my name still meant something to the men I had led in Burgundy, Montferrat, Savoy and Florence. To my relief, as we rode through the camp we were cheered and greeted like old friends. Perhaps they thought we had come to join them. We had not. The house used by Sir Andrew was marked with standards and flags and we reined in. The five of us had spoken as we had headed northeast and no words were necessary. Michael took the horses and the other three disappeared into the camp, their orders had been clear.

Sir Andrew emerged and he beamed. He had grown a little older in the short time we had been apart. The sole leadership of a company will do that to a man. "Sir John, my heart sings at this visit for it means, I hope, that you have forgiven me."

I clasped his arm in a warrior's grip and shook my head, "I was angry, Andrew, for I felt betrayed however you were not doing this to me but to win the love of your life. How is your lady?"

"She is well and we are to be wed later this month. The divorce has been granted by the Pope. Lord Visconti has been more than helpful."

We entered the house and servants quickly fetched in food and drink. A blazing fire in the hearth drew us there.

"I am pleased for you. Congratulations."

"Come, sit by the fire. These mountains chill a man to the bone, eh Sir John?"

I took off my fur and my cloak. I would need their warmth when I left this cosy nest.

"Did I hear that Robin, Dai and Giovanni are with you?"

"Aye, they acted as my bodyguards." Anticipating the next question I added, "They are seeking old friends. They will join us later."

"And what brings you here?" Sir Andrew's voice had become more guarded. He was a clever man and knew that my arrival was not just an accident.

"You and Baumgarten are raiding Pisan land. I am still employed by Pisa." I shrugged, "I may have to bring the company and drive you hence."

He laughed, "Yet you would be outnumbered by more than four to one."

It was my turn to smile, "And when would that stop me?"

"You say may. Does that mean you might not?"

I sipped the wine and it was excellent. I placed it on the table next to me and looked Andrew in the eye. "Do you enjoy serving Florence?"

"They are good paymasters."

"Suppose you could have the same pay from Pisa. What then?"

"You mean rejoin the White Company?"

"The White Company died on the foothills of Florence. Let us say we form a new company and start afresh."

He took his own goblet and drank deeply. I could see his mind working as he wrestled with the problems. His soon to be wife lived in Florentine land and the Florentines would not take kindly to his desertion. I attacked from a different direction.

"How goes it, serving with Baumgarten and his Germans?"

His face hardened, "They are animals and there is not a gentleman amongst them. General Malatesta has had to reprimand them on many occasions for they go beyond all common decency."

"If you served with Pisa then you would not have the problem of Baumgarten, except as an enemy."

"And that does appeal, Sir John. May I speak openly?"

"Of course, for that was ever my way."

"I do not lead this company as you led the White Company. We share decisions and this is not mine to make alone. You should know, as leader of the Pisans, that this raid is not going well. The Luccans hate Florence and they resist fiercely. Both Baumgarten and I have lost men and horses. The valley of the Arno would be a more profitable place to raid."

I now knew the land well, "San Minato?"

He looked shocked and then laughed, "God's blood but you are a mind reader, Sir John."

I shrugged, "It is where I would raid."

He stared into the fire, "Give me until the end of September. Come then to my wife's castle and I will let you know what my men have decided."

"Why not speak to them now, while I am here?"

He shook his head, "You have come, Sir John, when we are about to depart. We have been ordered by General Malatesta to camp on the Ceccina."

"That is even colder than here."

"I know," he said glumly, "but he has ordered Baumgarten to Val d'Elsa. He wishes us apart. At one time I would have thought it so that we would not combine and turn on him but now I know it is to keep us apart. The general, it seems, has learned that if you are to have guard dogs then they should be the same breed."

I spied hope in all this. My scouting expedition had not been in vain. The companies would be leaving Lucca and I now knew where they would be attacking.

"I will come to your home, Sir Andrew in September. Tell your men that all is forgiven so long as they return to the fold." I engaged his eyes as I might a spear with a poleaxe, "You get my meaning?"

"I do. Either we are friends or we are foes and I know which I would rather be. I shall be eloquent in my arguments."

Chapter 12

Our ride back to Pisa was uneventful but I learned much. Robin and the others had discovered that there was much discontent in the camp. They hated the Germans. There had been fights and deaths. It was clear why General Malatesta was ordering them apart.

"They will all rejoin us, Sir John, but the question is when?" Dai asked.

"By the end of September, I will have an answer."

"That is not long."

"Long enough. We need to warn San Minato of the imminent arrival of the two companies."

Giovanni gave me a sharp look, "We do not interfere?"

"Giovanni, do you think we would stand any chance of defeating either company at the moment? Besides, I do not wish to fight the White Company when they are about to rejoin us. No, San Miniato can defend its own walls. It is autumn and they will be gathering in their animals and crops. This warning we give them just makes them do it a little earlier. If they find nothing to raid then they will seek other masters."

The now secure doge and the chamberlain concurred with my view when we met in his palace. "I will order General di Jesi to take word himself to San Miniato." The doge smiled, "You are resilient, Sir John. Most leaders would have been disheartened by the setback of Cascina but you seem to have gained strength from it."

"That is because I learned from the defeat. Do not honey your words, doge, I was defeated. The reason was simple. I did not have all my company. I will regain that company and they will be paid by Pisa, correct?"

The chamberlain nodded, "Of course. Soon it will be winter and there will be no more campaigning. We will have the winter to prepare for the Florentines."

"It may well be, chamberlain, that Florence tires of this war and may sue for permanent peace. They have paid a high price for the two companies. They might see peace as a cheaper alternative."

"And that way you would lose money, Sir John."

I shook my head, "There are always men happy to employ swords for hire." Looking him in the eyes I said slowly, "We have until January to find a new employer for by then this contract will be over."

The doge peered at me, "You are saying that you would leave Pisa? You would serve Florence?"

"I think that you will find Florence, like you, tires of this war. It has swung back and forth but you must both realise that paying men such as us is expensive and if both sides hire a company, then there will be a sort of stalemate."

The doge smiled, "I think my friend, Bernabò Visconti, may have some work for you. We shall see."

There had been a time I would have dismissed an offer of work from the Visconti family out of hand but I was now more pragmatic and realised that I had to work with the devil if I was to continue to work in Italy and as Italy paid more than anywhere else then I would have to swallow my doubts.

"I shall consider all offers."

"Then I will make the arrangements."

"Thank you."

"Perhaps the wedding of my daughter Bianca to William might be such an opportunity."

William had not mentioned it but, then again, I had been away in Lucca for some days. It could do us no harm for the doge was both the richest and most powerful man in Pisa.

"And when will that be?"

"October."

"Then that will give time to arrange to reorganise my company and make it so strong that none will dare to attack Pisa."

I had already decided, even before I left the palace, that I would continue to serve Pisa after the present contract was ended. I doubted that it would pay as much as at present but it would feed and house us until we could find a paymaster who could afford to pay the fees I was now confident we could ask.

William was almost embarrassed that he had not spoken to me about his impending marriage. I waved away his apologies,

"You have your own life to lead and I know that no offence was intended. It means that you will live in Pisa?"

"Yes, Sir John, the doge has given us a fine mansion by the river."

"Then we will keep our money in the Pisan banks. I have a mind to employ the time expired warriors as guards for you and our money. Some of those who stayed with us after Figline did so because they are getting too old to fight and wanted the security I offered. I will reward that loyalty."

"But will that leave us with enough men?"

I realised I had not yet told him my news, "I am meeting with Belmonte soon and I hope to reunite the White Company." I held nothing back as I told him my news.

A week later we heard that both the White Company and the Company of the Flower had been badly handled in San Miniato and had departed after losing many men and horses to peasants and townsfolk who were prepared. The White Company were in Florence while the Flower Company just disappeared. With my usual companions I set off in the last week of September for the castle Sir Andrew had taken as his home. It was in Figline. The place seemed irrevocably intertwined with my fate.

We knew the roads well and managed to avoid, thanks to Robin's skills, any potential enemy. In fact, I think only a handful of woodcutters knew we were about and they would have had no idea who we were. When we reached the castle I saw that Sir Andrew's lady was both beautiful and gracious but I knew that she did not like the fact that we were in her home. Sir John Hawkwood brought only danger. She spent as little time as she could with us but when she was in our company she laughed and showed a wit that told me the couple were made for one another.

"I have spoken with my men, Sir John, and they are all happy to fight under your banner." I was pleased he said my banner for it meant he accepted my authority.

"That is good. And Baumgarten?"

"Have you not heard, Sir John? He has joined with your old comrade Albert Sterz, and their men are now the Star Company or the Stellar Company. I have heard both names used but the reality is that they have been hired by Perugia to make war on the King of Naples and Queen Joanna."

I rapidly processed that information. The two companies combined would dwarf the White Company but they were now far to the south and that suited me. "And you will bring your men to Pisa?"

"Would November be too soon?" He smiled, "It is cold along the Cecina and Pisa is warmer but I am not sure they would be welcomed."

"They will be welcomed."

We stayed just two days as I was mindful of a number of things, the passes would become harder to negotiate, William had his wedding but, most importantly, Andrew's lady wished time with her new husband to be. We left for the two-day ride back to Pisa.

While we had been unobserved on the way to the castle there were too many visitors to the castle for that situation to remain. People knew we were in Florentine land and, when we left, we were wary for we knew I had many enemies. Malatesta was not one of them. He had shown after his victory at Cascina that he was not vindictive. The mercenaries he had captured had been treated well and freed almost immediately, with their weapons. It was other mercenaries that were the danger. Baumgarten, Paer and Sterz were none of them my friends. We rode as though we expected to be attacked. The attack, when it did come, was closer to Pisa than was comfortable. I think anyone else could have been relaxed as we left Pontedera but we still rode mailed and with our two bows strung. The ambushers also made the unfortunate mistake of choosing the place we had ambushed the Florentine scouts. We were all looking for danger and when we saw the covey of pigeons take to the air and recognised the bend in the road then we knew.

Knowing that there would be an ambush and being able to do something about it were two entirely different matters. We had one difference this time. Michael was with us and he could hold horses. I looked at Robin who nodded. We reined in and I said, "Michael hold the horses and keep between them." I took my bow from its case and strung it.

The ambushers would be listening for the sound of our hooves to grow closer. There was no sound and they would be wondering why we had stopped. I nocked an arrow and began to move up the road. Dai and Giovanni drew their swords and lifted their shields up. Robin and I walked along the edge of the road, perilously close to the two ditches that paralleled it. I glanced to the left and saw that there was some tussocky grass and then shrubs before the thin spindly trees sprouted. I would be able to dive there if I needed to. I whistled and I heard Dai and Giovanni move their horses forward. The sound of the hooves would be reassuring to the ambushers but the whistle would make them wary. The face that appeared was just fifty feet away but I had no clear sight of it. Robin, on the other side of the road, did and the master archer drew and released before the head could dart back. I heard the sound of the arrow as it cracked through bone and then the dying scream of the man rang through the air. The ambushers knew that their plan had been thwarted and they burst from cover.

Thanks to Robin's arrow they had no idea of our formation and they had to step from cover to use their weapons. I drew back as the men appeared and when I saw the crossbow, I released. A crossbow is a cumbersome weapon but it does afford some protection to the user. My arrow hit the frame of the bow. Sadly for the crossbowman, the deflection drove my arrow into his eye. I drew another as the eight other men burst from cover. Like me, Robin recognised the danger of a crossbow to our riders and his arrow sank deep into the chest of the second crossbowman. The remaining seven were a mixture of Hungarians and Germans and they had lances and swords. It was tempting to dive into the bottom of the ditch but, instead, I drew back the bow and aimed at the mailed man on the right of the horsemen riding towards us. Robin would deal with the nearest one on the other side. I sent the war arrow at his chest. My lack of regular training showed and the arrow drove into the neck of his horse. The animal reared and veered at the same time forcing the men behind to take evasive action. Robin's bodkin did not miss and his rider fell. I nocked another arrow and sent it at the knight who rode with couched lance at me. My arm was burning with the effort but I pulled my arm back just a little further and released. The arrow was a lucky one. It managed, at a range of fifteen feet, to drive through the mail coif around the knight's neck and into his throat. His lance fell at my feet.

Dropping the bow I picked up the lance as the horse with the dying rider careered past me down the slope. Dai and Giovanni were now engaged and as I swept the lance around to fend off the next warrior, I saw that Robin had wisely ducked into the trees on his side of the road. Another arrow slammed into the side of one of the German men at arms and I rammed the lance up at a surprised Hungarian man at arms. His lance caught the side of my helmet and made my ears ring but mine drove into his thigh, through his saddle and into his horse. The lance was dragged from my hands and the Hungarian followed the fleeing horses down the slope.

His departure heralded a retreat from the survivors. Robin manage to hit one in the back with an arrow but the German kept his saddle. Peering down the road I saw that Michael had wisely moved away from the road and the three wounded mercenaries who had survived were heading towards Pontedera. I drew my sword and approached the men we had struck in case any survived. They were all dead. Three of their horses remained and we bundled the bodies of the knights onto their backs.

As we did so Dai said, "I recognise this one, Sir John. He was one of Lazlo's friends."

Giovanni pointed down the road, "And the Hungarian you speared was one also."

"Then this was an attack intent on revenge."

Giovanni said, "Perhaps but Baumgarten and Sterz both know your worth. They will know that you have retaken the White Company. I would not put it past either of them to let it be known where you were and encourage these men to have their revenge on you. It would suit their purpose."

Giovanni was an expert in the politics of the professional soldier. We asked the monks of San Savino to bury the dead men but took their horses, armour and weapons with us as well as their bulging purses. I realised as we entered Pisa's gates that I was now a target for enemies. I would need more than four men to watch my back in future.

The day we reached Pisa I found a papal envoy waiting to see me. He was staying in the palace but the doge was not the man he wished to speak to. It was me. When I was brought into his presence the doge gave a warning shake of his head and I wondered what was going on. The envoy, Cardinal Gil Álvarez Carrillo de Albornoz, asked for privacy and I remained in the room with just William as a witness. I knew the reputation of the Cardinal who was a most powerful churchman. When Pope Innocent had died there had been pressure for him to be elected but he declined in favour of Pope Urban. He was a warrior cardinal and both the popes under whom he had served had used him to raise armies and fortify papal towns.

He did not look like a holy man. He had the lean and hungry look of a wolf and when he spoke it was with authority. "Are you a religious man, Sir John?"

"I go to church, attend mass and I confess to a priest."

His smile had no warmth in it, "Yet you robbed from the church when you led your men in Burgundy."

I was not offended by the remark and I shrugged, "I confessed my sins and Pope Innocent forgave me. Since that time I have not taken from the church."

"Yet you used the abbey of San Savino as a fortress did you not?"

I thought it disingenuous to be criticised for doing just what the Cardinal was famous for doing, "The monks were safe in Pisa and the abbey remained unharmed and undamaged."

Seemingly satisfied and having got the rebuke out of the way he came to the point with a blunt speed I admired, "Sir John, Pope Urban has sent me with a holy mission. He wishes you to lead a confederation of free companies to stop the ravages of Bernabò Visconti. When you have succeeded then he wishes you to lead a crusade against the Turks. He sees you as a clever leader and the one man who has the ability to stop the advance of these enemies of Christ."

I now saw why the doge had given me a warning look. Even without his disapproval, I would be less than happy to undertake this commission and I certainly did not wish to fight the Turks. There would be no profit in it. However, I could not refuse outright and I would have to show both diplomacy and tact in any answer I gave.

"I am both flattered and honoured by the Holy Father's offer. Know that I am, until the New Year, bound to serve Pisa."

"This war would not be needed until next spring."

"And, of course, while I can answer for my own company, the others that you require will need to agree to serve under me." I knew that neither Sterz nor Baumgarten would agree."

"Then, Sir John, if I can persuade the other commanders of these companies to serve under your leadership then you will fight against Bernabò Visconti?"

I nodded, "If the Holy Father wishes to wage a crusade against the enemies of peace in Italy, then I will happily support him." My words were vague enough that I could argue, in the unlikely event that the others would serve under me, that I never actually agreed to lead a crusade.

I saw the cardinal frown at my words. I had not refused but my agreement was vaguer than he would have liked. However, he had little choice in the matter. He left the next day for Florence. It was fortunate he did for William and Bianca's wedding was set for the following week and I was supposed to be meeting with Bernabò Visconti. William and I sat with the doge and his chamberlain to discuss the situation.

"I have to say, Doge, that I think it will be hard for me to work with your friend Visconti if he is an enemy of the church."

Agnello smiled and the smile was born of a man who knew the world of Italy far better than I did. "Sir John, Bernabò is not an enemy of the church. You should know that we in Italy regard the church in Avignon as a travesty. Rome is where the Pope should live. Trust me, Bernabò is a good man. Not a man to cross, I grant you but then neither are you. The two of you will get on, of that I am certain."

There would be many guests arriving for the wedding. A man like Giovanni Agnello had such money, power and influence that any invited to the wedding would attend. I also knew that many would attend to view the guard dogs hired by the doge. There were fantastical stories about the mercenary companies and many visitors would be intrigued to see us close up. My men were not preparing for war, that would be the task for the New

Year, but they did practise every day and I impressed upon my captains the need for courtesy from our men. "Who knows, there may be a prospective employer amongst those who attend the wedding."

Only a handful of the company would attend the wedding and they were the ones closest to William. Giovanni, Robin, Dai and Michael would be with me. The distance prevented his sister's attendance. He would visit her with his new bride at some point in the future.

Bernabò arrived three days before the wedding. He slipped in with just a handful of men. He had enemies who might choose to assassinate him and riding incognito was his safest method of travel. I was summoned to his side the day after my men reported the arrival of the hooded riders. They had not known their identity but they recognised superior horseflesh and fine weapons.

Bernabò Visconti looked to me to be an old man but a hale and hearty one. The doge had told me that in addition to the fourteen children borne to him by his wife, he had fathered more than twenty illegitimate children. He still had the lean and hungry look of a predator, just an older one. I was wary when we spoke.

He beamed when we met, "Sir John, I have long wished to see the man who was such a thorn in my brother's side." He nodded, "And if I am to be honest, you spoiled my plans."

I knew not what to say, "It was unintentional, my lord."

He laughed and it was the laugh of a man who loved life, "Of course it was and rightly so. Montferrat hired you and you did all that was asked of you. I should have sought you out myself when you raided around Avignon. Pope Innocent was glad to be rid of you and that should have been recommendation enough."

The doge said, "Gentleman sit. Now is the time for you to talk. When the other wedding guests arrive on the morrow and the day after there will be ears to hear words which should remain secret, is that not so, Lord Visconti?"

"Giovanni you are a clever man and I am glad you are my friend for with your coin and men like Hawkwood here who serve you, then you might be a threat to my ambition."

Was that a warning? The doge did not seem to think so and he just smiled.

Visconti turned his wolfish gaze upon me, "When you did not take Florence's money, Sir John, you surprised me. I had thought, until then, that I had the measure of you. Clearly not. Tell me, why did you not take the coin and betray Pisa?"

"I gave my word and we signed a contract. Without such honour, a company is nothing for who would hire men who could be bought off?"

"You are right and it is one reason that I am here. I was pleased that you managed to avoid having to serve the cardinal." I glanced over and saw the doge shrug. "Yes, Giovanni told me. You should know that I have spies further south and they tell me that the Star Company refused not only to serve under you but to serve the Pope. The Cardinal is back in Avignon where he and Urban will have to devise another plan. You know that one day, you will have to fight the Star Company?"

"I do but Florence's bribe means that my company will need to be rebuilt and that takes time."

He looked at the doge who nodded, "And I have a commission for you, Sir John. Giovanni here has already agreed that you can serve me for a month."

I looked at the doge, who said, "We are safe for the while, di Jesi has built up the army once more and men do not fight in winter."

"Then, Lord Visconti, why do you need me?"

"I will explain what is needed and you can make your own decision. I am happy to abide by your judgement."

I knew that was not true. This was a test and future work would result. "Then speak, Lord Visconti and I will listen."

"I have just fought a long and costly war in the north. It has cost me half a million florins. Eventually, I will make back that money but for the present, I cannot hire the men I need. My sister's husband was Lord of Mantua." He paused, "Ugolino Gonzaga, you have heard of him?"

I had a vague recollection of having heard his name before but as I could not recall the context, I shook my head.

"He was killed and my sister is held prisoner in the town. I would have your company escort me to Mantua so that I can take her to Milan and safety."

"You want us to storm the walls of Mantua?"

He was patient and he said, "No, Sir John, I want you and your men to escort me to the outskirts of Mantua and I will enter, find my sister and then I will return to Milan."

I could not see why we were needed. "Why do you need us?"

"As a threat only. If I ride there with just my bodyguards then they may choose to bar their gates or demand ransom for her but if you are with me then they will fear that I might let loose the dogs of war."

"We would just be a threat?"

"Precisely."

The doge said, "I will be paying you, Sir John, and neither Bernabò nor myself expect you and your men to fight."

"And if they do not fear us?"

The Lord of Milan laughed, "Do not underestimate yourself, Sir John. They know you and your reputation."

"I need do nothing until after the wedding?"

"Of course not."

"Then I will speak with my men."

"Who will do exactly what you wish them to do." Visconti was an astute man and I knew it would be a mistake to underestimate him.

Surprisingly my leaders were all happy about the trip. I told them there would be little profit in it for us but they seemed happy about that. Robin summed it up succinctly, "Since Cascina, we have squatted behind Pisa's walls. The defeat was an honourable one but it was a defeat, nonetheless. This is the perfect opportunity to show the world that we are still ready to fight and we can march up to Mantua fearing no man."

It was decided and I left the arrangements to my men for I had a wedding to attend. It was not the wedding itself that was important but the people I would meet. I had fine clothes that I had rarely worn and I chose the best for the wedding in the cathedral. I was the nearest thing to family that William had and I was at the fore with him and my men. We must have looked splendid for we drew admiring glances from all the women both attached and unattached. It was good that my men and I were honourable for we could have bedded any of the women such was our appeal. The fact that we behaved like perfect gentlemen surprised many of the nobles who did not know us. The German and Hungarian companies had a bad reputation and most Italians thought we were all cut from the same cloth. At the wedding feast, we found ourselves sought out for conversation. My action at Figline in refusing to take the bribe now brought rewards. Those who ruled smaller cities like Padua and Bologna asked when our contract was up as their cities wished to hire us. We had many offers of work. Some would have been easy contracts for we just had to defend their cities and they were not seeking aggrandisement.

When we retired for the night I was more than pleased that William had agreed to marry one of the doge's daughters. The wedding feast had given me many more contacts and I knew that our ride to Mantua would only enhance our reputation. We would not raid and we would keep our swords sheathed. The rescue of a noblewoman would be seen as both honourable and chivalrous. I saw now that an alliance with Bernabò Visconti, which I would have thought impossible a couple of years earlier now seemed the most desirable of things.

Chapter 13

It was as we headed north that I saw another advantage to the task we had been given. We travelled through a part of Italy that was unknown to me. Lombardy was no longer a powerful kingdom but the city-states within it were all both rich and strong. We rode through it with men who knew it well. I rode with Bernabò while my leaders rode with Visconti's oathsworn. It was an education for us all. It was as we neared our objective that we learned that Baumgarten and Sterz had ravaged Rome to such an extent that the Pope called upon all good men to defend what had once been the holiest city from the mercenaries. A messenger came to us as we neared Mantua to tell us that Sir Andrew was leading the rest of the White Company to Pisa but he wondered if he should threaten the Star company. It was in Sir Andrew's nature to behave nobly. There was no profit in it for us and so I wrote a short missive and sent it with the messenger to tell him to await us in Pisa.

We stopped just on the north side of the Po at Borgoforte. As we had headed north we had paid our way and behaved impeccably. We could have pushed on to Mantua but both the Lord of Milan and I were agreed that we wanted a morning arrival and for the Mantuans to be pre-warned of our imminent arrival. As we ate Bernabò and I spoke.

"You are right to warn Sir Andrew to stay out of Perugia but I think that when you return from here it might serve us both for you to fight in the conflict."

"The stipend we have from Pisa ensures that we will protect the city but if we are to fight then we would need payment."

"And, as you know, at the moment I cannot afford to pay you but there may be a way. I know Queen Joanna. When the Marquis of Montferrat tried to take Piedmont from her it was I who went to her aid. What if Naples paid the White Company? What then?"

"Then I would consider it but know that the Star company is now the largest company in Italy. It has more than twice the numbers we do. Until we attract more men it is likely that we might lose."

"Hear my words, Sir John. If you are offered the contract then take it. The doge will agree to anything I ask of him and you will also have Pisan soldiers to aid you. If you march towards Perugia then Florence is threatened and that is no bad thing. Perugia has hired Baumgarten and he will have to obey their commands. Your presence will guarantee that Baumgarten ceases his raids and that will endear you to the Pope."

"I thought his holiness was no friend of yours, my lord."

"And he is not but I can use your good favour to my advantage."

I nodded, "Then if we are offered the contract, I will take it

In the end, our journey to Mantua was the easiest task we had ever undertaken. Not only was Visconti's sister released but my leaders and I were invited to dine with the city council who explored the possibility of our company being hired by them. Bernabò, his sister and his bodyguards had left for Milan and so we were able to negotiate without his ears listening to all that we said. William normally negotiated but I was the one, this time, who set the price. I asked for the almost impossible sum of one hundred thousand florins just to hire us for six months. They did not baulk at the price and said that while they did not need us yet when they did then they would happily pay the stipend I had demanded. We rode back to Pisa through an increasingly wintery Lombardy happy with our position. We now had allies in Milan and Mantua as well as Pisa. We had a potential employer in Naples and, despite Cascina, we seemed to be the most sought-after free company in Italy.

William, having married and enjoyed the time since his wedding with his new bride, was more than happy to throw himself into work. Not that it would have made a difference but he was happy with the new potential contract. He sent out his spies to Perugia and beyond. We needed as much information as we could get. Sir Andrew and the rest of our former comrades arrived on Twelfth Night. William had anticipated them and we had tents and homes for them all. He brought with him, information.

Sir Andrew had information that we could use, "The Perugians do not like us. One of the last contracts we took alone was to raid them. In doing so we tangled with Baumgarten's men and came off worse. Do we have enough men to face them in the field?"

"I do not know but unless Queen Joanna asks us for help it is a moot point. We prepare for war but if it does not come, we are still paid." I had only mentioned the Lord of Milan's plan to William. I was happy to have Sir Andrew back with us but that did not mean he enjoyed my total trust. Even if the queen did not request our help we would still march through Florence to Perugia when the summer came. We needed to keep those towns and cities that had been interested in hiring us aware that we had neither disappeared nor retired. The men would enjoy raiding Florence and as I pointed out to the doubters, I had not taken Florentine money nor had I made peace with them.

It was January the 14th when the emissary from the Neapolitans arrived. Giacomo d'Amalfi did not come by road but by sea and arrived less bedraggled than those who had endured the rigours of the road. He was something of a peacock but the man had a sharp mind. As politics dictated, he visited with the doge first but then wasted no time in seeking me out.

"Sir John, Queen Joanna implores you to bring your company and rid her land of the plague of the Germans and the Hungarians."

William was with me for he was now comfortably settled into marriage and could focus his mind on the task at hand. As was usual he scribbled on a wax tablet and took down the important words that were said. He remained silent.

"My lord, can I be clear here, do you wish our company to come to Naples and fight within her borders?"

The diplomat shook his head, "So long as Baumgarten and his locusts are gone the Queen cares not. She has been persecuted all her life by these savages from the north."

It was then I recalled that when younger she had been married to a young Hungarian prince, John. She had married him when he had been less than sixteen and after fathering a child some of the Neapolitans murdered him in a most gruesome way. The Hungarian royal family had naturally reacted badly to the murder and her lands had been briefly occupied by Hungarian forces. She had since remarried but I could see how that memory might linger.

"Captain Baumgarten has the largest mercenary army in Italy, Signior, and the best that we could hope would be to draw him from your lands." I could not risk a major defeat again and already I was contemplating refusing the contract.

"The Queen understands that, Sir John. The one hundred and sixty thousand florins you would be paid would be to fight for Naples for five years but specifically to keep the Star Company occupied far from Naples."

The sum was huge and I knew I could not refuse it. "We would not be able to march south until summer."

I saw the disappointment on the peacock's face but when he nodded, I knew that we were the only hope of salvation left to the Neapolitan queen. Bernabò Visconti had been less than honest with me. He must have known that the queen would send to me but he had made it sound as though he was doing us a favour. I would have to closely examine every syllable that Visconti uttered in future.

I glanced at William who smiled and gave me the slightest of nods, "Then you may tell the Queen that my company will ensure that the Star Company quits Naples and we shall keep them occupied for as long as we are able. We will have the contracts drawn up and signed before you leave."

He smiled, "What they say about you Sir John is right. You are the most business-like of captains and seem less like a mercenary than most."

It was a double-edged compliment and told me much. They had attempted to hire other companies. Perhaps they had tried Ambrogio Visconti's first. They were an Italian company led by Bernabò's son but I knew that Baumgarten would chew them up and spit out the pieces. There were others but I guessed they had baulked at the prospect of taking on the Germans and Hungarians of Annechin Baumgarten and Albert Sterz.

That evening we dined with the doge and the diplomat. I said little for I was planning. We needed numbers to persuade the Star Company to leave their pillaging and defeat us. I would need Pisans. I would need to speak with the doge. Perhaps I could offer him the carrot of plunder in Florence. The prisoners from Cascina had only recently been released and they had been badly treated. The mood of Pisa was one of anger. If we raided

Florence on our way south then I would be killing two birds with one stone. Perugia had hired the Star Company to defend its land and so if we threatened Perugia with a large enough army then Baumgarten would have to respond. All I had to do was to keep moving away from the threat and draw him away from Naples. That way I could fulfil my promise and avoid a disastrous defeat. By the end of the feast, I knew my plan and I just needed to refine it with my men and the doge.

After the Neapolitan had left us, I spoke with the doge who was more than happy for me to ask the nobles of Pisa to join me. I needed horsemen for Baumgarten was well endowed with knights. It suited the Pisan for it meant that trade would still continue and the economy that had already shown signs of improvement would continue. The nobles contributed little to the wealth of Pisa. I detected the hand of Visconti in all of this. It was almost as though he was telling Giovanni Agnello what to do.

That done it was time to plan with my men. I had promised that we would be close to Baumgarten by summer. That meant, however, that we would need to leave by spring. The raid on Florence would warn Baumgarten but it would be the attack on Perugia that would pull him north. I wanted treasure and success before we faced him. The men who had returned were not all mounted and so, with the promise of the Neapolitan florins, William began to acquire more mounts for us. If I was going to extract us from this battle then I needed the ability to move quickly. We sent Sir Andrew to buy them. He was desperate to show that he was contrite and regretted his decision to desert us. Having spoken at length to him I discovered that the reason had been one of the heart. He had been desperate to win his lady and now that he had and she was with child, he was keen to show that he was a loyal and valuable member of my company once more.

It was as we neared the middle of March and the spring equinox that I noticed Dai was becoming distracted. Dai was like my right hand. He seemed to anticipate my requests before I had even thought them but he began to be late when I sent for him or had to be told twice to do something that should have been second nature. In the past, I had been guilty, often to my cost, of ignoring subtle signs in those around me. After Roger and Elizabeth, I did not make the same mistake and I took Dai to ride down the Arno.

"Dai, you are the most loyal of knights and yet lately you are not yourself. What ails you? Do you wish more responsibility? Would you have your own men to lead? If so then ask and while I am loath to lose the protection of your lance I would rather have a knight on whom I can rely."

He shook his head and reined in his horse, "It is not that Sir John." He hung his head, "There is a lady."

It all became clear. I had another Sir Andrew situation. It was a relief and I smiled, "You are young and it is natural that you have urges. I had already planted my seed when I was your age."

"It is not that, my lord, I love the lady and she, I believe, loves me."

I was almost shocked for to me Dai was still a boy, "You would wed?"

He nodded. "I would. I have, thanks to you, money and there is a house I have set my eye upon."

I was confused, "Then marry. Where is the problem?"

"The lady is one of Lady Bianca's ladies." I waited for there had to be more. "Her name is Caterina Freganeschi and she is a daughter of the doge."

Like Visconti, the doge had many mistresses and while he did not have as many offspring as the goatlike Visconti, he had five daughters and a son. I recalled Caterina. She was older than Bianca and of an age with Dai. Whilst pretty she was not as beautiful as Bianca and the other ladies.

"Ah, but still I do not see the problem."

"William managed to marry Bianca because he is an older man with money and skills. I am just a sword for hire and, compared with William, a callow youth. I do not think that the doge would even consider me as a suitor."

"I am insulted, Dai. I am a sword for hire too."

He shook his head, "I am sorry, Sir John, I meant no offence. You are a hero of Poitiers and a great Captain."

I smiled, "I was teasing you Dai. I know what I am. I have made the best of what I am but I believe that you are wrong to disparage yourself. If this was combat would you hesitate before you struck or would you pull back your arm and put all your power into the strike?"

"Of course, I would not hesitate but this is not like combat."

"It is and you have nothing to lose. If you delay then some other might win her hand. Go to the doge and ask him. If, as you say, Lady Caterina is of the same mind then you have won her already."

I had given my former squire enough steel for him to beard the young woman's father and, as I had expected, the doge was delighted for Dai was not only a good knight he was very personable and well-liked. The doge even bought the house that Dai had set his heart upon and gave it to them with a handsome dowry. The result, however, was that Dai would not be coming with us on the campaign. He did his best to do as the others did but the wedding and the setting up of a home created a distraction and it was William who suggested that I leave him in Pisa.

"Sir John, he is one man and the last thing you need is a knight who is distracted by thoughts of home."

The one who was delighted with my decision was Michael. He would now watch my right side and he had the opportunity to show me that he was as skilled as Dai had been. With six thousand horsemen we left on the first of May for Florence. The date seemed propitious for it had been on that day we had attacked Florence and enjoyed such great success.

We headed up the Arno Valley and rode with such speed that we took all the lands and farms between Empoli and Scandicci without the need to even draw a sword. The whole of Florence mobilized; castles and towns barred their gates and the militia were mustered. After two weeks we had done enough. The treasure and animals we had taken were back in Pisa and we turned south to head towards Perugia. The Pisans with us were confident and eager for more victories. We had with us nobles and knights rather than militia and riding to war always changed the attitude of a warrior. I remembered my first campaign in England when, as an archer, I had marched my way to war. I had not enjoyed it. It took us until July to near Perugia and, once more we had been successful and collected treasure, armour and weapons. The Perugians, awaiting, no doubt, their mercenaries tried to slow us with pinprick attacks. They failed. However, as we closed with the walled city and castle of Perugia our Pisan scouts reported that Annechin Baumgarten was heading towards us and his army of almost twelve thousand dwarfed ours. I knew that we were attacking the papal warriors too. Cardinal Gil Álvarez Carrillo de Albornoz had managed to come to an arrangement with Baumgarten and I knew that I would have to tread carefully.

I sent Giovanni with twenty good archers to find us an escape that would not risk us being trapped. I was just being careful. I still hoped we could do as we had at Cascina and hold them but this time we were fighting Baumgarten and I had too much respect for his skills not to plan for failure.

We sent our horses to the rear with our squires. The Pisans were less than happy to be fighting on foot but I needed to make good use of our archers. Sir Andrew pleaded with me to be given command of a large number of our men and, in the absence of Dai, I reluctantly gave them to him. We had, therefore, three battles. The Pisans were on the right, Sir Andrew, the left and I held the centre. I had Robin behind my battle and Martin behind Sir Andrew. The Pisans used the crossbowmen they had brought. Here we had no river but we were waiting where steep hills rose to mountains to protect our rear. The enemy had their men mounted and they held couched lances. The one advantage we had was that they had few crossbowmen and hardly any archers. They had some Hungarian horse archers and hand gunners. We waited.

Sir Eoin and Michael were my companions that day. Dai was in Pisa and Giovanni scouting to the north and west of us. Michael and Sir Eoin's squire, James, held our helmets. We sat in a broken wagon we had found. I liked the view it gave me.

"This will be hard, Sir John."

"I know, Eoin, but we need not win. In fact, I had contemplated pulling back to Pisa for we have achieved all that Queen Joanna wished. The enemy bands have left her lands and now she can garrison her castles and hold on to what is hers."

"But you will not."

I shook my head, "We have given the Pisans confidence. I would not dash that confidence by falling back. We will hold them and make this a bloody battle that they cannot win."

"Will the Pisans hold? There is no General di Jesi to lead them."

Sir Eoin had managed to uncover the kernel of fear that was in my head. I felt I could rely on Sir Andrew for he commanded half of my men but the Pisans were an unknown force. I had already worked out that if they crumbled then I would simply wheel my right flank and Sir Andrew and I would fight a retreat up the steep slope.

"We shall see." I looked at Michael, "Much depends on you this day, Michael. I am relying on you to sound the signals as soon as I say."

"And I will be ready, my lord."

Sir Eoin seemed unusually pessimistic that day. Perhaps it was the Celt in him, "If they heed it."

Baumgarten was clever and in no hurry to attack. He waited. I wondered if this was like the attack at Cascina where men were slipping around our flank. I sent my best archers to scout although the delay helped us for not only Giovanni and his scouts returned but also Edward, one of the archers I had left with Dai.

I met with Giovanni and Edward along with Sir Eoin and Robin. The nature of our defences meant we had three camps and bringing Sir Andrew and the Pisan commander here might not be the wisest decision. Giovanni pointed to the north. "That is the safest escape route, should you need it, Sir John. There are no castles and we can pass Florence and be in the valley of the Arno before they know."

That was good news but Edward's presence was worrying, "But you Edward, what brings you here. I thought your injured leg kept you in Pisa."

"It did my lord but Master William sent me. The Lord of Milan visited and brought a warning. The city of Siena is preparing to attack from the south. He has heard of this through his son who was recently captured by the Cardinal."

I was suspicious, "If he is captured then how can he send a message?"

Edward smiled, "Lord Visconti and his son are clever men my lord. Part of Ambrogio's ransom was paid by Visconti. It was only a thousand florins but it gave them the chance to communicate. There were other matters that passed between them." He saw my look. "Master William only gave me the information you would need, my lord, and that which the Lord of Milan told him. Master William is clever."

I looked at Eoin, "Then the situation is even more dire than we thought. We cannot retreat for we are pinned by an army that has more horses than we do. We have to fight them." I shook my head, "Now we know why the delay. Siena marches towards us."

Before he could answer Edward said, "There is more, my lord."

"Speak."

"The Lord of Milan has a commission for you."

I laughed, "He thinks we can evade this cunning trap?"

"He does and both Master William and Sir Dai concur. Lord Visconti wishes you to raid Genoa in return for the passing on of this information. There will be no fee but Master William said that we would make a great profit."

This was madness and yet I could see that neither Visconti nor William would suggest it if they thought I could not deliver.

"Let us eat one loaf at a time. Sir Eoin, ride to Sir Andrew and tell him that when I order the retreat, he is to obey it immediately. He should keep his horses close to hand. Warn Sir Martin too."

"Yes, Sir John."

"Giovanni, I know that you are tired but take a fresh horse and deliver the same message to the Pisan contingent. Warn them that Siena attacks from their right and they should face their crossbows in that direction."

"Yes, Sir John."

Robin said, "We could slip away this night, Sir John."

"I know but I would lose my company not to mention my reputation. No, Robin, we are bound to this rock and tomorrow, come what may, we have to fight. We took the fortune offered by Queen Joanna and for good or ill we have to honour our commitment."

"Aye, well, she can have no complaints. The enemy has quit her land and we shall be sacrificed. I wonder if she will honour her side of the bargain and send the rest of the money to Master William?"

I shook my head, "If our company is no more then she need not do so. To earn the rest of that fortune we have to survive."

Robin nodded, "Then survive we shall. We have many sheaths of arrows and we will make them pay a heavy price. I shall have our horses kept as close as yours. Worry not, Sir John, while you and I walk then there is hope."

That night as I wandered my camp, encouraging my men and gauging their mood I wondered if I had overreached myself. The Florentine bribe kept coming back to haunt me. The company I had taken to war then had been the finest in Italy, nay in Europe and now we were the weakling who, when the battle was fought, would be fighting for survival and not victory.

Chapter 14

Battle of Perugia July 1365

The men I would lead, my battle, had embedded stakes before us. I had a line that was just two men deep but the reason was that I wished my archers to be closer and to hurt the enemy as soon as possible. Better than any other leader I knew the value of archers. We might escape if our archers could hurt the enemy enough. I would never give up hope for that was not in my nature but I missed Dai. I know many would wonder at that for he was a young knight and had come from humble beginnings but he had watched my back so often that he was almost a good luck charm and he was not here. I took comfort, however, from the fact that if we did suffer a bad defeat, he and William would be safe. Our freedom could be purchased. As I stood with the poleaxe in my hands, I could see that they intended to fight. The Sienese had appeared on our right and were in place, ready to launch what they thought would be a surprise attack. The Star Company's serried ranks of mounted men were ready and I could see their horses champing at the bit. Warhorses know when a battle is coming. They had waited the previous day and now they were ready.

I had sent the priests back to the healers once we had all been shriven. I saw Robin walking amongst his archers. His style was to banter and joke. Of my two archer commanders, it was Robin who was beloved. Martin was popular but Robin had grit and roughness that archers admired. I turned to Michael. He had grown much in the last year and his mail hauberk was supplemented with greaves and a breastplate. His open helmet was necessary to enable him to blow the signals. He had a shield strapped over his back and a good sword, "When you have sounded the signal then tarry not but fetch our horses. I will not have the luxury of time when I signal the retreat."

He nodded, "You are so certain of defeat, my lord?" He kept his voice quiet.

"I fear so. We might have held just one army that outnumbered us but two and one of them flanking us is too much. Here we have no river to help us. The ground suits our enemies but they will pay a high price."

The attack began at the ninth hour of the day. I wondered if the delay was to hope that the sun would rise and shine in our eyes. It did not for clouds filled the horizon and so the German horns sounded and the metal line lumbered towards us. Every man and horse in their front line wore mail and plate. It was like a steel leviathan. I hoped that the Pisans would stand. My men and Sir Andrew's would for they had faced this sort of thing before but the Pisans had not. I planted the end of the poleaxe in the ground close to my right foot. This might be a long battle and I did not want to tire too quickly. I was no longer a young man. I noticed the absence of both Baumgarten and Sterz from the charging line. I knew both men's livery and they were not leading the charge. I wondered when I would leave the fighting to others and direct it from the rear. I smiled and shook my head. When I did that, I would be an old man. I still felt as though I was the superior of any man that I faced in battle. Sir Eoin was on my left, three men down and Giovanni three men down on my right. Between us were the best and most loyal men at arms.

The thundering horses drew close. Far to the left, I saw a black cloud as Martin launched his arrows. Were the enemy closer there or had he released his arrows too early? I did not even turn to look at Robin. He was the most skilled of captains and he would choose the perfect moment. There was a slight dip three hundred paces from our stakes and the front line of horsemen briefly disappeared and then suddenly they rose, just two hundred-odd paces from us. It was then that Robin and his archers released their missiles. It was as though the enemy line had been punched by a giant. Horses and riders were scythed down but such were the numbers that the metal wall still came on. Then they struck the stakes. My men had placed them so that a man on foot could negotiate them but not a horseman and we stopped them.

Michael appeared at my side, "My lord, the Pisans are falling back."

I turned and saw that while not a retreat the Pisan nobles were falling back. Soon they would expose our flank.

"Tell Robin of the danger and have him use a third of his archers to guard that side."

Even as he left, I saw that Baumgarten or perhaps Sterz had anticipated our arrow storm and the ranks behind were not mounted but shielded and dismounted men at arms. Our arrows would not reap such a harvest. I shouted, "Ware dismounted men at arms!"

Along my line, I heard my men as they shouted that they had heard. Robin shouted, "Archers choose your arrows wisely and pick your targets. A florin to the man who hits either Baumgarten or Sterz."

I doubted that either leader would be foolish enough to lead this attack. The milling and wounded horses delayed the attack and enabled Robin's archers to hit a few more men. We were whittling down their numbers and I knew that if the Pisans had archers then we might have stood a chance but they did not and they relied on crossbows. When the horses had cleared and moved back the line of dismounted men advanced. To our left and right, I could hear the sound of the battle there but you fought one battle at a time and mine was to the fore.

Michael reappeared behind me. "Robin has done as you suggested, my lord, but the Pisans are marching back quicker than we might have liked."

"They face their front?"

"Aye, but they have mounted some of their men."

While that was understandable it was a potential disaster for all it took was one mounted man to have a faint heart and run to begin the avalanche of fleeing men. One stone was all it took to begin such a rock fall.

I turned my attention to the men before us. More arrows were being sent by my archers to our right rather than to our front for the shielded and mailed men were well protected. Robin's men still made hits and some wounded the men at arms. I even saw one die when bodkin arrow penetrated his helmet but we would have to use our pole weapons to hew them down. One advantage we held was that they had swords, maces and axes. Our front line had spears, pikes and pole weapons. We would strike the first blow in each encounter.

"Remember they cannot form a single line until they have cleared the stakes. Hit them hard!" It was a reassuringly loud cheer that greeted my words and I took heart. My battle was firm.

The first men to reach us were the younger ones and that meant they had less experience. They ran through the stakes and that meant that some died for in running they exposed a piece of mail or limb that was not protected by a shield and Robin's men did not miss. It took some time for even those few who survived to reach us. Each time I thought I saw one who would be the one I would fight, an arrow hit. The first man I eventually fought was a Hungarian. I knew that since my battle with Lazlo I was seen as the enemy of all Hungarians. They were a clannish people and the young knight who ran at me saw his chance of glory. He would kill Sir John Hawkwood! He held his shield before him and raised his sword above his head. It was a mistake and I brought the hammer side of the poleaxe down onto his helmet. The metal cracked and then his skull. He lay before me, between the stakes, another obstacle.

The next man at arms was also a Hungarian and he had seen the fate of his companion. Seeing how I fought must have made him think he knew how to beat me. He did not. He had an open-faced helmet and I saw his face. He thought to outwit me and raised his shield to cover his head. Caution should have been his watchword for I simply rammed the spike at his middle. The tip was sharpened and tore through the mail links, driving deep into his body. The sharpened edge of the axe head widened the wound and as his guts spilt out, he tried to clutch them and fell on the body of his compatriot. He would be a long time dying.

I knew that the next warriors would be harder to beat for they would be the older men, the veterans. I had fought alongside some of these men and they would not make such foolish errors as the first two I had slain. It sounded like a weaponsmith's workshop as swords and axes clanged and sparked together. It was why we used good horns for their sound had to rise above the cacophony of battle. Without looking I knew that Michael held his sword in one hand and the horn in the other. It was a German who came at me next. I vaguely recognised him as having been in the White Company. Perhaps he had left with

Albert Sterz when we had split. He held a mace next to his shield. He intended to break limbs. I had no shield to stop his blows and if he hit, even my left arm, then I would be a dead man. It was the weapon of a soldier who knew that a sword had less chance against plate and mail than what was, in effect, a bone-breaking, metal headed club. My only advantages were the long reach of my poleaxe and the fact that he had to negotiate two bodies: one dead and one dying. He chose to step to my left, his right and that was clever. It kept his shield between us and if I turned then another could attack my unprotected right side. I could not allow that and as he passed the stake close to my left, I lunged as he looked down at the ground to ensure he did not slip. It was a momentary lapse in concertation but a costly one. The spike slid over the top of his shield and through his mail. He tried to turn but I pushed even harder and twisted. When his left arm dropped, I knew that he could not raise his shield. As I pulled my poleaxe back, he showed his experience. He turned and headed back to his own lines. He knew if he stayed then he was dead. As it turned out he lasted but ten strides and then a goose feathered flight blossomed from his back.

 Even as I started to turn, I saw Sir Eoin die. He was fighting two men and, against fellow mercenaries, that was simply too many. He rammed his pike into the stomach of one only to have his helmet and head hacked in two by a war axe. I took consolation that one of the first knights to join me had a quick death. Already the line close to where he lay was bulging as the Star Company took advantage to drive into our lines.

 "Robin, ware left!"

 I suspect that my captain of archers had anticipated the potential break in his line for forty arrows flew, using a flat trajectory to slam into the advancing Germans and Hungarians. The gap was sealed with the dead and dying. We had been fighting for more than an hour. We were evenly matched men and I knew that I had been lucky to slay three.

 Michael's voice came in my ear, "Sir John, the Pisans have broken."

 I said as the next Germans negotiated the stakes and the bodies, "Have the squires bring up the horses and warn Robin that we will sound the horn soon."

"Aye, Sir John. Sir Eoin is dead."

"I know and there will be others that will join him."

Two Germans approached me. Perhaps they had seen the success of the tactic with Sir Eoin and each thought that the other would be the one to perish. I knew not but until Michael returned, I would have to find some way to defeat them. Our line was now broken and there was no one within three paces on either side of me. The men behind me had advanced and the next warriors to me were archers who would, no doubt, be nervous about being charged by mailed men at arms, no matter how skilled they were. Another German ran to join the two who were advancing with deadly intent towards me. I moved slightly to the side for that way there were three dead bodies to protect my right and I could swing my weapon left to right. The three men had to come around the stake and face me. That meant their right sides were exposed to my archers. There were no shields to protect them. As they turned, I swung my poleaxe in an arc. As I expected they raised their shields in their left hands and the archers who were just twenty paces behind me released their arrows. At that range, it mattered not if they wore plate for the bodkins drove through all metal as though it was not there. The one on my right was protected by the two falling bodies of his companions but even as the archers nocked another arrow, I rammed the spike at his chest for he wore no breastplate. The tip scraped through his breastbone and into his body.

I heard the shout of joy from the enemy as they realised that the Pisans had broken. I heard the sound of horses and risked a glance behind. Michael had our horses but even as I shouted to him to order him to sound the horn I saw, to my dismay, that Sir Andrew had thought we were getting our horses to charge. He and his men were mounted and charging towards the Star Company.

"Sound the horn!"

"But Sir John, Sir Andrew…"

"Will hear the horn and should follow us and if not…"

I swung myself onto my saddle. I would use my poleaxe like a lance. I saw that Giovanni had survived. Robin ordered his men to launch arrows into the air and then they ran for their horses. It was a clever tactic. The advancing Germans and

Hungarians, not to mention the papal contingent, had to raise their shields for fear of being hit by the deadly shower of missiles. It halted them and that was enough time for our archers to mount and for Giovanni to take the lead. As we headed north, I saw that the majority of Sir Andrew's battle had heeded the horn and were following us. Few of his archers appeared to be missing. Sir Andrew and the foolish men who had followed him were now embroiled with the Hungarians and Germans. They would either die or be captured. Either way, they were lost to me. At least their sacrifice bought us time.

When I looked to the other side, I saw that the Pisans were heading for the castle of San Mariano and they were closely pursued by the Sienese. It felt like a defeat but, as with Cascina, part of me knew it was not. I had to be pragmatic about this. Our contract had asked us to ensure that the Star Company was not raiding Naples and in that, we had succeeded. More, we had hurt them and it would take time to recover their numbers. True, we had lost more men than I would have liked but I was proud of myself that at least a thousand men were following me and as the great majority were my archers then I was happy. I hoped that Pisans, who had not followed us were safe but I knew that as nobles they would be ransomed. My greatest fear was the fate of Sir Andrew and the men at arms he had led. If they had not been killed, they would be captured and while cities tended to let them go free the Star Company was a different matter. I could do nothing about them and I concentrated on the men who rode with me.

Giovanni had scouted out the route home well. We ascended to a Tuscan village. It was remote and afforded a good view of the valley. We used gold to pay for food and wine. The healers tended to the wounded and the squires, who had not been called upon to fight, took the duties of sentries. I sat with Robin and Giovanni, Michael served us food and wine.

"What happened to Martin?"

My other captain of archers was not with his men and when Robin shook his head, I knew the worst before he spoke, "He made the mistake of staying too long when Sir Andrew, that foolish knight misread the situation and charged. He and ten archers were slain by Hungarian horse archers. Had he obeyed his own orders and the horn he would be alive. I shall miss him."

Robin had not said all that was in his heart and the grumpy old archer was hurting. I left the subject alone. When he wished to talk, he would, or not. Robin was his own man.

I changed the subject and spoke to Giovanni, "This talk of Genoa, while we were preparing for battle, I thought little of it. What exactly did Edward say?"

"Just as I told you, that the Lord of Milan wished us to raid Genoa and William thought it was a good idea."

Michael said, "Sir John, Master William would not make that suggestion if he thought we might die for nothing. There will be money."

I waved a hand, "With less than a thousand men?" We could not do it.

Robin came out of his reveries and took one of the legs of fowl offered by Michael, "You know how it is, Sir John. There may be less than a thousand here but how many others are making their way back to Pisa. Do not count until we have been back for a couple of days. One thing, if we do raid quickly then none will be expecting it. Baumgarten will waste no time in telling the world that he destroyed our company."

I snorted, "We slew more of his men than he did ours and but for the Sienese, we would not have quit the field."

"But quit we did, Sir John, and we both know that whoever holds the field tells the tale."

Giovanni was wise and correct. Men who hated and feared my company would mock us. My fear was that men would not offer as much coin to hire us. The Neapolitan gold meant we were well off for a while but I had expensive tastes and there was not enough gold in the world to satisfy my need.

The Florentine nobles, now freed of the need to hire mercenaries also saw an opportunity to wreak vengeance on the company that had humiliated them in the past. They rode from Florence to waylay what they saw as a demoralised, dispirited and defeated army. They waited for us where the Arno River and the road were almost close enough to touch and the ridge of mountains made the road twist and turn. We still had our Italian scouts and Robin had used the death of Martin and his archers to make his own company even stronger. They rode ahead of us and spied the Florentine nobles who waited for us in a bend of the road. They were largely mounted nobles but they had brought retainers with handguns and crossbows. Robin had estimated that there were less than one hundred paces between the river and the tree line that marked the start of the mountains. It was a bottleneck and they were the cork.

"They are equal in number to us, Sir John."

I nodded for I knew what he meant. We were the professionals and while they might have more men at arms and knights than we, they were not the same quality. "Giovanni, have the lances we still have given to our best knights, Michael fetch one for me. I shall lead."

As they rode away Robin said, "You need not, my lord, for no one doubts your courage."

"And I do not do it for my company. I know I do not need to prove it to them. This is for the Florentines who think, if they send their popinjays and peacocks to fight us, that I am a spent force. They will feel the steel of my lance and learn to fear me again."

That made sense to Robin, "We will flank them. We need a quarter of an hour."

We were not in a town with a church bell chiming the quarters, halves and hours but we knew what fifteen minutes felt like. In any case, I knew it would take roughly that time to organise my lines. Michael brought me my lance and I donned my helmet. I let my shield hang from its strap around my shoulders. I placed myself in the centre of the road and as my men, now with lances, helmets and shields joined me, I arranged them to make a column of men thirty men wide. I turned in the saddle, "The rest form up behind us. Michael, have ten men who do not have spears act as the rearguard behind the wagons with the wounded. The squires can ride there. Today they draw swords although if my plan works, we shall not need them."

Michael grinned and drew his own sword with a beaming smile, "Aye, Sir John."

I had left enough space for Giovanni. I needed to ride into battle with someone who knew how I fought. With Dai still in Pisa, that left, now, just Giovanni although William Hammer

Hand and John of Ecclestone managed to get as close to my side as they could.

I had no visor on the sallet helmet and said to the front rank, "We do not need speed, just a solid line. Do not tarry to take prisoners or treasure. Strike to kill and unhorse. There will be time in the future to show these Florentines the folly of their impudence." I raised my spear and spurred my horse. We trotted forward.

As we turned the bend, I saw the Florentines ahead of us arrayed for battle. They had a camp and were making merry as though this was a holy day. To them it was sport. They were mailed and helmed but not mounted. Their hand gunners and crossbowmen sat with their weapons piled and when we appeared they sounded their horns and raced to their horses. We kept the same steady canter and our lances pointed to the sky. The attention of the Florentine nobles was upon us as we moved inexorably closer to them and they tried to form lines. The hand gunners grabbed their weapons and fuzes. I saw them blowing them into life. The crossbowmen were using their spanning hooks to draw back the strings on their crossbows. Some nobles were struggling to mount their horses and there was little order to them. When the arrows descended from the woods and hillside then there was chaos. I heard the bang as some handguns prematurely popped and the smoke added to the confusion. Some crossbows cracked as their operators sent hasty bolts at us for we were now less than two hundred paces from them. Men began to fall as arrows plucked riders from horses and sank into the brigandines of those on foot.

When we were just eighty paces from the disorganized milling mass of men, I lowered my lance. The men on foot had one escape route, the Arno, and many discarded their weapons and hurled themselves into its waters. Here it was one hundred and fifty feet wide, some might survive the crossing. They knew that facing the charging lances and warhorses they stood no chance at all. Robin's arrows had ceased but they had done their work and we ploughed into riderless horses and nobles who were trying to draw swords.

Giovanni and I were slightly ahead of the others for we had the better horses, I was riding Ajax, and had allowed our mounts their heads. The two of us struck at almost the same time and two surprised nobles were knocked from their horses. Whilst the two strikes we made were not necessarily mortal the horses' hooves would be. The crack of metal on metal rippled between the mountains and echoed back. The din seemed louder than the noise when the Star Company had attacked us at Perugia. I marvelled at the effect of the valley sides, river, and hills. The sound aided us and those nobles at the rear joined their crossbowmen in trying to cross the river on their horses. I knew that many would perish. Riding a horse whilst wearing mail in a river took skill. I pulled my hand back and my lance took a young noble in the shoulder. He screamed like a vixen when the head penetrated the mail and tore a hole in his left arm. He would probably decide that hiring mercenaries was a safer way to fight a battle.

Then we were through their men and at their camp. They had brought wagons with provisions and, ignoring my own command at the start of the skirmish, I reined in. The Florentines were defeated. I had expected more resistance but the fighting was over and Florentine nobles were on their knees begging for mercy. We took their horses, their swords, their wagons, tents and their treasure. It did not compensate for the defeat at Perugia but we were richer and our reputation somewhat recovered. I was happier as we headed down the Arno Valley to Pisa.

Chapter 15

I had sent riders ahead to warn the doge, William and Dai of our imminent arrival. The result was that doctors were waiting to tend to the wounded and the city knew of our travails. Dai met us at the gate and as he rode with us to our quarters, he told us what he knew, "Many Pisans escaped the battle. Half are holed up in San Mariano and others have been arriving in dribs and drabs to the city." He smiled, "Some thought you perished but they do not know you as I do."

"And Baumgarten?"

"As far as we have heard he remains in Perugia. So far he has not headed back to Neapolitan land."

I nodded. That meant we had hurt him and the Queen of Naples would be happy with the result of the battle. It was not always about victory. "Tell me about Lord Visconti's suggestion."

"His brother is attacking Genoa in the north of that land. As you know there is little love lost between Genoa and Pisa. The doge's use of us to gain him the city did not sit well with many noble Pisan families. This raid suits both the Visconti family and the doge for if we can hurt Genoa then the doge may be seen as a more acceptable ruler."

I looked at Dai, "You are now tied to the doge, as is William." I wondered about his loyalty and his judgement.

He smiled and I saw the young boy who had followed me for so many years in that smile, "I am of the White Company and that will always be my first loyalty. I am thinking like the soldier you trained, my lord, and this makes sense. I have sensed the mood in the city. It has worsened since the Pisan army began to return and the doge needs a victory of some sort. The Genoese do not expect an attack from Pisa. Since they destroyed the power of the Pisan fleet generations ago, they think they are safe. There are few castles and defenders."

Giovanni nodded, "Sir John, the victory over the Florentines was good but if we can raid Genoa with impunity then it will show the world that Perugia was an aberration. It will put heart in the men." He waved a hand behind him, "We have the

Florentine horses we captured and we can leave in a day or so. None will expect it."

My two senior knights were right and the thought of a plunder raid appealed. I knew that the weight of the deaths of Martin and Eoin weighed heavily on my mind as did the loss of Sir Andrew. "Make it so. I will speak with William and the doge."

When I arrived at the palace there was already a meeting going on with the chamberlain, the doge and General di Jesi. They all looked serious. "Sir John, things did not go as we had planned." It was the chamberlain who spoke and his face was the gravest.

I nodded, "The nobles who accompanied us did not follow their orders. They retreated before I gave the command and they did not follow our line of march."

Di Jesi said, with venom in his voice, "Perhaps they feared being abandoned as they were at Cascina."

I laughed, "General, you were with the Pisans that day and they were militia you did not control. My men, good men, sacrificed their lives to try to save your command. Where were you?"

His eyes narrowed, "Do you question my honour?"

I walked close to him so that our eyes were locked, "I do and what do you intend to do about it?"

When his eyes dropped, I knew that I had won but the chamberlain quickly intervened, "My lords, we cannot fight amongst ourselves. We have a situation and it needs to be resolved. What if the nobles decide that they have had enough of the doge?"

Di Jesi said, nastily, "And if the Florentines choose to attack us then we have no defence. You have let us down and placed us in great danger thanks to your arrogance."

I looked from one to the other. I had taken enough from Pisa. I did not need to stay here. Bernabò Visconti would pay my company.

The doge must have recognised that possibility for he said, "Sir John, I still believe in you." He glared at the other two, "It was my friend, the Lord of Milan, who sent you to Naples. What shall we do?"

I liked the doge and both William and Dai were now related to him. I nodded, "Firstly the Florentines will not attack, general. They tried to ambush us on the way home and we slew them. They have no army. I could march into Florence now and there would be none to stop us. As for the populace? From what I have seen of the fighting spirit of Pisa you could defend the palace with two brooms and a blind caretaker. The doge's palace guards are more than capable but, before I leave for Genoa I will leave behind enough men to keep you gentlemen safe in your beds." They did not hear the sarcasm in my voice.

Pellario Griffo shook his head as General di Jesi burst out, "You are leaving us to raid Genoa?"

The chamberlain said, patiently, as though explaining to a child, "The Genoese have abused us for years and now is the time for us to have some revenge. Can you, General di Jesi, take our militia and defeat the Genoese?" The silence was eloquent. "Sir John is acting on the doge's orders. He is right and if we sent you, General di Jesi, would we win?"

He turned and headed for the door, "I will not stay here to be insulted." He stormed off and his petulant exit made me smile. When I had first met him I had been taken in by his age and apparent experience but having fought with him I saw that all was an illusion. He was no leader.

"When will you leave, Sir John?"

"My men are tired and we have hurts but if we are to catch Genoa unawares then we need to strike and strike quickly. Two days are all we shall need. I intend a rapid campaign of no more than a month. By December we shall be back here." I paused, "And then we shall decide what it is we wish to do."

The doge said, "You will not fight against Pisa." It was a plea and not a command.

"As our likely employer will be your friend, Lord Bernabò, then you would have a better idea than we, would you not?"

He smiled, "Then Pisa is safe." He was about to dismiss me when a thought struck him, "We had planned the wedding of my daughter Caterina to your knight Sir Dai. It was supposed to be on November 30th."

"It can still go ahead. I will ensure that we will be back by then. What I would suggest, doge, is that you use some of your wealth to hire more palace guards and to use, as William does, spies. If you can discover who these malcontents are then they can be eliminated."

Pellario Griffo asked, "You would have them murdered?"

"There are many ways to eliminate an enemy and not all involve death but, to answer you honestly, I would kill if it kept my home and my family safe."

The doge's nod and smile told me that he approved.

I needed to speak with William. He had chosen Pisa as his home and we had made it ours too. If the doge fell from power where would that leave us? William knew the city better than I did. He had made one brief journey to England and Bordeaux; for the rest of the time, he had lived in Pisa.

His house was beautiful and reflected the wealth of William's father-in-law. Stepping through the door was like entering a palace. William and his bride greeted me. I liked his wife, Bianca, she was both beautiful and funny, in my view a rare combination. She made me welcome when I entered the house and insisted that I stay to dine. Michael was busy running errands for me and I accepted. When I lived in Pisa, I did not dress for war but wore fine clothes and expensive hats and shoes. I felt at home in the palatial dwelling of William and Bianca. While his wife spoke to the cooks, I took the opportunity to speak openly to William. He had trained his servants well and once we had our wine they knew to stand beyond the doors. We sat before a crackling fire and spoke quietly like two old men in an English inn, heads close together and straining to hear the other's words.

"Is the doge safe, William?"

"There is a faction who seek to overthrow him. They do not like his warlike policies and they fear the influence of Bernabò Visconti. However, for the present he is safe and so long as we live here then they would not be so foolish as to try to remove him from office. They are patient men and will wait until our company is far from Pisa."

I was relieved and sat back in the chair, "And this Genoese affair?"

"It makes perfect sense and I do not think that you will encounter much opposition. The Lord of Milan and his brother press on the northern borders of the city-state. It is her navy that gives Genoa her power and they have the bulk of their army either facing Milan or guarding their port against attack. The land is ripe for raiding. It is autumn and they have crops and animals gathered. There are few soldiers to worry about and you can easily avoid the castles all of which guard the ports."

"So we will make money." He nodded. "How safe is it here?"

"I have thought of that, Sir John. Should we not do as they do in Florence and have our own bank? There are men we could hire who are not necessarily right for the company but would be perfect to guard a bank. We have the coin to build such a building and there are Pisans who might avail themselves of our service. It might be another way for us to make money."

I nodded for I knew the type of men he meant. Basil of Tarsus had employed such men. Von Landau had killed them it was true but that was because the Jew had to disguise his business. John Braynford had the right idea, both his home and his warehouse were fortresses. "I think it is a good idea. It will take time to build, I know, so until then, keep our treasure here and I will leave men to guard it and you. If what you say is true then we shall not need every man in the company."

We watched the fire for a while, each wrapped in his own thoughts. I knew that William would be planning a bank so safe that none would even dream of robbing it while I was working out how to rid Italy of Baumgarten and Sterz. I feared none of the other leaders. Ambrogio Visconti and Johann Hapsburg were the other leaders of mercenaries. Neither was a threat to my company for I was a better leader and my company was better. The Star company was our rival and, as they had shown at Perugia, had such great numbers that even I could not defeat them, at least not yet.

"When we return from Genoa, I wish an increase in our numbers. We lost good men at Perugia."

He nodded, "Sir Eoin and Sir Martin were sad losses. I hear that Sir Andrew and fifty of our knights are held in Perugia. They will return to us eventually."

"We pay no ransom, William, for once we begin then it is a slide towards disaster. All can be replaced. I like Sir Andrew but he is a little too reckless for my liking. He sees himself as a knight errant. Robin and Giovanni have better attitudes. They have skills and they sell their skills. They care not whom they fight but they fight with honour."

"I agree, Sir John, we pay no ransom and I have already let it be known that the Company of St George is offering new contracts." He hesitated.

"Speak, William, you know there are no secrets between us."

"If you were to ask my opinion, Sir John, the company should be called Hawkwood's Company for it is yours and such a name would attract Englishmen. They will always be the core of your army."

"Army?"

He laughed, "We have grown beyond a company, Sir John. Our company is greater than the army of many of the city-states. Genoa, Naples, Venice, they may all have larger armies but for the rest?"

I had not thought of it like that and I now saw why Bernabò Visconti sought my help. I was a lever to move rocks that were in his way. Such knowledge was important. I now had my own lever to use against him. He needed me more than I needed him.

When Bianca returned and we sat at the table, all talk of war and the company was forgotten but Bianca had grown up listening to business and politics. Talk about lace gowns and fancy headgear were for her ladies. When she sat with her husband and his warrior friend she spoke of politics. However, her opening gambit concerned Dai.

"Your former squire has made a good choice of a bride in Caterina." I was not surprised that Bianca knew of her half-sister and my knight's liaison. She had, after all, been one of her ladies in waiting. The niceties of legitimacy merely meant that Bianca would be given a greater share of her father's money than her half-sister. "She is a clever one is Caterina but I hope that Sir Dai," she shook her head, "Such a strange name, Dai. I hope that he treats her well."

I smiled, "He has fallen in love, Lady Bianca, and he will be true to her. Dai may come from common stock but somewhere in his past he inherited noble blood."

"You do yourself a disservice, Sir John, surely you are the model upon whom he bases his life."

I shook my head, "I know that I am not honourable. If he has picked anything up from me it is how to survive." I thought it better to stay away from my character and its many flaws. "So, how go the preparations for the nuptials?"

"The last day in November is not the best day for a wedding but Caterina is practical. She knows that it will, perforce, be a pale shadow of my wedding and she is content just to be wed. I think she would be happy to be married in a small country church. Our father has been generous with the house he has given her. It is not the palace that I was given but it is more than she might have hoped." She shook her head and laughed, "I just hope that the archbishop does not mumble as much as he did when he married us. I was next to him and I could barely hear his words." She was, as I came to learn, a great mimic and she did such a good impression of the old priest that both William and I fell about laughing. Encouraged by our response she proceeded to give us insights into all the Pisan nobles and their wives. She was funny but she was savage in her demolition of their characters and traits. I knew that she loved William and that was a good thing for while she made a good friend, as an enemy I would fear my back.

I took just eight hundred men on the Genoese raid. We slipped out of the city by the east gate so that any spies thought we were heading to raid Florence. Our purpose could not be hidden but our direction could. We rode to Lucca where we picked up some local guides and then we headed, through the passes in the mountains to drop down to the coastal road. The towns that lay to the south of us we would raid on the way back. We simply rode north taking everything in our path. The castles were, as William had told me, intended to keep enemy ships from raiding their ports. Their defences faced seaward and we raided and plundered warehouses filled with goods ready to be taken by sea. We simply left the castles, with their inadequate garrisons to impotently shake their fists at us. Such was our success that I was able to send fifty men a day back to Pisa with what we had taken. When they returned north, they raided the towns we had skipped. It meant I rode north with a band of men five hundred strong. Over the month that we raided the only constants were Robin, Giovanni, Dai and Michael. It proved a good system as the men who returned every couple of days were refreshed and ready to raid. The tip of our human spear was kept honed by the rotation of men.

We only stopped when we reached Chiavari just twenty miles from Genoa. The Genoese had brought their army from the city and faced us on the other side of the river. They had also brought their fleet and I knew we had done all that we could. It was the last week in November and we were due to return in any case. We burned the Lavagna side of the port. It was the side with the warehouses and after we had emptied them of all of that was of value we set them on fire. The smoke and the wind masked our departure so that by the time the Genoese realised we had no intention of fighting them, we were ten miles down the road and although their fleet followed us, they had no means of fighting us.

We reached Pisa on the 28th of November. I was tired and had enough of riding but we had taken more than a hundred thousand florins in plunder. The merchants of Pisa made a great profit for we sold our plunder to them and, as we had burned many ships on the way north they could sail to French and Spanish ports, not to mention Byzantine ones, and sell their goods at a great profit. The only losers were the Genoese. That we had done a favour to the Visconti family was clear when expensive presents were sent to Dai, William and myself with the news that Genoa had been forced to sue for peace and Milan had grown ever more powerful. It was the Genoese raid that showed me the potential of my company. Even without payment from a city, we could still enrich ourselves. While Pisa was our home and we enjoyed the protection of the doge then we were untouchable. There was a symbiosis between my company and Pisa. So long as that remained, we would go from strength to strength.

The wedding, as Bianca had predicted, was a shadow of her own but Dai and Caterina did not seem to care and my former squire looked as happy as his bride. At the wedding feast, I was seated between the chamberlain and the doge. William was on the other side of Griffo.

"You have heard of the fate of your former associate, Albert Sterz?"

I shook my head. As far as I knew the Star company was raiding the lads of Florence.

The doge said, simply, "The Perugians executed him. I think that he was blamed for your escape. They thought he colluded with you."

"But that is not true!"

The chamberlain shrugged, "He was blamed and that was enough for the Perugians to kill him."

William said, quietly, "I see the hand of Annechin Baumgarten in this. He now has sole rule over the Star company."

I knew not why but I was sad. Sterz and I had wrenched our company from the hands of Arnaud Cervole in France and while we had gone our separate ways we had never actually fallen out. When we had divided the company in Montferrat, he had accepted that he left with fewer men because the English stayed with me. It was a lesson for I now saw that if I lost when in the service of a city-state, I would need a plan to escape rather than stay and face their wrath.

Chapter 16

It was spring by the time the bank building was finished and by then we had the twenty men who would guard and run it. William chose the brains who would count the coins and I chose the brawn who would ensure that we kept it. Even before it opened its doors, we were a success and nobles and merchants flocked to us to protect their gold and treasures. Even more important to me was the forty lances who had come to join us. Some had left other companies and that heartened me. Despite our couple of defeats the way we had handled the potential disaster showed these warriors that we had a backbone and did not fly in the face of danger. Robin now had sole command of the archers while I divided the men at arms and knights between Giovanni and Dai. I then chose four good men at arms and their squires to be my personal bodyguards. Dai and Giovanni would have other duties.

The presence of our company also relieved much of the pressure on the doge. He had heeded my advice and now knew his enemies. He had them watched. We, therefore, enjoyed that rarity for a mercenary company, relative peace.

When Bernabò Visconti visited us in spring it was for two reasons. Firstly, he wished to thank me for what we had done in Genoa and he gave us five thousand florins as a sort of bonus. I think he expected me to keep it for myself but that was not my way. I had made enough gold over the last couple of years to be able to share the gift with my men. In the scheme of things, it was diluted so that it was a trickle but that endeared me to my men who saw that I was behaving democratically. The other reason was to warn us that he had heard that Genoa had hired the Star Company to attack Milan.

"And you believe you can defeat them, my lord?"

He smiled and each time he did so he reminded me of a wolf about to devour a sheep, "If it comes to that but first, they have to pass either Florence or Pisa." He left the sentence hanging, allowing me to draw my own conclusions.

"And you believe that Florence will do as she did before and pay them off so that they do not come through Florence."

"Exactly, and Pisa will not pay, will she, Giovanni?"

The doge and chamberlain were with us and the doge shook his head, "We have our own guard dog in the shape of Sir John here."

I saw the scheme then as clearly as if it had been written on parchment. The Lord of Milan needed to do nothing for we would fight the Star Company. It would not be in Pisa itself and that meant we would march to war and fight them in the open field. It would be a battle without a paymaster but a battle we could not, this time, afford to lose. We had to win.

I looked from the doge to Visconti. I wondered if this plan had been hatched out when first I had spoken to the Milanese lord. He might not have known the precise details but he had moved his pieces around the chessboard quite brilliantly. He had hovered in the background like a puppeteer with his marionettes. He had not been tainted with defeat and his victories had come as a result of our efforts yet he had paid us a paltry sum. I did not resent his manipulation of us but I would learn from it.

"And when we have defeated Baumgarten, my lord, we will, no doubt, be rewarded by Milan."

"Of course and may I offer Pisa the company of Ambrogio Visconti, my son."

The doge beamed, "A very generous offer, eh Sir John?"

I nodded but it was a double-edged sword. I would have to use them in such a way that they were not vital to my plans, "Indeed it is, my lord, so long as your son understands that I will command."

"Of course, of course. That is clearly understood." He paused and looked guiltily at me, "You know, Sir John, I have often been an enemy of the church. The Pope excommunicated me not long ago."

I had also suffered that supposedly terrifying sanction and it had been rescinded. It was not as bad as people thought. I frowned, for I was not sure where this was going, "But you have now been reconciled, have you not?"

"I have but there was a price to pay." There always was. The church did not become as rich as it was without charging for such services. "The price was that I join the league to rid Italy of the mercenary companies."

I could not help myself and I burst out laughing, "So you are using the mercenary companies to do your bidding and yet you join a league to rid the land of us?" He nodded. "And who else is in this league?"

"The Emperor, and most of the city-states." He looked at the doge, "Only Pisa and Florence have yet to sign and I believe that there will be pressure, Giovanni, for you to do so."

"Do not worry, Sir John, Avignon is far from here and I know how to prevaricate. This will end in nothing."

"My friend is right, Sir John, for the Pope does this to force the companies to go on a crusade against the Turks."

"And that will never happen. Even if we were banned from Italy then Castile, Aragon, Burgundy, all of them would happily pay for our services. They may not be as rich as Italy but we would earn a crust."

Visconti seemed relieved, "Then you do not hold this against me?"

"You did what you had to do and I appreciate this piece of honesty," I emphasised the word, *this,* to let him know that I was aware of his machinations. Thus far they had not harmed me but if they ever did then he would pay the price. I was not a man to be crossed.

Ambrogio brought his company to Pisa to join us. Between us, we had four thousand lances. He was young and seemed willing to not only serve under me but also to have me as a sort of mentor to guide him. I could see that his father had chosen this career for his illegitimate son. He was young and I wondered if it was just his father's money that drew men to his band. I saw that most of his men were good warriors and I was happy for they swelled my numbers and meant I had a better chance of defeating Baumgarten.

We used his Italians as scouts and secreted them in the hills to watch the roads that led from Perugia to Pisa. If he went through Florence then we would not hinder his passing but when we heard that Florence had paid forty thousand florins to him not to attack them then we knew he was coming through Pisa. That meant he intended to do battle with us and I mobilised my army as spring drew towards summer, the campaigning season. We marched up the valley towards San Miniato for there we could use the river and the hills to funnel the Star company towards us. Word came from the scouts that the Star company was forty miles away and that meant we had two days at the most to prepare. When last we had fought him, we had used stakes and he would, no doubt, be expecting us to use the same tactic. He would have planned for such an eventuality. I would have to improvise something better this time. I also decided to use some of Robin's archers the same way we had when we had defeated the Florentines. While the men embedded stakes, I walked the field with my three captains as well as Ambrogio and Michael.

"I want a channel dug from the river this afternoon so that when the tide is high, during the night, it will flood the ground behind the place we have buried the stakes."

Giovanni nodded, "The stakes are not the obstacle then?"

"They will slow them and mean that they will not use horses but the real obstacle will be the muddy ground just after. They may wonder why we do not stand immediately behind the stakes but as we will have fewer archers, they may decide that is the reason."

Robin said, reasonably, "And where will we be?"

"You and a third of your archers will be three miles up the Elsa valley." The Elsa fed the Arno. It was not wide but the trees, three miles up the valley would allow my men to hide. I would have you, when the battle begins, bring your men down the valley. I want Baumgarten engaged before I launch you on his left flank. You, Ambrogio, will form a line with the rest of the archers. Some of your men will be given a bow so that Baumgarten sees what he expects to see, two ranks of men at arms and knights and then two more of archers. The reality will be just one line of archers and your men at arms."

I looked at their faces and was pleased by the smiles and the looks of approval on their faces.

"The final lure will be that I shall be in a wagon, just behind the muddy ground. That is for two reasons. One, I want them to know where we are and two, I want a good view of the battlefield. It will become a rock we can defend. Michael will be with me and he will use our horn to the best effect. Finally, our squires will all be mounted behind Ambrogio's last line. I want them to think we have more men at arms than we do so that when I sound the horn for Robin's attack, he braces himself and his shields for a frontal assault."

The trap set I joined my men as we dug the channel across our front. It was three feet deep and four hundred paces long. The rising water would fill it and then overflow. The soil we had removed and placed around it would become soaked and sink back. When the river level was lowered it would appear as a slightly muddy depression and not the slippery bog I planned. It was dark by the time we were ready to break through to the river and that suited me as it meant it was unlikely that any spies would know the effect of our digging. They would assume we were making a defensive ditch. When the last two feet were removed then the Arno rushed into the gap and headed south towards the Elsa. The frothy flow gradually subsided and then spread itself out on either side, coming perilously close to some of the stakes, threatening to loosen them. That done we went to our camps to eat. We had sequestered food from the people of San Miniato. They gave knowing that to refuse risked our retribution after the battle. I think that they were just pleased we had sited our defence a mile to the west of their town. It would not be involved in the battle and they would be spectators from the town's walls.

Robin and his chosen men did not camp with us but they slipped away south down the Elsa valley. I did not worry that they would be seen. Robin had picked only the best and they knew how to move like ghosts. I made my wagon into a chamber. With furs and blankets as well as oiled cloaks for a roof, Michael and I slept well. Around us, I heard the banter from the various camps and it was clear to me that my men relished the chance to have revenge after their last defeat. The ones I worried about the most were the new men, Ambrogio's. If they became the key to victory then we had lost. I was using them as support. If they did well in this battle then I might risk them a second time and give them a more prominent position. For this battle, it was my company would win or lose. To that end the password that night was *'White Company'* to which the reply was *'Hawkwood's men'*. I did not know it then but the passwords became our name in the future, after the battle of San Miniato.

I was no longer a young man and I rose well before dawn to make water. Not wishing to waste my urine I went to the boggy ground. As I expected at that hour you could still see patches of water but I knew that they would soon disappear as the greedy grass drank. The scouts watching for the Star company had told me that they were camped four miles up the valley. They had protected their camps with stakes and would not be here before nonce at the earliest. I added my water to the puddles and went back to the wagon. The night sentries were cooking ham on a skillet over an open fire. I could never resist the smell and I wandered over to them.

They were all Englishmen and greeted me warmly, "Come by the fire, Sir John, warm your body and we will serve you fried ham. The bread is yesterday's but that is not a problem."

Unlike the other nationalities, the English liked to fry bread in the fat of the ham. Sometimes there was so much fat that when you bit into it then fatty juices ran down your chin. I had been brought up on such fare in England serving with the archer company. By the time the sun was up we had devoured the ham and the bread and washed it down with ale warmed with a poker from the fire.

I stood, "After such a feast we few could face these Germans and win!"

They cheered and I saw faces from the other camps turn. The story would spread and my men would be encouraged. I went back to the wagon where a patient Michael waited with my war gear. His horse was tethered to the wagon for Michael would be busy that day. I had a gambeson to don and then my mail. I had bought the best of plate armour and Michael fitted the back and breastplate, greaves, cuisse, poleyn, faulds, vambrace and spaudler. My sallet with the visor lay at my feet as did the poleaxe I would use. My bodyguards were similarly armed. They had but one task and that was to keep my enemies from me so that I could judge our attack more effectively.

The enemy when they moved, came cautiously towards us. Their mounted scouts rode to just beyond arrow range and I saw them assessing our defences. The nearest they could get to the stakes and then the boggy ground was more than one hundred and fifty paces.

"Michael, have a dozen archers walk to the boggy ground. I want to discourage their scouts from coming closer."

If the ten or so scouts thought of venturing closer then the twelve archers nocking an arrow was enough discouragement to send them, after ten minutes or so, back to the rest of their company. They would have seen the stakes, the wagon and the camps. We all know how to estimate numbers from the fires we saw burning and they would know our numbers. It took an hour for Baumgarten to bring his company and start to form his battle. He would not make the mistake of a mounted attack. I saw mounted lancers ready to exploit any weakness he found but the four hundred or so of them were on the flatter ground close to the river and the right flank of the Star company. He had hired Genoese crossbowmen and their pavesiers. I also saw that he had many mailed men with shields. He had found the antidote to archers and stakes. His plan was clear, at least to me. He would use his crossbowmen to send their bolts at my men at arms while men, protected by shields would remove the stakes. With the obstacles cleared they could march forward and use his superior numbers and his mounted lancers to overwhelm us. He would see what I wanted him to see. He would see that he outnumbered us. Robin and my flank attack were clearly not in his planning as his left flank was made up of feditore, Italian warriors wearing little mail but fast enough to attack our flank if we gave them the opportunity. I had a plan to eliminate them too. An attack on foot took time and I used that time. Summoning Michael, I spoke in his ear. He nodded and mounting his horse rode to the rear of our lines. By the time he returned, tied up his horse and mounted the wagon the Germans, Hungarians, Genoese and feditore were ready to march.

I shouted, "Shields!" Michael picked up my shield and held it so that it protected both of us. I looked to the right and saw Giovanni wave as he ordered his men to raise their shields. On the left, Dai did the same. We had locked shields rather like the ancient Romans who had fought this way, probably on exactly the same spot hundreds of years earlier.

The range of the crossbows was similar to that of a longbow. The difference was that archers could release their arrows in the sky to descend. The Genoese used a flatter trajectory. The dozen archers I had sent as a discouragement to the scouts saw the Genoese approach. When the pavise stopped then they knew what was coming. They each sent three quick arrows and then ran through our lines to join their fellows. The arrows came as a surprise and when three pavesiers and one crossbowman fell to their arrows our line gave a cheer. It was a small victory but battles are won by many such small victories. The way the Genoese fought was predictable. They used the pavise as a shelter and then stepped out and sent their bolts at their enemy. It meant they sent a ragged but continuous rain of missiles at an enemy.

   I raised my hand and then dropped it. It was the signal for our archers to release. They knew their range exactly and the arrows descended. Genoese crossbowmen are well paid and they wear mail and helmets. The pavesiers were not. It was hard to see the full effect of the falling arrows but I spied enough men falling from behind the pavise to know we were having an effect. The Genoese bolts began to diminish in number and when I heard a horn then I knew they were being withdrawn. We had neutralised the threat and Baumgarten did not wish to waste expensive Genoese when there was no need. I raised my arm to stop our arrows. From my elevated position, I saw there were twenty odd bodies lying where the pavise had been. As both crossbowmen and pavesiers wore the same tabards it was hard to tell who had been killed.

   The long line of Hungarian and German men at arms and knights began to advance to the stakes. This time an arrow storm would find less to harvest. The ground I had chosen meant that my archers were on a slightly higher piece of ground and could see over the heads of the men at arms. My wagon obstructed a small part of the enemy advance but my archers would have a clear enough view to judge their moment. The next time I used a wagon I would position it behind the archers. I was constantly honing my craft. Each battle I fought reflected the improvements in my skill.

   The Star company came on steadily. They methodically removed the stakes. It took time to do it properly as one man had to use his shield to protect the two others who pulled and heaved the wood from the ground. My archers ensured that they did not do without risking an arrow and bodkins struck some of those who were not as well protected by a shield as they had thought. They made progress, however. I saw the horsemen on one flank and the feditore on the other begin to edge slowly forward. I had a self-satisfied smile on my face for I saw Baumgarten's plan. His mailed fist would punch their way into the heart of my men at arms and then he would launch two flank attacks while we were disordered. It was a good plan but I had it countered. Baumgarten must have remembered how his last battle had not been as successful because he had not enjoyed an obstacle-free patch of ground. Bodies were removed as were the stakes. The lightly armoured men who did so, they were probably squires, paid a price but the Star company was clearing the ground ready for their horsemen to pour in.

The feditore and the horsemen were now almost in arrow range. "Michael, signal the squires." The signal for Robin was to be three blasts on the horn. He gave a single blast and I saw the enemy line stiffen as they looked for the danger. When the young squires, using spears rather than lances suddenly galloped towards the feditore it took the whole of the enemy line by surprise. Still in the stakes, the men at arms braced themselves and the horsemen stopped. The ones who did not stand were the feditore. They did not see squires, they saw men at arms and in their loose formation, they had no defence. They ran and I heard the cheer from my squires as they galloped after men whose backs were to them.

Baumgarten was quick thinking and I saw him ride to his horsemen and lead them to charge across the battlefield to rout my squires. The squires had done all that I had hoped and were not to be wasted. "Michael, sound the recall!" They might have hated me for ordering it but the squires, almost all of them, obeyed. The half a dozen who carried on with their charge paid with their lives. The rest of the squires, flushed with success rode back to the cheers of our company. The men at arms continued their attack and Baumgarten showed his ability to adapt. After he reached our right flank, he steadied his line. He was going to charge my right flank with horsemen instead of feditore. My vantage point now proved crucial. I saw that the German and Hungarian soldiers had almost reached the boggy ground.

Baumgarten had used one of his men as a leader and he raised, one handed, his halberd. He was a strong man. I knew it was the signal to attack.

"Michael, now is the time."

The three blasts on the horn were clear and echoed across a battlefield that only had the sounds of arrows cracking into mail, plate and flesh. Baumgarten might have wondered what trick I was playing but he had patently not even considered that his horsemen were in danger. The men on foot had opened a wide gap in the stakes to allow an arrowhead of horsemen to charge through. Michael dropped the horn and raised his shield. I gripped the poleaxe in two hands and the German and Hungarian soldiers found the boggy ground. It was as I had expected. Having rid themselves of the obstacle and formed a solid line they ran at us. Men slipped and fell. They brought down men behind and my archers wasted not an arrow as they sent bodkins into men floundering on the ground like fish stranded at low tide. At the same time, Robin's archers arrived, dismounted and slammed arrow after arrow into the unsuspecting horsemen. Although some of the horses wore mail hoods their rumps and flanks were unprotected. Horses and riders fell. As some looked behind them then the archers behind me were able to send arrows at men who were no longer sheltered behind shields. Had the battle ended then it would have been a victory. Baumgarten was determined to win and, as his horse was slain and he tumbled from its back he showed both his skill and his courage by standing, grabbing his shield and drawing his sword. The horses now also found slippery ground and the ground was also littered with bodies of wounded men and horses. The equine attack slowed and then stopped. The riders emulated their leader and they dismounted.

Robin's archers continue to harass the enemy but as soon as the disordered and disorganized Star company engaged our men at the fore then they had to rein in their arrows for fear of hitting our own men. This would now be a battle between our men at arms and my men were ready. We had run the last time but we were now whole and the enemy was hurt. They roared as pole weapons struck mail, helmet and swords. I heard Baumgarten shout and it was my name he shouted. He intended to rid himself of his nemesis, if he killed me, he hoped the battle would be over. The enemy surged towards my wagon. I had become the magnet to which the enemy line was attracted. If I survived, we would win and if not, then my company would be defeated. The elevation of the wagon afforded me some protection but Michael had to bravely put himself in harm's way to stop the missiles thrown at me. My bodyguards all held pole weapons and when the first of the enemy reached us their swinging poleaxes, halberds and pikes wounded and drove the first attackers back. The two ends of the wagon were protected by a triple line of men at arms and knights. This was where Ambrogio's men might make the difference. It meant we had more mailed and plated men in the front ranks than we normally did.

When two Germans fell next to the wagon an enterprising Hungarian used the two bodies to attempt to spring up at me. I could have swung but the timing would have to have been perfect. Instead, I thrust at his flying body with the spike on the end of the poleaxe. It slid up his breastplate and as he was not wearing a gorget it drove into his throat and he fell back. A second and a third tried to clamber up on either side of me. Michael was forced to hold the shield above me to allow me to swing. I swung from left to right. The hammer side caught one of the men in the side of the helmet. It stunned him and knocked him to the side. The second took the full force of the axe head and it made a dent and a crack in the side of his helmet. He was not just stunned but knocked unconscious.

We were paying the price. Two of my bodyguards, Hugh and Edgar both lay in the bottom of the wagon bleeding their lives away. The two bodyguards had done their job for three men lay dead but they had paid the ultimate price. I saw men beyond the front ranks of Germans and Hungarians falling to arrows sent from their side and rear. Robin had a wise old head on his body and knew that men paid more for frontal armour than their back and the reinforcements that Annechin Baumgarten was relying on were being decimated. He and some of his men had managed to get to the front and now that there were bodies laid before the wagon, they were able to climb on them and be on a level with me. We did not make it easy for them. Michael had dropped the shield and taken up Hugh's halberd. There were now four weapons poking, stabbing and hacking at those who tried to climb. His halberd tore through the cheek and face of one German. No matter how brave you are such a wound ends your combat. I rammed the spike through the eye hole of the helmet of another. When James fell it allowed Baumgarten to jump into the wagon and occupy the space vacated by the wounded bodyguard. I was forced to turn to face him. He held a shield and a sword. He was no longer a pole's length from me and I was at a disadvantage. I turned the weapon so that it was held before me like a staff. I used the butt end, with the small spike to strike at his shield while I whipped the hammer head around to hit his arm. He was not expecting me to do so and I saw him wince as the hammer hit his lower arm. Our heads and bodies were well protected beneath our plate and mail but not so our arms and legs. I saw him pull his head back to butt me.

Ambrogio's voice came from behind me, "We have them on the run. Now is the time to attack! Charge!"

He was not obeying orders but as Charles, my last bodyguard, had fallen there was just Michael and me on the wagon and we faced four men. An arrow flew dangerously close to my shoulder and slammed into the helmet and head of a Hungarian with a war axe. The head butt did not reach me as the flight of the arrow made Baumgarten react and move back. I lifted the axe head a little and brought it down to the dent I had made in the German's armour. He punched with his shield and it made me almost trip over Hugh's body. The German saw his advantage and, raising his sword came to end the combat. I was already moving backwards and so I simply dropped to one knee. The haft of the poleaxe rammed against the end of the wagon, or a body, I knew not which and pointed the spike at the German. He was committed to the blow and as the sword came down to split open my helmet and skull, he impaled himself on my spike. He was killed, not by me but the Hungarian who had climbed on the wagon and was trying to get to Michael. He inadvertently pushed Baumgarten so that the spike went through his plate, mail and deep into his chest. Michael's swinging halberd ended his life. I stood and taking my poleaxe chopped off Baumgarten's head. The helmet fell from it and I lifted it up by the hair and held it above my head. It was enough. The arrows continued to rain upon the defeated Star company and their leader and best warrior lay dead. They fled.

We were in no condition to follow and we allowed them to leave. Perugia and Cascina had been avenged and my company, the White Company of Sir John Hawkwood had regained both its honour and reputation not to mention the treasure of the Star company. Although we did not pursue the fleeing men, Robin and his archers mounted their horses and captured their baggage. The florins they had been paid by Perugia were there. The Star company had no bank. We made a small fortune and Italy was free from the Star company. Without Sterz and Baumgarten, they were a spent force. They would still hire out their swords but not for the one company that threatened our supremacy. Italy was ours for the taking.

Chapter 17

We had lost men but the most serious losses had been my bodyguards who had been the best men in the company. We honoured them by burying them with the others in the monastery of San Savino. Dai and Giovanni were unscathed as was Robin. The ones who benefitted more than any others were our squires who now had confidence oozing from them. My problem would be to rein them in. The other success was Ambrogio. He had acquitted himself well and having helped defeat the Star company thought he could take on the world. His disobedience to my orders had not ended in disaster but it might have done. We returned to Pisa and after we deposited our treasure in our new bank we spent well in the city. All resentment to the doge and the men he had hired evaporated like the morning mist and our defeat at Perugia forgotten. We were heroes. Now was not the time to sit on our laurels. While Ambrogio took his company off to fight against the Queen of Naples under the banner of the Hungarians who hated her, we rode up the Arno to Florence. We were ready to fight and the horses we had taken from the Star company meant that we had a force that was all mounted. We reached the walls of Florence before the Florentines could begin to mobilise their army. We squatted outside and heard the wails, screams and cries from the women. They were terrified.

Under a flag of truce, I rode into the city with Dai, Giovanni and Michael. Our safety was guaranteed by the hostages they presented to us. It was the first time I had breached the walls and I confess that I marvelled at the beauty of the Tuscan city. I saw people who had come to watch us recoil as we passed. Many made the sign of the cross for we were seen as soldiers of the devil. At the palace, we were greeted by the doge and General Malatesta. It was the general who did the speaking.

"Sir John, Florence does not wish to fight you. It is harvest time and we do not want our crops to die while we fight you and your men. We would rather pay you a stipend not to fight against Florence for five years." I said nothing for no sum had been mentioned. "We would have the promise of no attack made by the company no matter who leads it."

I smiled; I had achieved what I had wanted to. The name of the company was now seen as the threat. "How much would the stipend be?"

"Six thousand florins a year."

Whilst not a huge sum, it was a guaranteed income for five years and would pay every soldier without the need to war. "And Pisa?"

"We promise that while you serve Pisa, we will not attack our neighbour."

I nodded, "Then if you would consign this to paper then we will agree and once you have fed my company we shall leave for Pisa."

We headed back down the Arno valley like conquering heroes. The hard fighting against the Star company was now a distant memory. We had a winter to rearm, train and recruit for I had plans for the spring. Our arrival back in Pisa pleased everyone. The city had guaranteed peace for the next five years and with the defeat of Genoa by both Visconti and our company, the Pisan fleet was rewarded with greater trade. It was also a time for my men to take wives. With both Bianca and Caterina enjoying their first pregnancy, other knights and men at arms chose to use their treasure to buy homes and to marry. We were no longer vagabonds but heroes who had saved Pisa. Pisan fathers were happy to have a son in law who was a member of my company.

Perhaps it was the sight of Dai and William so happy at being fathers that made me decide to travel back to Bordeaux. Taking just Michael and a small chest of treasure I took a Pisan ship for Marseille. I would travel overland to Bordeaux. My leaders worried about me and asked me to take more men. I shook my head, "I will travel incognito and besides, I have a mind to hire men in Marseille. It is not a long journey and I am confident that I will spend a joyous Christmas with my family."

William gave me gifts for his sister, the mother of my sons, and we took ship in October. The voyage was not a pleasant one. It would have been far worse in the Atlantic but even the Blue Sea could be rough in October.

We landed far enough from Avignon and the Burgundy Valley for me to be reasonably anonymous. However, I was not a fool and, using a name I had from William, I sought out a man who would provide me, for a fee, with reliable men. The innkeeper of a small tavern, Jean le Dupont was a villainous-looking man and had I not been told by William that I could trust him I would have walked from his inn as soon as I saw his face. It was not just that he was an ugly brute of a man, he had been scarred in a knife fight and his face was crisscrossed with the evidence, it was his brooding eyes. He must have won and I would have hated to see the man he bested. Surprisingly he knew my name despite the fact that the tiny inn in the back streets of Marseille was far from the world of condottiere.

"Your reputation precedes you, Sir John." So much for my anonymity. He saw my face and smiled, "I doubt that many other men would recognise you but I met your Master William and he described you. In my youth, I hired out my sword but not as successfully as you." He touched his face, "The men alongside whom I fought were less than honourable." He smiled, "They are all dead now and I make a good living. Not as good as yours I might add but good enough. What can I do for you? You need men to fight in Italy?"

Shaking my head I said, "I need horses and men to travel to Bordeaux. I will return in January and the men can return here then."

"Bodyguards." He nodded, "I have just the men for you. You arrive at a fortuitous time for few men travel in winter and fat merchants who normally use me are safe inside their homes." It was getting late and he stood, "I will have a room made ready for you. I will put it all on my bill."

He knew that I would pay whatever he asked and, to be truthful, my safety mattered more than the extra florins he would put on my bill. The purse of Annechin Baumgarten had been a fat one. Surprisingly for such a low tavern the room we were given was well apportioned and I did not have to duck too much. The toothless crone who took us there also offered the services of two whores if we needed them.

We hesitated and she laughed. Her cackle seemed appropriate, "Do not worry, my lord, my days of making the two backed beast are long gone. Jean keeps pretty young things here for men such as you and they are clean."

I smiled not only at her words but the appalled look on Michael's face. As far as I knew he was still a virgin. "I thank you, mistress, but food and wine are what we need."

"A wise man and your purse will be fatter for that. The food here is good. I am the cook and happy to lick my fingers. You will not be disappointed."

We unpacked and then descended. We travelled without mail and plate. I had no fine clothes but the serviceable clothes we would need for a hard ride of four hundred miles. I might have taken the land route from Pisa to Bordeaux but that would have meant passing through Genoa and Savoy. I knew that I would not be popular in either county. The crone, her name was Bella, served us wine and told us that the food would be ready in an hour. I was happy about that for it meant we were to be served fresh food and not the leftovers from the previous day.

Jean returned before the food and he had with him four men who could have been his brothers. Their hands bespoke violence and none of them was without a scar or a broken nose on their face. They were not big men but they had the lean and hungry look of killers. They would do although I wondered what Elizabeth would say when we arrived at my manor.

"These are the men I have chosen. They are all willing to spend two months away from their home. You will pay them all a florin now and a second when they return." He smiled, "I will pay their wages between and you shall pay me," he hesitated, "it will be on your final bill. This is Arnaud, Georges, Guillaume, and Pierre. You can trust them with your lives." He laughed, "You will have to trust them for the lands through which you travel have bandits aplenty. They have all done this before and know the inns that are safe. You will pay for their rooms and food, of course. The horses are mine and while they will ensure that they are not mistreated you will pay for their food and stabling." He paused, "Is that satisfactory?"

"It is." I took eight florins from my purse. "I will pay two florins to each of you." I smiled, "I am a generous man and I would like to return here looking as I do and not like Jean."

They all laughed and took the coins. The one called Arnaud said, "I like you, Sir John. This might be more interesting than escorting merchants. From what I hear you can handle yourself."

He nodded to my boot, "Anyone who carries a bodkin dagger in his boot has my approval. We shall see you in the morning." They knuckled their foreheads to their captain for I now saw that was what Jean was. His men were not called condottiere but he had the same relationship with them that I had with my men.

He sat next to me and poured some of the wine from the pichet into a goblet he had picked up, "And the fee for my men, my horses and my accommodation is fifty florins."

I saw Michael's eyes widen. It seemed a fortune to him but I nodded and handed the coins over. A man like Jean could not afford to have clients die. The money guaranteed our safe arrival in Bordeaux and return to Marseille.

Jean smiled, "You are a wise man, Sir John."

The food was good and the knowledge we acquired was priceless. Jean ate with us and we learned much about the politics of this area. Sir Hugh Calveley and Bertrand du Guesclin had led their own mercenary companies against King Peter of Castile. An ally of England, he had asked for the help of the Black Prince and the man I had followed at Poitiers now campaigned on the Castilian-Gascon border. It meant there would be men in Bordeaux either heading for Castile or returning from it. Either way, I had the chance to hire English men and, especially, English archers. I was pleased I had stopped in this inn for I might have just gone to my manor and not headed into Bordeaux. I wanted to see my sons but Italy was where I made my living and a mercenary captain who did not recruit was asking for trouble.

The first eighty miles were along the coast and the weather was benign. It gave me the chance to get to know my bodyguards. They knew their business and Michael and I were cocooned and kept safe. One always rode twenty paces ahead of us and one ten paces behind. One held the reins of the sumpter with supplies and the fourth rode next to me. They changed the order each day and I admired that for it showed that they would not be complacent. The rider at the fore had to be alert to danger the whole time.

The danger would come, Arnaud said, when we headed into the mountains of the Languedoc. There we might encounter both snow and cold, not to mention bandits. He smiled and I saw that he had lost teeth. "The bandits know us and we normally manage to avoid conflict. Last summer we were escorting a fat merchant and his pretty young wife. Perhaps the wife proved too attractive but one band thought to rob us. We left their heads on their spears. We shall see, eh, Sir John?"

I learned much about our four companions as we headed west. They had all been soldiers but, by their own admission, not good soldiers. When they were not fighting, they found that they were bored and took to stealing and robbing. They had lived for a while as bandits until Jean had found them and turned their skills to his advantage.

Arnaud liked to talk although his eyes never stopped moving, "We have a good life, Sir John. We pay no taxes and only Jean tells us what to do. As he can best all of us then we are content. You respect a man who can defeat you. We know our limitations. One day we will meet an enemy who is bigger and stronger than we are and we shall die. It is the way of the world. From what we have heard it is the same in your world. You have taken on the Pope and defeated him."

I shook my head, "Not quite true and I have lost battles."

"We were soldiers and we know that a lost battle does not always mean a defeat. We have seen men passing east to join you. They were not the kind of men to follow a loser. To be truthful the four of us have often thought of joining a free company for the rewards are great but it is the obeying of orders we would not like. You have hired us but if we have to fight then you will not be the one to tell us when enough is enough."

He was right, of course. My company obeyed every command and any who chose to disobey their captain would be released immediately. Theft and violence towards a brother in arms was also similarly punished.

The journey became colder as we ascended and I was glad that my cloak was not only lined but had been well oiled. Even so, the inns that Arnaud and his men found for us were havens for their warm fires and hot food enabled us to travel on. As we descended towards Gascony the weather changed once more. Still chilly, the flurries of snow changed to rain and we knew we were nearing the Atlantic. We also passed companies of men marching south to fight in the Castilian wars. They knew not me for there was no mark or livery about my person and the four bodyguards discouraged conversation. It was a sign that England was flexing its muscles. France had always been a happy place to raid and to fight. Now, it seemed, Poitiers had made Edward, the Black Prince, even more ambitious and he was looking towards Iberia.

As we neared Bordeaux, I broached the subject of accommodation. "I am more than happy for you to stay at my manor. There is a fine warrior hall and good food."

Arnaud nodded, "And it is a generous offer but, if you are not offended, Sir John, we will seek rooms in Bordeaux. As our contract states, you will pay and we can be more ourselves in such a place. We are rough men."

"I am not offended. If you mention my name, you may well get a reduced rate. Let me know where you are staying. We plan on staying in Bordeaux for no more than a month but who knows when circumstances might change. I will keep the horses at my manor for there is a good ostler and they can graze on grass. It is better for the horses."

"You are right, my lord, and I can see why you have been so successful. Your attention to detail is impressive."

They entered the gates of my manor but then slung their bags over their shoulders and headed up the road to Bordeaux. I knew what they intended. They would find an inn that needed their services and earn extra coins by keeping order in the inn they chose. They were men after my own heart and earned a coin whenever the opportunity arose.

Roger of Norham had been a fine man at arms but since he had married Elizabeth, the mother of my children, he had grown a paunch. He and Elizabeth also had children of their own and fatherhood suited him. Elizabeth too was no longer the pretty and slender maid I had bedded. She had also filled out but like Roger, looked well on it. Their greeting was warm but guarded. I had given them no warning of my arrival and, in the past, I had sometimes been less than polite. I smiled to put them at their ease.

"I am here to spend Christmas with my sons and to see if I can hire more archers and men at arms. You need not put yourselves out for us. Michael and I will, if you wish, keep to ourselves."

Elizabeth kissed me on the cheek, "Nonsense, Sir John, this is your home and we are merely caretakers. We are pleased that you are here and the boys will be too."

I looked around, "Where are they?"

Roger spoke, "We hired a tutor for the children. They work at their studies until an hour after noon. Then they are allowed to play. They will be here soon."

"And have you begun to train them to be warriors?"

"Ralph does that and they are coming along well. Sometimes the boys can become a little spirited and use more violence towards one another than is acceptable. Ralph chastises them when they do so."

"I would not have their martial spirit spoiled."

Roger nodded, "Speak with Ralph, Sir John. When they have finished their studies and eaten, they usually practise for an hour in the yard with Ralph."

"Good. I shall watch. Our chamber?"

I did not expect the master bedroom even though this was my house. However, it was a well-built house and there were a number of large chambers. We were given a large one with two beds within. I was happy.

We had finished eating when the boys raced in. It had been some time since I had seen them and they had grown. I must have changed for they did not seem to recognise me. However, they had been drilled well and given good manners for they bowed, seeing that I was a lord and John said, "Good afternoon, sir, and welcome to my father's home."

"Your father?"

Thomas, anxious to impress said, "Aye, my lord, Sir John Hawkwood, the hero of Poitiers."

An embarrassed Elizabeth said, "This is your father, boys, and he has come to spend Christmas with us. Sir John, these are my children by Roger."

She introduced me to her three children but I merely nodded. I had come to see my sons and I could not wait to be alone with them. As they ate, in silence, I inspected them. They had grown since last I had seen them but they were still too small to take with me. I had hoped that they could be pages but I could see that such a journey would have to wait another year. Having seen them I was more determined than ever to take them in hand and mould them into warriors. I would speak to Ralph. I had hoped that Roger of Norham would have used his knowledge and skill to make them into soldiers but I could see that he had changed. This was not the man who had fought at my side for so many years. Marriage had brought him happiness and contentment but it had also changed him.

Ralph had been another man at arms who had served me and married. He had chosen to stay here in Bordeaux rather than come with me and the company. The difference was he was still a warrior. He had no paunch and I saw that his arms were still well muscled. While my sons dressed for their training, I spoke with him.

"It is good to see you, Sir John. How are my old comrades?" I told him of Dai and his knighthood and then of the deaths of Martin, Eoin and the others. He made the sign of the cross and nodded, "It is the fate of all those who go to war. I am content to be here with my wife and my family. I train your sons and guard the manor. I will die in my bed."

"I need to speak to you about their training, Ralph. Roger tells me that they have been chastised for coming to blows."

He looked shamefaced, "Aye, that was Sir Roger's doing. Boys will be boys. John is bigger but Thomas gives as good as he gets. I would have just had them shake hands when the spat was done but their mother and her husband asked me to reprimand them. I am sorry, my lord. I have my position to keep."

I felt myself becoming angry and then forced myself to stay calm. Elizabeth was doing what she deemed to be best but I was lord of the manor. "I will speak with them and your place here is assured. I am the only one who will turn you out. You have them for one year more, Ralph, and then I will take them back to Italy. This time next year you will bid farewell to your charges. I want them to have the skills necessary. Can they ride?"

"Aye."

"Draw a bow?"

"A bow, my lord? I am no archer. I teach them sword, shield, and spear. I show them how to wrestle and use their fists. That is all."

"Is Long John still here?"

Long John had been an archer who had married a Gascon. Ralph nodded, "Sir Roger uses him as a gamekeeper. He hunts and provides game for the manor."

"Then send him to me when we have seen the boys train. I would have them know how to use a bow. They may never be archers but they should understand what makes an archer and, besides, it will make them stronger warriors."

He understood, "You would have them made into you, Sir John."

"I would."

The boys came out and a servant girl brought some warmed ale for Michael and me. "Let me see what you can do."

I saw what Ralph meant. John was bigger and slightly stronger but Thomas was determined and full of guile. They used wooden swords but neither held back. I knew there would be bruises. I had them show me, when the sparring was done, how they could throw a spear and then they rode their ponies, which they saddled themselves, around the yard. After they had finished and unsaddled their ponies, I watched them groom their animals. The boys had potential. Ralph had done his work well.

I handed him a florin, "You have done well, Ralph and I want you to continue to do as you have. Now fetch Long John. Michael and I will speak with the boys."

Left alone in the stable we sat on some bales of hay. "Michael here is my squire. One day he will be knighted. This time next year I will come for you to take you with me and you will learn the art of war. Michael will teach you how to be a squire so that I can knight him." I saw their faces light up with excitement. "It will not take place overnight. You have years of training ahead of you. What you need to do is to become stronger. Heed Ralph's words. Long John will also teach you to use the war bow. That will be the hardest thing you ever learn but you must persevere. Do you understand?"

"Yes, father."

I nodded, "Until you come with me to Italy then call me father but once you are in Italy and in the White Company, you will call me Sir John like all the others. Michael here will tell you that all men are treated equally in the company. Just because you are my sons does not mean that you will be given preferential treatment, if anything you will have to prove yourselves even more." I saw their faces fall, "However, when you are great captains then there will be great rewards. You may hate me at first but when you are older you will thank me for having made you great captains."

They bombarded me with questions about Italy and the company. Michael helped me to answer them. They had exhausted their supply of enquiries by the time Long John arrived. I was pleased that he still looked like an archer. When he had stayed in Bordeaux, I had been disappointed, as had Martin his friend, but now I was glad.

"Long John, in addition to your gamekeeping and hunting duties I would have you teach my sons to use a war bow. You practise at the mark each Sunday with the other archers?"

He looked a little embarrassed, "Sir Roger does not enforce it. There are three men in the village who join me each Sunday but…" his voice trailed off.

I nodded, "That is my fault. I have been absent and Roger of Norham needs reminding of his duties. From now on all the men in the village will train and if any are suitable you will tell me so that I may take them into the company. John and Thomas will work with you. By the time I come, next year, I would have them hit the short mark with every arrow and be able to make a good attempt to hit the second mark. Is that clear?"

"It is my lord."

I took a florin from my purse. Annechin Baumgarten's gold was being put to good purpose. "This is for you. I will return in a year." He nodded, "You are still happy here?"

Smiling he nodded, "I miss my comrades and I was sorry to hear of Martin's death but I have a wife and two children. I am content." He held up the gold coin. "But if these are the rewards archers can earn then I am envious."

"If you wish to make money then come and serve for a year. You could make enough to buy your own farm." I saw him thinking about it. "You have a year to train my sons and when I return, if you wish to come with me for a short contract then you will be more than welcome."

I had planted a seed and I wondered if it would grow.

When the boys had gone to bed and while Elizabeth saw to her children I spoke to Roger. I kept Michael with me. "Roger, are you happy here, in my home?"

He heard the tone I used and said, warily, "I am, my lord. is there a problem?"

"There is. You may be happy to grow a paunch like a priest in a comfortable sinecure but I am not happy that men do not practise with a bow each Sunday. I like not the lack of discipline here at my home."

"But, my lord, Gascony is at peace. We have not had to muster the men since I came here."

I felt myself becoming angry and I took a deep breath before I spoke, "I care not if there is never a muster. I may wish my men to come to war with me. Do you understand? The men of the village are my men. They are not yours. You are a caretaker. The house in which you live is comfortable and I thank you for taking care of that but you also take care of my manor. I will return in a year for my sons. You have until then to show me that you are capable of managing my affairs here." He nodded and I paused, "If not then you and Elizabeth, along with your children, will be thrown from my land and I will give it to another. Understand?"

He was white and he nodded, "Aye, Sir John, and I am sorry."

"The word sorry flows from your lips with such ease does it not, Roger? I forgave you when you slept with the mother of my children. Any further disappointment will not be forgiven."

The next morning I knew that he had spoken with Elizabeth for, red-eyed she came to me, "Sir John, my husband is a good man. Do not throw us into the streets."

"And, if he improves his management then he will not. When I take my sons with me, I have no need of either of you. Think about that, Elizabeth."

"You are a cruel man, Sir John."

"No, I am not. I am a hard man and I expect those around me to live by my rules. This is a beautiful home. It would be a shame to lose it because of indolence. I do not demand the income from the manor. You and your husband live well and it is a life I have given you. Earn it."

I knew that I was being a little vindictive and the reason why. Roger and Elizabeth had betrayed me and while I had forgiven them in my heart, I knew it would never be complete forgiveness. It was a trait I did not like in myself but a man does not choose his character. It is moulded by life.

There was a chilliness between me and the couple but I cared not. I enjoyed the time I spent with my sons. Arnaud sent a message to tell me that they were staying in the White Cockerel. It was the roughest inn on the waterfront in Bordeaux and I smiled. The Bordelaise would have a harsh lesson in how to behave. Michael and I visited Bordeaux just before Christmas. I presented myself to the Seigneur in the castle there. We also visited the inn and I saw that it was now an orderly inn and my four bodyguards looked happy.

When we had visited Bordeaux, I had made purchases for Christmas. They were for John and Thomas. I bought them short swords and scabbards. I gave them to the boys on Christmas Day. That Elizabeth was unhappy with the gifts neither surprised nor upset me. I impressed upon the boys that they were not toys and only to be used under the supervision of Ralph. The Christmas feast was less than I had hoped. There was a chilly atmosphere around the table and if it had not been for my squire and my sons would have been miserable. I began to think of an earlier departure than I had planned. Fate intervened in the form of Sir John Chandos who came to visit with me around about Twelfth Night.

Sir John was an old comrade in arms and we spoke the same language. While his escort was entertained in the warrior hall, I sat in the small antechamber next to the hall. A blazing fire made it comfortable and Michael attended.

"The prince has sent me."

I nodded for I knew what was coming, "And how is he?"

"Ready for the crown but he will exercise his mind with this Castilian adventure."

"Ah, he has ranged further afield than is normal, eh?"

"He has and he finds himself fighting men such as you and your company. Bertrand du Guesclin is proving to be a challenging opponent."

"I have not heard of him, my lord. My experience is largely in Italy."

"Where you have earned a mighty reputation and, I hear an even mightier fortune."

"It has been earned at a great cost, my lord."

He held up his hands, "I did not say you had not. The prince would have you serve him."

"My company is in Pisa and we are contracted to the doge of that city."

"But you are English. Most of your men are English. Surely you owe it to your country to fight for her."

"My lord, this war is not being fought because England is in danger, it is to help one of the prince's allies. Besides, I am not certain you could afford us."

His eyes narrowed, "How much does your company charge?"

"Five thousand florins secures our services and then we take a monthly stipend when we fight."

He laughed and shook his head, "But that is when you fight for foreigners. This would be for your future king."

"My lord," I said, reasonably, "we are mercenaries and have to earn a living. Even if the doge would release us, it would take more than two months to fetch my men here and I do not think that you could afford to hire us. I have to, reluctantly, decline the offer." There was no reluctance at all for there was nothing in it for us and if we left Italy then another company would assume our position and we would lose all that we had gained.

He stood and I saw anger written on his face, "You are like the men I spoke to in Bordeaux. They seek coins to fight for England. You have no honour, Sir John Hawkwood, and you are no Englishman."

I stood and faced him, "I have fought and killed men for less, Sir John, but I will forgive the slur. I ask you to hold your tongue and say nothing more for you will regret it. I have honour and I am a true Englishman. I think Crécy and Poitiers proved that. The prince has a short memory; he lets warriors go in time of peace and they have to earn a crust where they can. If England is threatened then send word to me and I will come but as you have the beating of the French, I do not think that is likely, do you?"

After he had gone, I turned to Michael, "Saddle our horses. I need to ride and clear my head for I am as angry as I have ever been." The boys would be at their lessons until noon and I wanted the fresh January air on my face.

We galloped over my fields and through the woods. Soon I had recovered my composure. I knew now what my fellow countrymen thought of me. All my service to England was forgotten. Prince Edward wanted men to die for England and then they would be well thought of. I wheeled my horse and headed for Bordeaux. We walked them through the streets and I rode to the quay. I had come for English archers and men at arms. I spoke to the captains of the English cogs and discovered that many men had landed. They were the ones Sir John Chandos had tried to get to fight for the prince. I knew why they had come; it was for money and they sought employment with the free companies. I would hire those that I could, buy horses and then head back to Marseille. I had done everything in Bordeaux that I wished and my mind was now set. I had a plan for my return. I knew what the White Company would do come the spring. I had Sir John Chandos to thank for that. He had annoyed me so much by his words that it had sowed the seeds of a plan in my head. We headed for the White Cockerel and there was a smile upon my face.

Chapter 18

We found more than twenty archers and ten men at arms and their squires who were willing to join the White Company. Twice that number chose the shorter journey to Castile where they would join Sir Hugh and his men. No wonder Sir John had been angry. He had tried to hire the archers and men at arms for the Black Prince but the lure of gold was too much and the very men he had tried to hire would now fight against England and Castile. Arnaud and the others were quite happy to leave the inn. They had clearly made a small fortune in the time they had been there and the establishment now attracted a clientele with fuller purses. They had made enough contacts to know where to buy horses good enough for the journey home to Marseille. The ones who were most disappointed were John and Thomas who wept when I told them that we were leaving. They had grown fond, not only of me but also Michael.

"What have we done to offend you, father, that you discard us and leave us here?" He managed to imbue the word *'here'* with so much venom that I saw his mother recoil.

"You have done nothing that is wrong, you should know that the two of you are the only reason I have stayed as long as I have, I swear that next Christmas I shall return and you will come with me then. You have a year to grow as much as you can and to learn all that Ralph and Long John have to teach you." They nodded. "And your Christmas gift next year will be your very own mail hauberk. How about that?" It was a bribe and one Elizabeth clearly disapproved of. I cared not.

We headed east and this time we did not need the four bodyguards for we were an armed column that made hamlets and villages close and bar their doors when we passed. I did not begrudge the bodyguards their payment for they were the most excellent guides and shortened our journey to Marseille by two days. When we bade them farewell in Marseille, I was genuinely sad. They were hard men and had rough manners but they were my kind of warriors and I would have been happy to employ them.

I used my position to commandeer two Pisan ships to carry my men and horses back to Pisa. The captains were happy to do so as they would otherwise have had empty ships. As they told me a ship handled better when it had a cargo. We left Marseille in the first week of February. I divided archers, men at arms and horses between the two ships and Michael and I sailed in the larger of the two which had a cabin we could use.

The winds did not cooperate with us and the first day saw us tacking back and forth to make what seemed to me, minimal progress eastwards. The second day was almost as bad and I began to wonder if we should have risked the land route. On the third day, we woke to see three Genoese ships heading for us. They had what the captain called the weather gauge and he prepared to flee south and west to try to outrun them.

"Why run, captain?"

He looked at me as though I had lost my mind. "Because they have armed men aboard their ships and I do not wish to lose my livelihood."

"And you will not for they do not know that we too carry armed men. Do you know how far an English archer can send an arrow?" He was a Pisan and the war bow was an unknown weapon. He shook his head. "With the wind three hundred paces and even into the wind more than two hundred. Keep heading east but make it more south and east. When they are within range, we shall launch such a shower of arrows that these Genoese will think that we have a hundred men aboard each vessel." He looked dubious. "I have hired this ship and your consort. I am employed by Pisa and its doge. I do not ask, I command. Now close with the other vessel so that I may give my instructions."

While we closed, I had the men at arms and archers prepare for war. The archers had plenty of war arrows and I did not think there would be too many mailed men at sea. I cupped my hands and sent over my commands. In the time it took to do this the Genoese had closed to within half a mile of us. They were hunters and knew that their three ships could act as sheep dogs and make us go where they wished. They had expected us to run before the wind and it had taken some time for them to realise their mistake. They would still catch up to us but it would take them slightly longer than they might have anticipated. Our consort sailed on our steerboard quarter so that her bowsprit was protected by our stern. The two cogs each had a bow castle and a sterncastle. The archers were divided between them and I stood with my men at arms and Michael in the waist of the ship. I saw sunlight glinting from spears, pikes, halberds and helmets on the Genoese ships. They would have crossbows and they would be in the bow and stern castles of the three ships.

I went to the sterncastle because I wanted to judge this perfectly. The wind was from the north and east and I intended to use it. The captain had told me that we could still make progress sailing a couple of points into the wind. The crossbows would not be able to reply if we loosed when we had the wind behind us and it was in their faces.

"Now, Captain."

The captain, reluctantly, turned the steering board so that we were almost into the wind. Our consort was closer to the leading Genoese ship and I had given clear instructions to their archers. They were to clear the quarter deck and sterncastle. The archers on my ship would do the same to the bow castle. Twenty-two archers would be able to send a hundred arrows in a very short time. I had never fought the Genoese at sea and I was interested in the result. The Genoese were masters of the northern Mediterranean. If my plan worked, we might make Pisa the new ruler.

I swept my hand down and the twenty-two arrows on the two ships flew. This was not like the land for the target was moving in a number of directions and I did not expect a spectacular result. The flapping sails partly obscured my view but as the fifth flight descended the leading Genoese ship suddenly veered to steerboard as the men at the steering board were slain. It brought the ship broadside on and the sixth flight took the sailors racing to get control of the ship as well as some of the men at arms and crossbowmen. I saw men hit by our arrows and thrown over the side. Some lay over the side of the ship and I doubted that they had a crew to save the ship. The other two ships would have to go to her assistance and that meant they could not follow us.

"Now, captain."

The captain turned his steering board and headed south and east. The wind caught our sails and as the undamaged Genoese ships tried to avoid their stricken leader, we made good our escape. Michael shook his head, "That was very easy, Sir John,"

I nodded, "They have never experienced English archers at sea." I pointed to the tops of the masts. "If we had a small fighting platform there then we could have destroyed all three." I cupped my hands and shouted, "Well done, archers! There will be silver for you when we land!"

It was a good start. We had not expected to fight but we had and we won. When we landed, two days later, both the new men and the ships' crews were all in good humour. My reputation had been enhanced. I confess that as we rode to our home, I felt reinvigorated. The anger when I had been insulted by Sir John Chandos had been replaced by pride. I was a good leader whether on land or sea. I cared not what my fellow English thought of me. England was no longer my home and here, in Italy, I was the master.

That evening Michael and I dined with William, Dai, Giovanni, and Robin. My inner circle were keen to hear my news. I did most of the speaking although Michael, who had grown in confidence over the last months, chipped in now and then.

"You were right to refuse Sir John Chandos, Sir John. The cheek of the man. Why should we die in Spain for a prince who cares not for us?"

I smiled at Robin's anger. He had been the most patriotic of men at one time but he had seen men discarded when war was over and left with no money often having lost limbs in the service of their country. "And now, my friends, I have a plan."

William said, "Before you tell us that, my lord, you should know that Ambrogio Visconti took his company to Naples. He was soundly defeated and now languishes in a Neapolitan dungeon."

I beamed, "Better and better! What happened to those of his company who were not killed?"

"They are spread to the winds, my lord. I am sorry but why does that make you happy?"

"William, I have a mind to make us the only company to rule in northern Italy. Perhaps in time, we can extend the land we control but let us take this one step at a time. Spread the word that the White Company will employ as many of Ambrogio's men as we can. We shall need them."

I had intrigued Giovanni, "We have plenty of men already, my lord. We lost few in the battle with Baumgarten and the men you have brought will fill those ranks."

"Because, Giovanni, I intend to attack first Perugia and then Siena and to do so will need many men. Both cities revelled in our defeat to Baumgarten. We will now make them rue their premature joy. I intend to make them pay a fortune when we defeat them. The only mercenary band left of any size is that of Heinrich Paer. I pray that Perugia hires him so that we can rid Italy of the only competition to the White Company of Sir John Hawkwood. We will go from strength to strength and our competition will simply disappear." William's spies had told him that Heinrich Paer had survived our ambush and the arrow in his shoulder had not killed him. He would seek vengeance.

William nodded. He had been scribbling while I spoke and he said, "Genius, Sir John. How came you about this plan, for you are right? If we are the only mercenary company then we can charge what we like. We have the support of Pisa and Milan. We care not if the Pope hates us for he is powerless."

"The plan came when I spoke to Sir John Chandos. He was so keen to employ our company that I realised the power we held. He was terrified of Sir Hugh and Bernard de Guesclin and yet he was unwilling to pay us what we needed. There is no money in Castile, but Italy? I will speak to the doge on the morrow for he should know what we intend. He will add more florins to our pay and we can hire even more men."

"And when do you intend to start this war, Sir John?"

"Come May we will march on Perugia. We will raid their lands and bleed them dry. By the time it is high summer we shall move on to Siena. This will give us time to hire the men from Ambrogio as well as others who will come from the other companies. When they hear that the White Company is recruiting then I expect a flood."

Outside that room, none knew our intended target. We just said that the company would be raiding in the spring. The obvious target was Florence and we did nothing to stop the gossip. As men arrived to ask for contracts, they brought news of the other companies. The Germans who had been in the Star company had now joined Heinrich Paer and a small number of them had been hired by Siena. Spies told us that despite our secrecy Siena expected our attack but Perugia was arrogant enough to think she was too big a target for my company. The recruits we had were mainly English. A handful of Germans and Hungarians came with them but most of those nationalities chose to join Paer in Siena. The Italians who had followed Ambrogio Visconti joined us. His father visited Pisa just a fortnight after our return.

"Sir John, you have heard that my son has been taken by Naples?"

I nodded. "If you wish me to give a reason, my lord, it is that he overreached himself. We had a relatively easy victory over Baumgarten and he thought it would be simplicity itself to do the same in Naples." I saw his eyes narrow, "What you need from me, my lord, is the truth."

"Aye, you may well be right. He was young and what I have learned of you is that you are the master of your craft. Would you be able to rescue my son?"

Shaking my head I said, "I am not your son and know that there is little for us in Naples. It is a longer journey and we have made plans already."

"Florence?" I said nothing but smiled enigmatically. It would do us no harm if Bernabò Visconti thought that we were raiding Florence. He took my silence and smile for assent. "I did not get to thank you for your help with Genoa. We make good allies."

"We do. And your son?"

"I will see if I can buy him back. The war with Genoa refilled my war chest but I had hoped to take on the Emperor. Now I shall have to use the coin to buy back my son."

"The Emperor?" I wondered if the father was copying his son and overreaching himself too.

"He is not popular and his adherence to the Pope in Avignon means that he is weaker. That adventure will have to wait. I will watch your war with Florence with interest. This time you may not be betrayed by treachery."

"That is for certain." I still wondered if the whole betrayal had not been engineered by the Lord of Milan; certainly, his brother had been involved. I would never know for sure but in my heart, I believed it to be true.

He left a few days later but I was already busy organising the lances and battles we would use. I liked the idea of integrating new men into veteran companies. William knew the size of purses but I knew the character of men and I was the one who formed the companies. The archers were easy and Robin appointed vintenars and centenars from the men who had served us the longest. I had three battles: Dai's, Giovanni's and the one made up of Germans and Hungarians led by a new recruit, Otto von Lipseck. Some of the squires were also promoted to become men at arms. Their charge against Baumgarten's horsemen had shown me that some were ready.

It was early April when we had more visitors into Pisa. Sir Andrew led a hundred horsemen and their squires through Pisa's south gate. I had thought he was still in captivity in Perugia and I was pleased that he had been released but I wondered at his arrival. Had he come to challenge me for the control of the White Company? Was he passing through or was there another reason?

While his men were settled by Dai and Giovanni, William and I entertained the knight who seemed to have been aged by his time in captivity. "I am pleased that you were released, Sir Andrew. Was it expensive?"

He gave a cynical laugh, "Aye, my lord. It cost me all."

I poured him a goblet of wine. There was more to tell, "We are friends here. Let us hear your story."

"Monna is dead." His words made the spring morning suddenly icy. His wife had been young. Had that been what he had meant, everything? "She was with child and the ransom so high that she had to spend longer than she should to meet the ransom demand. The money was sent but by the time I was released and found my home she had lost the baby and her life." He looked gaunt as he said, "I did not even get to say goodbye. She slipped away two days before I reached my home. That was before Christmas. I sold my lands, the few that remained, and used most of it to have a mausoleum built and the last I used to hire the men I brought. Most were held with me and they hate Perugia with a vengeance. We would all join the White Company and serve under you, Sir John."

"And obey all my orders?"

"All of them. I know I let you down the last time I followed your banner but the price I paid has made me a chastened man. I thought that war was noble and fought by men with honour. Our incarceration has made each of us realise the truth. The knight with lofty ideals died in Perugia's dungeon and you see a warrior reborn. I will obey every order you give me, Sir John."

I nodded for I believed him. I looked into his eyes and saw the hatred that burned there. It had replaced the love I had seen when his wife had been alive. "William, have the contracts drawn up. Sir Andrew, you will lead your own lances. I now have five battles to command. You have a month to prepare for war. We leave at the end of this month."

He nodded, "I heard, to Florence?"

I knew that I could trust Andrew and I wanted to give him a reason to live, "No, my friend, but keep this in your head. The men shall not know." I saw his eyes narrow and I said, "We ride to Perugia."

I watched the fire enter his eyes and the youthful smile I had known was replaced by a curling up of the lips, "Then I shall have vengeance and the Perugians shall pay for my loss."

"Remember, not a word. We want Perugia to be surprised when we descend on their sheepfold."

"I told you, Sir John, the old idealist is dead and I will be as close-mouthed as any."

One effect of the arrival of the men we thought we had lost was that the stories they told of Perugian hospitality created antipathy amongst the whole company towards the city-state. We had lost to the company they had hired but mistreatment of mercenary prisoners was rare. They thought we were going to fight Florence. When they discovered that it would be Perugia then they would be like greyhounds straining at the leash.

Each day saw me rise at dawn and not rest until long after the sun had set. I had lost two battles and I did not intend to lose a third. I wanted everything to be just so. When, in the middle of

April, Bianca gave birth to a healthy son, Giovanni, we all took it to be a good sign that our venture would go well. With Dai's wife well into her pregnancy, my former squire was also anxious to defeat Perugia and Siena and then be at his wife's side. Sir Andrew's story had been told around our campfires. We all accepted that we might die but for our families to suffer was unacceptable. The timing of the birth was perfect and when we left Pisa, to head along the Arno valley in the last days of June, there was an air of confidence that rippled down the column.

Chapter 19

Robin commanded the archers as well as two dozen Italian scouts and it was they who cleared the road ahead of us. We wanted the whole of the region to think we intended to raid Florence. The Florentine scouts we found were scattered to the winds by my archers and I knew that the city of Florence would be preparing for war as those who survived the encounters with my men fled to tell them that the White Company was heading east. On the ride from Bordeaux to Marseille, I had been able to formulate my plan. If we had ridden directly for Siena then Perugia would have been warned. This way Siena would think we had forgotten their flank attack that helped Annechin Baumgarten win his victory. We would ride to within fifteen miles of Florence and then head for Arezzo and the Perugian road. Siena would be wary as we passed through the northern parts of their land but reassured when we continued on our way eastwards. I planned on using my archers and Italian scouts as a screen so that no word of our advance would reach them. We had more than seventy miles to travel once we turned south and my plan was to do that in under two days. I wanted shock and surprise to be our allies when we fought the Perugians.

It was as we neared the lake, we called Trasimene and the Italians, Trasimeno, that Sir Andrew rode next to me and pointed to the northern shore of the lake. There the hills we had just crossed rose steeply to the north. "You know, Sir John, that the Romans fought a battle here against the Carthaginians under Hannibal. Twenty-five thousand Romans were killed or sold into slavery for a loss of fewer than two thousand men. Do you think this is an omen?"

I laughed. Sir Andrew had enjoyed a classical education but my more practical one told me that such ancient battles bore no relation to modern ones. "If it was an omen then why did we lose at Perugia after we passed the lake the first time? No, Sir Andrew, it is an interesting story but it bears no relevance to what will happen when we return to Perugia."

I saw disappointment on his face. Michael asked, "Will not the Perugians simply shelter behind their walls?"

"They could but if they did so then we would simply raid the land between here and there. They would lose all the food that would feed them through the winter. They will fight us and they may even think that they can win but they cannot, Michael, for they have no mercenaries this time."

By the time we reached Perugia our horses were exhausted for we had ridden them hard but we had complete surprise and we camped, encircling the city. I remembered every detail of the battlefield and we camped in exactly the same position we had when last we had fought here. This time we would not use stakes for I wanted us to be the more mobile army. With the city effectively cut off on three sides the only escape route for them was the road south. If they took that road then it would take them closer to the lands ruled by their enemy, Queen Joanna of Naples, and I did not think that they would risk it.

I had my leaders join me in the farmhouse we had appropriated. Our campfires would ring the city and add to their fear although as we were more than half a mile away there was little likelihood of either army trying a night raid. I had four new bodyguards; I had hired them in Bordeaux. They stood guard outside the farmhouse to afford us privacy.

"My plan is to do things differently this time we fight. Sir Andrew, I want you and your men mounted. Wear your livery and have your men do the same. The Perugians must recognise you. I want you and your lances to be on the left of the battlefield. They may well expect you to repeat the mistakes you made the last time." I saw his face colour but this was no time to consider his feelings. "I want you to draw their eye. They will expect you to seek vengeance. You will hold yourself until there are five blasts on the horn and then you drive into their flank." He nodded, "Otto, I wish you to play a part too. I want you on our right flank. When you hear two blasts on the horn fall back as though you are retreating, or even fleeing. Move quickly with your backs to the enemy for two hundred paces then turn and face them."

"My men will not like that."

"They will do as I have ordered for just as I want them to think that Sir Andrew and his horsemen are reckless so I want them to think that there is bad feeling between your men and the rest. Robin, you will have two hundred archers ready to shower death upon the Perugians who follow after our German and Hungarian warriors. When I sound three blasts then all, apart from Sir Andrew, will advance."

Robin drank deeply from the goblet of wine, "A complicated plan, Sir John, but a good one. They will be looking for us to do as we did last time."

I nodded, "And that is why our squires will wait on their horses. They showed, the last time, that they can be controlled. Michael will lead them if we need to repeat the tactic that confused Annechin Baumgarten."

Otto and Sir Andrew were mollified when they knew their place in the grand plan. Robin refilled his goblet, "And the archers?"

"Make the ground before us a killing ground. You and your archers will be before us so that when they launch their attack at you, you can do as Otto and run as though you fear them."

He snorted, "That will be the day."

After we had eaten Michael and I went to prepare our weapons and our armour. I know I could have ordered servants to do the work but the day I did that would be the day that something would not work the way it should. Michael had already cleaned it using a bag of dried sand and now, after I had checked each fastening for any sign of wear or tear, he polished it. While he did that, I went over every single mail link. It was time-consuming but necessary. The hauberk was well made and there was no damage. I had chosen an open sallet. I wanted to be able to see the whole battle. The nasal on the helmet was only small but it offered protection for my nose and eyes. I had a new arming cap for the padding on the old one had suffered too many blows over the last year or so. A new one would give me the best protection. Then I took the whetstone and sharpened my daggers, sword, and, lastly, the poleaxe. I like the weapon but it took skill to keep the spike sharp. I knew that after another couple of combats I would need the hammer part of the head to be replaced. I dismissed the thought immediately. Better to have a new one made, perhaps with a longer langet. That done I watched as Michael checked his own equipment. There was less of it but, like many of the White Company, he polished his mail so that it shone. It marked us better than any livery.

Many men would have then summoned a priest to confess. I decided that I would not die the next day and I kept my sins to myself. Since I had been an apprentice tailor I had been used to rising early and the older I got the more I needed to make water. I was awake before any of the others. I left Michael happily sleeping and slipped out, passing my sleeping bodyguards. When they woke and found me gone, they would be angry. For my part, I enjoyed the fact that I could still move silently. I went to the pot we used and relieved myself. I strode to the camps that lay between me and the enemy walls. There was no ham being fried and I was disappointed. However, I could not smell baking bread drifting over from the city and that made me smile. The Perugians, even those who would not fight, were suffering thanks to our attack and that gave me satisfaction. Generally, the people in the towns and cities did not suffer as a direct result of the fighting, yet they enjoyed the benefits of victory. Sir Andrew had told me that when he and the others were taken into Perugia, they had been spat upon and had rotten vegetables hurled at them. That they now had no freshly baked bread was a small victory.

The men were in good heart. The flight from Perugia had hurt their pride. All around me came positive comments.

"We will show them today, eh Sir John?"

"This night we shall dine well in Perugia's walls."

"I hope they have full purses!"

I returned to the farmhouse and poked the embers of the fire into life with fresh kindling. I had an appetite already. There was stale bread and I cut a slice and placed it on the end of my longest dagger. We had found fresh butter in the farmhouse. I would have hot food before Michael rose. I hoped we would have time for breakfast but if the Perugians attacked first we had to be ready. I had learned long ago to eat when you could. The golden bread turned, I toasted the other side. As the fire grew hotter so the toast would cook more quickly and I was soon spreading farmhouse butter on hot, toasted bread. As food goes it was about as simple as you could get but as the melting butter dripped down my chin, I wondered why I did not eat it more often. I had just smeared butter on the third slice when Michael rose. I saw the sky becoming lighter outside. I would have to dress for war and view the Perugian lines.

"You should have woken me, my lord."

I shrugged, "I can still make myself toast, Michael. Dress me now and then prepare breakfast. I need to show myself both to my men and the Perugians."

My bodyguards had heard our voices and rose. Soon the farmhouse was filled with the sound of creaking leather and the chink of mail and plate. I was ready first and while Michael dressed and then began to fry ham I stepped from the farmhouse. In the short time since I had made water the camp had woken and was now a busy place. I smiled, we were not the retinue of some English lord that waited for commands and instructions. We were the White Company and every man had a share in the profits of war. It made them do things without being asked. We needed no trumpet to rouse the men. When I needed them then they would all be ready. Food would wait until they were dressed for war.

I heard horns inside the city. Bells rang and I knew they too were preparing for war. The difference was that our men were camped where they would fight. Andrew, Dai, Robin, Giovanni and Otto had slept amongst their men. The Perugians would need to emerge from their city and march to their positions. It would take time. This battle would not be fought for some hours. The morning was pleasant and, after striding along my lines to show myself, in my white armour, to both friend and foe alike I returned to the farmhouse. "Have a table fetched forth. This is a fine morning and I would dine in full view of Perugia's walls and my men."

The men on the towers and walls of the city would see me and report it. It was a small thing but it would weaken their resolve just a little. To see your enemy dining in full view of your walls without a care in the world would put doubt in their minds.

Sir Andrew rode down and dismounted while I was eating the fried ham nestling beneath the clutch of eggs Michael had fried for me.

As his squire took his horse the knight said, "A fine breakfast, Sir John."

"Come and join me." I lowered my voice, "And then you can tell me what brings you from your position."

He sat next to me in the seat vacated by Michael, "One of the scouts from the east brought us a rider who had tried to escape the city. He was heading for Siena."

I nodded, "And he did not use the obvious gate which would have been the one to the west. So Siena and Perugia are still allies."

He nodded as his squire handed him a platter of fried salted ham, "And they may not fight this day."

I knew what was on his mind. If the Perugians stayed behind their walls then allies could come to their aid. It would suit the Sienese to fight the battle on Perugian land. "Then, if they have not attacked by noon you take your battle and ravage the land to the east. Take all that you can. We will see if burning farmhouses puts steel in their spines." I did not think that the Perugians would wait until noon to attack but Sir Andrew had been defeated and taken prisoner. I was giving him something to plan to stop his mind from dwelling on the past. I never dwelt on the past, I learned from it.

It was nonce when the gates opened and with trumpets, flags and drums the Perugians marched from the three main gates. There was no rush from my men. They finished their food and then, taking their weapons strode to their allotted positions, marshalled by vintenars and centenars. The enemy host milled around as their different units tried to find their own muster point. They wasted time and energy in doing so. It gave me the chance, as I sat on my horse, to view the army we faced. There were no Genoese crossbowmen with their pavesiers. Instead, it was militia crossbows we faced. They could be cut down by arrows. Their feditore began to form up on the two flanks. The centre was held by nobles although I recognised the armour and livery of some German and Hungarian soldiers. Not all had joined Paer. Some who had fought with Baumgarten had hired their swords to the Perugians. The army we faced outnumbered us but not in quality. They must have emptied the city of every male who could bear a weapon. They had even enlisted boys as slingers. Looking beyond them I saw few men on the walls. My plan would work.

Harold, one of my new bodyguards said, "Sir John, do you allow them the time to form up?"

I nodded, "I do for it does not do to interrupt an enemy when he is making a mistake."

"A mistake, my lord?"

"His strength is in the centre and his feditore are inclined to run either forward or back as the mood takes them. I would have strengthened the flanks with nobles. They are not a free company, Harold, they do not have the discipline of our men." Dismounting I said, "I have seen enough, Michael. Take my horse to the rear and fetch me my poleaxe and standard. Today we will fight alongside Dai and his men."

I chose Dai for his position was the most central and it would encourage his men if I joined them. The Perugians would come for me and my standard. With no stakes before us and ground that they knew well it would encourage an attack.

I was proved right and it was an hour before noon when the attack began. They had some bolt throwers on the walls and I saw the reason for the men standing there. The bolt throwers were at extreme range and I was not afraid. Used since the Roman times they made an alarming crack when the bolt was released and I knew that, at close range, a bolt could travel through several men. Had we been advancing then the bolts might have done some damage but the ones that did reach our lines were easily stopped by shields. It did more damage to the Perugians than to us for some fell amongst their waiting men and they soon stopped using them. We waited as did they.

I waved Robin over, "They need some encouragement."

He nodded, "Aye, Sir John." He had organised his men well and he shouted to three of his centenars. They walked forward towards the Perugians with their men. It made them load the bolt throwers again and it was laughable to watch the bolts sent at the loose line of men. The crack told the archers when the bolt had been released and of all my men, they knew how to judge the flight of a missile. There were jeers as each bolt was easily and contemptuously avoided. When the three hundred archers were two hundred and fifty paces from the enemy Robin stopped and ordered the nock and the draw. Even as the Perugian crossbows began to send their bolts at them the arrows descended. Robin sent just five flights and then I heard his stentorian voice as it commanded his archers to retreat. Five of his men had been wounded by bolts and they were helped back.

As he passed me, he said, "They have left seventy men on the field, my lord and they are not very good crossbowmen. If you wish I could take all the archers and end this battle in under an hour."

I shook my head, "Even five wounded archers is five too many. We stick with the plan."

It was like prodding a wild animal with a stick. As the dead Perugians were taken away their horns sounded and I knew they would attack. I did not need to issue a command. Shields were pulled around while pole weapons and swords were readied. Archers nocked arrows and we waited. I watched the Perugians as they raced across the ground to get to us before the arrows could do their worst. They ran with shields held aloft knowing that archers used a plunging trajectory. As soon as they were in range the arrows descended. Their shields and their speed saved most of them and that seemed to encourage them to run at us harder. I had my four bodyguards flanking me and Michael with my banner and his horn behind.

"Brace!"

It was a simple command but all heeded it. With one leg behind and, if they held one, the haft of the pole weapon rammed in the ground every man at arms and knight waited for the weight of those behind to support them. Even Michael leaned into my back.

When Baumgarten's men had attacked us, they had come steadily and as one line. The Perugians did not. Encouraged by the static nature of our defence they hurled their bodies and weapons to try to break our lines. I did not even have to move to skewer my first victim. He simply ran into the spike of my poleaxe. His spear rammed my breastplate but the bodies behind held me firmly in place and the padding I wore beneath saved my body from harm. The clash and crash of weapons on mail were deafening and any orders that might have been given were a waste of breath. I swung the head of my poleaxe and deflected a spear. One of my bodyguards lunged with his sword and stabbed the Perugian in the neck.

I deemed it was the time for the first signal. "Michael, two blasts on the horn."

I knew that Sir Andrew would be readying his men. With the whole of their line engaged they would have forgotten the horsemen on their flank. They had crossed the open ground and suffered few losses and now they were holding the White Company. As Otto and his men fell back, I heard a cheer and we began to echelon back. As the feditore, sensing victory, hurtled after Otto von Lipseck, Robin's archers suddenly unleashed a wave of death in the form of arrows. It was as though the attack had been punched. The inevitable happened, as we echeloned back and Otto reformed his line so the Perugians emulated us and their line was stretched. To militia and those who were unused to war, it would feel as though we were all falling back. In truth, we had barely been hurt. Our lines held firm and our archers were now reaping a harvest of those trying to come to the aid of those in the front rank.

"Michael, signal Sir Andrew!"

I had rarely used a cavalry charge and the reason was simple. It was too easy to put barriers in their way added to which horsemen who are charging rarely like to stop. My plan negated both those objections. Sir Andrew was attacking the flank and rear of the Perugians and if he did not stop it mattered not. The thunder of hooves from the east made even those close to me turn their heads. It cost three of them their lives as my bodyguards and I struck at them. The thundering hooves grew closer and with it the cries and screams of men who were being ridden down and lanced by men with nothing but vengeance on their mind. As Sir Andrew and his men rode past me the Perugians broke and I shouted, "Sound the advance." The regular single blast on the horn was the signal to move forward. We did not need to run, we could adopt a steady gait. Sir Andrew and his men would wheel when they passed Otto and his men and then ride for the gate. Men on foot could not outrun horses. We accepted the surrender of those who dropped their weapons and that was the majority. One who tried to keep running when we chased them was felled by a tap to the helmet. He would be taken prisoner and have a bloody coxcomb for his trouble. By the time I reached the gate, I realised that I was no longer a young man, the battle was over and Perugia was ours. My defeat had been avenged.

Chapter 20

Many of the Perugian horsemen escaped us. When they reached their city, seeing Sir Andrew coming for them, they continued to ride through the city and left by the south gate. The rest were taken and we disarmed them. Their leaders greeted us in the Great Hall. I allowed Sir Andrew to accept the surrender of the town although I was the one who negotiated the ransom for the city which was high. We stayed for two days and then leaving Otto to command the city we left to head towards Siena.

The Sienese knew that we were coming. The fleeing Perugians had ridden ahead to tell them of the disaster. We gathered plenty of treasure and supplies and then, instead of heading directly to Siena, rode to the south of Lake Trasimene. Siena was close enough to Florence to represent a threat to both our flanks and supply lines back to Perugia. Our route would still approach Siena but from a safer direction. Otto would stay at Perugia until all the ransoms were paid and we had defeated Siena. If he objected to being left out, he wisely said nothing. As we rode towards Siena we ravaged and plundered as we went. This land had been free from attack and was rich. The purses of the merchants bulged and we went slowly enough to extract every florin we could. The stipend from Florence not to attack them and the pay from Pisa to defend it were enough to pay our men. Everything on the Perugia, Siena raid was profit.

With our now confident Italian scouts and Robin's archers, we had a screen of men who warned us of any danger. Sir Andrew and his five hundred mounted men at arms were our vanguard and such was their zeal that they managed to clear the minor obstacles that lay in our path. Perhaps the Sienese thought that we were heading home and had forgotten them for it was not until Montalcinello, thirteen miles from Siena, that they finally sent an army to stop our progress. It was, in many ways, the perfect place to stop us for it guarded the southwest approach to Siena. There was just one road through the Tuscan hills and they gathered a huge army. The Perugians we had defeated and fled had joined them and they filled the horizon before us. They would make no attempt to attack us. Our victories had ensured that they would fight a defensive battle. They had made pavise behind which their militia could take shelter. They had two mounted battles on each flank and, behind the crossbowmen, they had gathered their feditore. The last lines were dismounted mailed men at arms. What I did not see were the Germans and Hungarians of Heinrich Paer. We were fighting citizens. That they would give us a hard fight was clear to me. They knew that defeat would result in financial ruin and with winter ahead they did not want us to take the bread from their table.

I gathered my leaders in the small house that overlooked the town. It was not the largest house in the village we occupied but it had the best view of our opponents.

Had Otto been with us he would have been nervous for he was new to us but the others trusted both me and their own abilities. "We have a wall of steel before us and they expect us to make a frontal assault where their crossbows, darts, javelins and handguns will take their toll. They expect us to bleed before them and then take our treasure back to Pisa."

Robin nodded, tearing some flesh with his teeth from the mutton we had cooked, "And that would be the clever thing to do for we are rich men already and what does Siena have that we need?"

He was being typically Robin. Playing devil's advocate he wanted us to attack but he wanted me to give the reasons.

"They have the pride they robbed us of and they need to be taught a lesson. Does anyone around this table think that Perugia will be quick to send men against us in the future or will they do as Florence has done and buy us off?" I was answered by silence. "We will do as we did at Cascina. The plan did not work then but it will work this time. We use our archers to duel with their crossbowmen. Hopefully, the feditore will obligingly charge us but I do not think we will be so lucky a second time. Then we will withdraw and first, Sir Andrew on the left and then I on the right, will make feint attacks. We will ride up to within two hundred paces and turn. Their horsemen will respond with a counterattack. We will dismount and rest and then Dai and Giovanni will do the same. After a pause, Sir Andrew and I will repeat our charge and then Dai and Giovanni. But between the last two charges, Robin and his men on foot will advance and weaken their centre again.

Dai nodded, "You want them to use up their bolts and powder and exhaust their horses. Then we attack?"

"Then we attack. The archers will be supported by a thousand lances on foot. They will advance and then Sir Andrew, Dai and the squires will launch a cavalry attack from our left and Giovanni and I will do the same on the right. We will hit them together. Their apparent strength is their horsemen on the flanks that guard their weaker warriors. I want them tired before we charge them. Our strength lies in the arms of our archers who can defeat the crossbowmen and then the feditore. Their centre will crumble when we launch our flank attacks. We begin our archers' attack on the tenth hour of the morrow and the first cavalry attack will be at the eleventh. When horsemen have attacked, they return to our lines, water their horses and, those who are able, change horses for the second attack."

Many of my more experienced lances had more than one horse. I would ride Michael's horse for the first feint and my spare for the second. My best horse, Ajax, I would leave for the final attack.

Their nods of approval told me that they saw how we might win. Our last attack would be launched in the afternoon when they had the sun in their eyes.

I had men moving about early to confuse our enemies although in truth we were just eating breakfast. Their horns told me that they expected an early attack. In fact, it was just our squires who made it seem like the whole company was roused. From my vantage point, I smiled as I saw the enemy standing to and saddling their horses. Ours would remain grazing and without saddles until the last moment. Those who do not go to war do not understand how hard it is to stand in armour and wait for a battle. It exhausts both men and animals. Men are also exhausted mentally. The men we fought were not mercenaries. They did not wear mail and plate every day as we did. Waiting for an enemy to charge would make them nervous. Their bowels would demand to be emptied and men leaving the battle line for the most mundane of bodily functions could appear worrying as their fellows would wonder if they would return. We ate a leisurely breakfast and dressed half an hour after the nonce. I smiled as I saw Sienese riders dismount and let their squires walk their horses. The plan was working.

When we formed up at the tenth hour the Sienese and Perugian horns sounded and they mounted. We did not mount. I had already decided not to wear a helmet until the final attack. It was one weight I would not have to carry. The archers marched forward so quickly and began to release so rapidly behind the line of shielded men at arms that the enemy warriors were taken by surprise. Stepping from behind a pavise to loose a bolt sounds easy but if every crossbowman has four or five arrows heading for him then they are going to suffer more casualties. The crossbows cracked but it was not a thunderous crack suggesting all were released at the same time. It was a regular crack that bespoke a few men being able to release. Robin pulled his men back having lost a handful. Before the enemy could relax, I mounted Michael's horse. He stood behind me.

"Sound the charge."

I spurred my horse to ride towards the enemy. I heard the horns sound and, as they saw no archers within range the crossbowmen stepped from behind the pavise to lose at us. I saw the smoke pop from a couple of handguns and then when we were just two hundred and fifty paces away and the enemy horsemen riding towards us, I held my hand up to stop us. The men had been given clear instructions and they all halted. We had the enemy confused. A few bolts came at us but like the first ones sent at us were wasted. I raised my lance and led the men back. Sir Andrew, having seen my signal, did the same. Their horsemen were confused and, expecting a trick were still standing, stranded between our two battle lines while we dismounted.

As soon as we reached our lines, I took my men behind Giovanni's where, hidden by their horses, we dismounted. There was laughter and banter at the ruse we had pulled off. Michael brought me my spare horse and then led his to be watered. Those who had spare horses had their squires fetch them. It was less than an hour later that our second feint charge was made. This had exactly the same result except that the two groups of horsemen attempted a countercharge rather than an advance. Dai and Giovanni extricated their men without them coming into contact and a few arrows from Robin and his men discouraged the enemy horsemen further. When our men returned, they waited behind us. The Sienese and Perugians had remained mounted and the sun was now as hot as it would get and made armour hot to the touch. Horses needed as much water as could be found.

When I made our third attack, I only waited thirty minutes and it was clear that they thought that this was the real attack for bolts and handguns were all used and a pall of thin smoke drifted between our lines. This time the enemy horsemen attacked sooner but it was child's play to sweep my lance to the side and lead my men back. The enemy tried to pursue but when a dozen men and horses were hit by arrows they returned to their own lines.

When I dismounted this time, I drank deeply and waved Robin forward, almost immediately. We really had them confused and I saw the horsemen preparing to attack not us, but Robin and his screen of men at arms. Six flights of arrows had been sent in the enemy's direction before the horsemen made a move. Their horses had made three charges. Most of our horses had made one or two at the most. I saw that the Sienese and Perugian horses were tiring and Robin and his men fell back without loss.

Dai and Giovanni's next attack was made and this time the horsemen just watched them come knowing that it would not be carried through. Few of their crossbows loosed bolts. I mounted my best horse, Ajax. He wore a mail shaffron and a thick trapper. I donned my helmet. I saw our archers choose their best arrows and hold them in their left hands. I knew what they would do. When they reached the point at which they would release they would ram the ten arrows in the ground so that they could release their missiles as quickly as possible. Unseen by the enemy Giovanni's men now formed up behind us and half of our squires behind them. After half an hour as I led my horsemen forward, I saw the crossbowmen watching us but their weapons were not in their hands. We cantered as we had on the previous occasions but instead of halting two hundred and fifty paces from the enemy, we spurred our horses. At the same time, the archers and dismounted men at arms ran forward. The enemy soldiers were caught napping. Some riders had dismounted and the crossbowmen and hand gunners were spectators. As soon as they saw the archers running, they reacted but it was too late. The archers stopped two hundred and fifty paces from the enemy and then death dropped from the skies. The horsemen tried a belated counter charge but some were on foot and the line that came at us was slow and it was ragged.

My lance took one man in the chest and was then torn from my grip. I drew my sword and swept it across the chest of the surprised knight whose lance was held too low. Our lines were solid and theirs were not. The men at the fore were our best riders and we reached their second line intact while theirs was a broken shambles of a line. Giovanni and my squires were spreading out behind us so that the impact was spread over a wider front. The centre of the Sienese and Perugian line had more holes in it than a pauper's underwear and the crossbowmen had broken taking with them, as they fled, some feditore towards the dismounted men at arms. Our ever-enveloping lines sent the enemy cavalry back to their own lines and the wild panicked horses galloped through to head for Siena. As we neared the dismounted men at arms we slowed. Our horses were tiring and I wanted as many of those on the battlefield eliminating rather than chasing those in flight.

We were stopped only by the dark. Half of the enemy army had escaped. They were mainly the cavalry and the dismounted men at arms who had managed to reach their horses. I knew that many of the feditore and crossbowmen who had escaped would be in the hills but it was not worth pursuit. We stopped in the enemy camp and devoured the food that they had brought with them. We had defeated them and the road to Siena was now open.

Although the rest of the company, my leaders apart, seemed to believe that the Sienese would simply surrender we did not. The men we had fought and defeated had been hastily cobbled together to slow us down. The real battle would be at Siena. Heinrich Paer had ten companies of mercenaries with him. They would not be fighting on horses but in their best formation, on foot. Their two-handed swords, long axes and pole weapons would hurt us and I wanted as many of my men to survive as possible. Over the last couple of years, our losses had been too high. The English men I had led from France into Italy had been whittled down until less than two hundred of the original company remained alive and all of those were leaders. I needed to keep as many men alive as I could. We did not race to Siena. We had wagons with plunder and food and we did not need to exhaust men and horses in the summer heat. We also raided as we rode. There were farms, hamlets and towns dotted along the valley and we made just five or ten miles a day, stopping at captured villages and farms. We ate well and our plunder grew. Our horses were watered regularly and they grazed not only on grass but the crops that would normally have been harvested in a month or more. Siena was paying a high price for her treacherous attack.

By the time we reached Siena, the Sienese must have wondered if we were ever coming. However, they were prepared and we saw their army camped before the city. They had planned well and as well as Heinrich Paer's men, all of them mailed, plated and well-armed I also saw some Genoese crossbowmen. This was not Grimaldi's men but the small company were professionals such as we. I also saw Enrico Montforte and his Florentine horsemen. They had been the ones we had defeated in Savoy but who had then turned the tables on us at Cascina. I would not underestimate them.

We camped but I made it a defensive camp. They had two leaders whom I knew and both were capable of a John Hawkwood plan or ruse. We embedded stakes before us and dug a shallow ditch as well as using the wagons as a wooden barricade. I rode with my leaders along our front as my men made us defensible.

Their core was made up of their professionals. Paer's men were camped in the centre with the crossbowmen before them. I saw that they had emulated us and had laid stakes before them. The Florentine horsemen were on the right and the Sienese and Perugian nobles were on the left. Behind them were the militia and feditore. There was a huge number of them and unlike Perugia, there were many men on the walls. We were outnumbered and this time there were enough enemy mercenaries for the disparity in numbers to make a difference.

    We reined in and dismounted. I knelt to feel the ground. It was hard and dry. While that suited cavalry the enemy had prepared for that and a frontal charge would be a mistake. Robin was my most practical warrior and he took a swig from his ale skin, "Whichever way you look at it this will be a bloodbath. To get to the Sienese whom you could slaughter, Sir John, you must get through men who can fight as well as you. The Genoese will be hard to dislodge and will not be as easy to kill as those we found at Montalcinello."

    Sir Andrew, who was always the one for a reckless charge said, impatiently, "So we squat like toads and starve them out?"

    Robin was not one to mince his words, "Or perhaps do as you did, my lord and charge the enemy so that our men are captured and spend time locked in a dungeon. Let me see…" He snorted and put the stopper back in his ale skin with a finality that made Sir Andrew recoil. No one, save me, perhaps, would have taken on Robin. He was too strong a man.

    I spoke firmly, "Now is not the time to turn on each other. There is always a way but we have yet to see it. Let us return to our camp. Michael, the pig we slaughtered at the last village, have it butchered and put on to cook with some of the wine we took. While the meat is made tender, we will drink some wine and talk through what we can and cannot do." I looked at Robin and Andrew who still glared at each other, "As friends."

    I knew what had created the animosity. Eoin and Martin had been close friends with Robin and their deaths had affected him. While Eoin's death could not be laid at Sir Andrew's door, Martin's could. I had been able to forgive the reckless knight but Robin could not. Their backgrounds were as different as any. One had grown up, like me, fighting for everything in life while the other had been a pampered lord with ideas of chivalry which we did not hold.

    It was a warm evening and there was still heat in the sun so we seated ourselves in the shade of a stand of trees. As Michael organised the cooking of the food the other squires brought us wine then hurried off to follow Michael's orders.

Dai and Giovanni were both thoughtful knights. They had been with me as long as Robin and when they spoke, I always listened. Dai nodded towards the enemy camps behind the stakes, "They expect us to make a sneak attack on them."

Giovanni nodded, "Aye, they hope that we will rush across the open ground before dawn and get at them."

"Yes, Giovanni, but what if, instead of sending a mass attack we send perhaps four hundred men. Three hundred archers and a hundred men at arms. We get to the stakes and then the archers send three thousand arrows into their camp. Men would not be wearing mail and although we could not count on all the arrows hitting flesh, enough would so that they would be angry. The next two nights are perfect for there will be no moon."

I saw Giovanni nod and smile, "Aye, for Robin's men are seen as devils for they cannot be defeated easily. The weather, at this time of year, often brings clouds at night. I see how your plan, Dai, could work, it is cunning."

"It is but there could be a refinement. While the hundred men at arms could act as a defence for the archers, the four hundred men would have to cross almost three quarters of a mile. You can bet that Enrico Montforte has horsemen ready to ride at a moment's notice. We will also have a hundred mounted men at arms. They will be ready to charge any who come to punish the archers."

"I will lead the horsemen, Sir John."

"No, Sir Andrew, you will not. I will for I would not lose a single man. Dai, it is your plan, you choose the one hundred men. Robin, would you lead the archers?"

He snorted, "Who else? It is a good plan, Dai, and I will choose the archers. Do we go this night?"

I shook my head, "No, we let them wonder what we plan and besides I want the men we send to be well-rested. The five hundred men who will make the attack spend the day resting. The others can move around as though they are planning to attack. That will be your task, Sir Andrew, and Giovanni. You need to do as we did at Montalcinello and keep them alert. The survivors from that battle will tell them what we did." I smiled at the humour of it all, "We use a ruse to make them think we use the same trick but we will not. The legend of the White Company will grow."

One thing I had learned since I had begun to run the company as Hawkwood's men, was that you had to have a good chain of command. My leaders each knew their task and when they had selected their men, they told the others what they would be doing. It meant that once I had spoken then I needed to do nothing more. When I rose the next day, I did so late. Perhaps those on Siena's walls might wonder why Sir John Hawkwood was not stalking the battle lines. They might become suspicious and wonder if I was planning an attack on another part of their land or even their walls. As I enjoyed a leisurely late breakfast, I reflected that Siena's defenders should have been more aggressive and brought the fight to us. This stalemate suited us for I knew what I would do. Their battle plan appeared to be to react to whatever we did. When that was done, I went with Michael and we inspected our horses. The exertions of Montalcinello had been hard on horses and men. I wanted to see if any lasting damage had been done to the horses. After a good inspection, Ajax appeared sound in limb and eager for war. Michael groomed them, and I gave my warhorse the treats he liked.

I had the luxury of time and so I sat and wrote two letters. One was to my sons and one was to John Braynford. I knew that I was not as good a father as I should have been and that annoyed me for after the way I had been treated by my own I had been determined to try to be a better father. I had obviously failed. The letters took me to lunch to write and I had that rarity, a lunch with my leaders. Wine or beer at noon always makes me sleepy and the heat encouraged me to sleep in the afternoon. The Italians all enjoyed such a rest but to we English, it was alien. I woke when the sun began to head west and I felt refreshed. After preparing my weapons for the night attack I went to speak to the men I would be leading. My four bodyguards would ride as close to me as a second skin. I needed the rest to be spread out and appear a greater number than we were. I told them that we would be using spears. Lances might be too cumbersome but I knew that any men who came after us would not have time to dress and arm for war properly. A long spear would give each of us an edge.

Sir Andrew was quite animated as, when we ate after dark, he told us of the tricks that they had used during the day. Mounting men and suddenly galloping towards the walls of Siena had resulted in horns and panic. I confess I had heard the horns as I had sat writing. Giovanni had then mustered the archers, mounted them and ridden them to within three hundred paces of the crossbowmen. He had laughed when he told me that rather than horns it elicited the bringing out of more pavise and shields. It was a lesson for the real attack. They had shown us what they had planned. When the archers had ridden back the defenders had stood to, expecting another attack. They would be tired and tired men make mistakes.

That night we kept the same fires as the night before and all but the five hundred men who would be moving out to be the killers in the night. Dai and the men at arms wore no mail but went out in gambesons and brigandines with arming caps and coifs. They carried smaller shields than normal. We had taken many round ones from the feditore at Montalcinello. In the dark, we might be confused for their own men. Our archers had short swords and just fifteen arrows in their belts. All were war arrows. As silence fell, Dai and Robin led their men out towards Siena's walls. I allowed them a start and then the one hundred men I commanded led our horses in a long line. We were helped by the fact that the Sienese kept their horses well away from us. I think they feared we might cut them out. That meant their animals would not neigh when they smelled ours.

We crossed the open, shrub-covered ground in darkness. We were invisible but the campfires of the sentries not only marked their position but also spoiled their night vision. It was not cold at night, in Italy but the Italians found it so. English and German sentries were quite happy to forego a fire if it meant they could see their enemies approaching.

Robin had a good sense of the range and when he stopped, I knew that we were in killing range. Dai and his one hundred men stood behind the archers and we led our animals to the right of the archers and men at arms. I wanted a good view of the arrow storm. It seemed inconceivable that no one saw the shadow that appeared before them but, apparently, they did not. Robin gave no commands but he nocked an arrow and then drew. I had been an archer and knew the effort needed to do as he did. The creaking of his bow was the signal for the others and it was that sound, four hundred yew bows creaking as they stretched that alerted the Sienese sentries.

"What is that?"

As the second flight was sent, I said, "Mount."

Screams rent the night as the first four hundred arrows plunged to earth. In the dark, at least half would miss and the other half might not cause a mortal wound but as men stood or emerged from tents and the next arrows fell so there were more targets and men were hit. From the back of my horse, I saw the confusion and mayhem that resulted from the attack. Horns sounded and I caught an order to mount cavalry.

Robin shouted, "Done!" as the last flight was sent.

"Michael, sound fall back." The archers grabbed their bows and took to their heels passing through Dai and his men. Then Dai and his men began to walk backwards. I heard horses and I shouted, "Dai, run!" Lowering my spear I shouted, "Follow me! Michael, stay close to me." The command was for his protection. I had four bodyguards and they would ensure that he remained unharmed. I saw men rushing out from their camp to wreak their revenge on the archers who must have slain friends and shield brothers. It was when they heard the hooves of our horses that they stopped but for half a dozen of them, it was too late. I speared a feditore who wore just a gambeson and carried a spear and shield. Then I saw the horsemen. I wheeled my horse, "Ignore the men on foot. Take out the horsemen." The men on foot had no chance of catching Dai and his men.

Our move caught the men on foot by surprise and they were forming a shield wall for an attack that never materialised. We were an arrow point aimed at the horsemen with me and my bodyguards in the centre. We tore into half-dressed mounted men at arms and a couple of knights. They had swords in their hands and one or two had shields but we were all armed with spears and simply skewered the horsemen. I did not want to risk getting too deep into their lines and I shouted, "Michael, sound the retreat!" As the horn sounded, I hurled my spear at the nearest horsemen and it caught him in the shoulder making him rein in. Drawing my sword, I wheeled my mount and lay low over the neck of my horse. We galloped. The whole of the Florentine camp was like an angry disturbed wasps' nest. They would follow us but I was unconcerned. Robin was too good a leader not to have a reception prepared and, sure enough, as we neared our own camp, I saw that the men were all awake and ready to fight. Arrows soared over our heads to fall onto the horsemen who pursued us. I wondered if I had precipitated a battle. If so, we would win but when I heard the horns recalling the men pursuing us, I knew it would not. We had not won the battle but, as with a game of chess, we had made the opening moves and we held the advantage. The question was could I turn that advantage into victory?

Chapter 21

We had a few men stand to and keep watch all night but they were not needed. When we rose the next day the Florentine dead were still being carted from the camp. A German, under a white flag, came to ask permission to collect the bodies that lay betwixt our two camps. I, of course, allowed it. It was in our interests to do so. The sight of so many dead bodies would demoralise the enemy and the clearing operation could only help us. It was in the afternoon that I held my council of war.

"Thank you, Dai, the plan worked far better than we could have hoped. Tonight they may plan a revenge attack. Robin, have your archers go out after dark and lay traps to warn us. We attack in the morning at first light."

Sir Andrew said, "You know already how we will fight?"

"I saw, by the light of their fires, that their stakes are too close to the walls of Siena. It means that they cannot defend in depth. We know that their strength lies in the mercenaries in the centre. I plan to draw their eye there. I will lead a thousand lances and, supported by Robin and half of the archers, we will advance on their centre. Sir Andrew will lead his men to make an attack on the extreme right of their line but only when my battle is engaged with Paer's men. Giovanni will do the same on the other side of the battlefield. Each of you will have the rest of Robin's archers. They can ride with you until in range. The squires can hold the archer's horses. Dai, you and your men will be behind Robin's archers. Once we are engaged then you will pass through the archers and join my men. The battle at the fore will be bloody and I cannot see either side winning quickly." I shrugged, "Giovanni and Andrew we will win or lose this battle with your efforts. I will just hold their attention but you two will win this war."

Michael was with us, "And the rest of the squires?"

"We will keep as a reserve. You, Michael, will lead them. I know I am giving you great responsibility and you are little more than a youth but you have a sharp mind and I think that, like Dai, you have learned well by following me." I saw my squire grow before my eyes. It was a risk but I now had four bodyguards. A squire was a luxury and what I needed was another man at arms. By testing Michael's skills as a leader I might make not only a man at arms but another leader.

We went through the plan and the signals until I knew that we all understand what we had to do and when. I knew that if everyone did as I had told them then we had a good chance of victory. Thanks to Perugia and Montalcinello we had already won but victory the next day would make it complete.

I used Dai's squire, John, to accompany me with the horn. It would be good for him to experience the pressure that carrying the standard and horn entailed. After I had told him of his task, he and Michael went off so that my squire could ensure he understand everything.

That night the Florentines did try to return the compliment and raid us. Thanks to Robin's traps they were heard and sent scurrying back to Siena even before I had risen. The putative attack was just an hour before the time I was due to rise and so I remained awake and ate an earlier breakfast than I had planned. Michael too was nervous and he rose when he heard the commotion. He helped me to dress and then went to the horses. He wanted his horse to be as well prepared as he was. Unlike the Sienese we needed no horns and drums to waken us and the company rose and readied for work as though they were bakers on the early shift. I had been at Poitiers and heard the bravado and false courage of knights and men at arms who were trying to impress others. There was none of that in my company and it felt like a monastery with monks going through a familiar ritual that was their daily routine.

Before first light, we were all in position. The two battles of horsemen walked their mounts to their allotted positions. They were both echeloned back and they hid the mounted archers behind them. When the sun rose fully the Sienese would know that we had two blocks of horsemen ready to attack but the closer block of dismounted men at arms and archers would be seen as the more imminent threat. We walked to our starting position and waited for dawn. Their night guards had seen our movement and they did sound their horns to rouse their camp. The ones who had attacked us would be tired. Of the twelve bodies my men had recovered, eight of them were German and so it was likely that Heinrich Paer's company had been responsible. They would be the ones I would be facing.

 We had four hundred yards to cover before we reached our enemy and as they still had stakes embedded then I knew that they would not advance. That suited me. When we were all gathered, I pointed my poleaxe and we advanced. This time I wore a small buckler attached to my left arm. It would help me to deflect any bolt that came in my direction and as I wore a helmet with a visor it would take a lucky strike to hit my eye and my plate would stop other missiles from penetrating too deeply. I knew that a bolt might hit, say, the plate on my upper arm but the plate, the mail and the padded sleeved gambeson would slow down the tip. The silk on the gambeson would prevent the wound from being too serious and I could fight with a bolt in my upper arm or even my leg. We all understood the risks.

 We stopped when we saw the Genoese step from behind their pavise and before we reached the stakes. Planting my poleaxe in the ground I held my buckler directly before my face and then turned to the side. The first bolts slammed into my buckler and pinged off my plate armour. They sounded terrifying but I trusted in the weaponsmith who had made my armour. The ones with poorer made armour were the ones who cried out. Then I heard cries from ahead and knew that the Genoese, emboldened by their success, had been tardy in retiring. Robin's archers did not miss and when no bolt came in my direction for a count of ten, I lowered, gingerly, the buckler. As I did so Robin and Tall Tom slid alongside me and stood, less than two hundred and twenty paces from the enemy. Here an arrow would drive through a pavise. I watched the duel before me. Thanks to our night raid and the first volley, my archers outnumbered the crossbowmen by more than two to one. As they could send an arrow six times quicker then the duel was a short one. I later learned that ten archers had been hit, five mortally but the Genoese, the ones who survived, fled. In their flight, they disrupted the lines of the Germans and Hungarians behind them. In that time my archers reaped the reward and their bodkins drove through plate, mail and helmets. As soon as they were able Heinrich Paer, I saw him before me, reorganised their lines and they began to advance towards their stakes. They would be the ones disrupted by them and not us. Our archers passed through us so that they could send more arrows from behind us and Dai's men. I knew that we had to fight the mercenaries and not yield an inch. I was no longer in charge of this battle. I trusted my leaders and like Hannibal, Caesar, Alexander, I was trusting to my plan and like those great generals at Cannae, Alesia and Issus I would fight where the fighting was hottest. That was what leaders did, they led.

It took the enemy some time to negotiate the stakes and that gave us the opportunity to fill the gaps from the fallen men so that Paer and his men would face a solid line. They hurried towards us because our archers had yet to send another flight of arrows over our heads. That was a mistake for the first eager Hungarian reached me and two of my bodyguards alone. I parried his halberd and my two bodyguards rammed their own weapons through his body.

Heinrich Paer saw more men fall and shouted, "Form lines!"

In the time it took to stop and steady themselves my archers began their song of death as the arrows they sent seemed to sing rising and falling to crack and draw a cry of pain. Paer was not in the front rank. He had chosen to organise his men. I fought a German with a two-handed sword and an open-faced helmet. My bodyguards also had opponents. Standing on either side of me, my flanks would be guarded but it would be my skill that defeated the swordsman. I blocked his first overarm strike by catching his blade between the head of the hammer and the spike. While the edge of the sword would begin to lose its keenness, my newly forged weapon was unharmed. More importantly, the bottom of the poleaxe was embedded in the ground and the ground absorbed most of the force. The effort would begin to drain him. As he pulled back the sword for a second strike, I simply lowered the spike of the poleaxe and it gouged a long line down his cheek. It was an irritant rather than a winning blow. Behind him, I saw Paer studying my moves. He expected his man to lose but he would learn from the warrior's death. The swordsman chose a different strike and he pulled his blade back to use the tip to drive at the eye holes in my helmet. It came at me like the strike of a snake but my buckler came to my aid and, blocking the tip, I rammed my poleaxe at his left shoulder. His sword scratched and screeched across the metal buckler and even scored a line on the armour protecting my shoulder but it did no harm while the spike did what it was intended to. It found the gap between the spaudler and the besagew. The gap was small but the tip easily slid through the plate protecting the armpit and the one guarding the shoulder. It tore through the mail and into the arm. I twisted when I saw his bloody face contort in pain and then drove my weapon to his right. The besagew fell off and he began to tumble. Hugo, on my right, had killed his man and he brought his halberd down to chop into the swordsman's neck.

As he fell Paer and two more men stepped into the gap to face Hugo, Harold and me. It was a matter of honour and the other two allowed Heinrich Paer to face me. He had a pike which was a handspan longer than my poleaxe. It was lighter than my weapons for it had no hammer. He nodded and said, "You are all that I have heard. You are cunning and skilled but today you will meet your match. And I will have my revenge for the arrow that laid me low for a month."

There was a time for silence and a time to talk. This was the latter. Sir Andrew and Giovanni would be studying the battle and choosing their moment to charge. I could not see the effect of Robin's arrows but they could. So long as we were not falling back then all was well.

I lifted the visor and after I locked it open, I nodded, "And it is good that this comes down to a battle between us two. Perhaps we should have arranged this combat and save the other men we will slay this day."

He laughed, "I know what you did to Lazlo Kaepernick. You will not trick me so easily and I have seen you fight. You know not my skills."

That was true but I knew my own and what he did not know was that I still had my archer's arms and the strength that went with them. I knew that one shoulder would be weaker than the other and it explained why he had chosen a pole weapon. I knew he was a good swordsman. The wounded shoulder impaired him and I would use that weakness to my advantage. He nodded and slashed the pike to rake down my face. It was a clever move and delivered quickly; he had fast hands but I pulled up the poleaxe and with it, the buckler. The pike scraped off the small platter sized shield. I then used the butt of the poleaxe to swing horizontally at his face. There was a small, sharpened spike and it had been embedded in the earth. It was not clean and any wound would become poisoned. I took him by surprise and he stepped back. As he did so I jabbed the spike at the side of the German fighting Hugo. I drew blood and before Paer could take advantage I took the on-guard position with the poleaxe held diagonally across my chest. This was not a game of cat and mouse for in such a game the cat would have no chance. It was more of a contest between a lion and a tiger. Both were killers but they had unique skills as well as shared ones.

    He adopted the same grip and punched at me. The weaponsmith had followed my instructions well and the langet, the metal protection for the head, was longer on this new poleaxe. As our weapons clashed together, I punched hard with my two hands and the langet cracked against the wood of his pike. My superior strength and the blood from the men I had wounded and slain made the ground slippery when he stepped back. He was off balance and when I brought my axe head down, he struggled to block it. Hugo had killed the man I had wounded and the driving back of Heinrich Paer allowed Hugo to follow me into the gap and Paer found himself with a stake perilously close to his back. It hampered his mobility. I swung my weapon to use the hammer. He partly deflected it but it still struck his injured shoulder and I saw him wince. It was the one that was still recovering from the arrow wound and it had hurt. Harold, on my other side, brought his war axe down to slice through the arm of the Hungarian he was fighting. It seemed we were winning.

    Suddenly, from behind the ever-diminishing numbers of mercenaries came men wearing the livery of Perugia. They were coming for me. I watched arrows fly from behind me strike some but it seemed they had committed their reserves.

    My bodyguard's voice was urgent, "Sir John, we are in danger of being surrounded. We must fall back."

    There are times when you walk away and times when you throw the bones. This was a time for a throw. I raised my weapon as I saw the glance Paer gave to the Perugians. He was losing and they were his salvation. I brought the hammer down to the exact spot I had just struck. I saw the dent but this time there was no block and the metal cracked, along with a bone. The arrow that had hit him north of Florence had come back to haunt him. The pike fell from his hands and he shouted, "I yield, I yield."

I nodded but I had no time for self-congratulation as four Perugian knights hurled themselves at me. Hugo stepped forward and skewered one but paid for it with his life as a Perugian sword drove up under his arm. I was not fighting one man but several and so I swung the poleaxe in a long swing. I was rewarded when the axe head bit into the helmet, cheek and skull of a Perugian. As Harold was struck in the arm by a bolt from Siena's walls, I lunged with the spike at another knight. When I did so I heard the horn. My horsemen were making their attack. The Perugians charging at us thought that they had won for I was isolated and if they killed me then victory was theirs.

I shouted, "John, sound the charge!" I hoped that Dai's squire was still alive and when the horn sounded close to my back, I knew that he had obeyed orders. "Guard my prisoner."

I stepped over the wounded Paer and thrust the spike at a wild-eyed Perugian as our line, which had absorbed so much pressure, began to advance. His sword clanged off my helmet but my spike drove between the breastplate and his faulds to split mail and enter his lower body. I pushed and ran, using my strength to hold up his body and making it into a human battering ram although, by the time I dropped it, his body was already dead. Now the stakes that were intended to stop us aided us and we ran through them. We were the professionals and there was no thought of vengeance, honour or chivalry. When a body was before me, I eliminated it the speediest way I could. Those with open helmets were speared. I used the hammer with a closed helmet. My handy buckler deflected sword thrusts. True, some weapons hit me but my armour was the best. I would be battered and bruised after the battle but I would be whole. The Perugians were like wild men. Paer's men, seeing their leader defeated and knowing our skill just surrendered so that the Perugians were not actually reinforcing anyone for the men behind me had no one to fight.

Dai made his way next to me, "My lord, there is no need for this madness! You risk your life against men who have lost their heads. We have won."

I said nothing but raised the poleaxe high above my head and brought it down to split the skull of a Sienese man at arms who thought he was beyond my range. Dai did not know but I was making a point. I wanted this story to become a legend so that I would not have to do it again. I wanted to slay as many of the Sienese and Perugians as I could. I wanted every Italian to be terrified of Sir John Hawkwood.

Realising the futility of further words he joined me as the two of us drove the men at arms back to the walls of Siena. When I saw Michael, still mounted on his horse, his mail and tabard bloodied and his sword notched then I knew we had won. The squires had done well and some would win their spurs. The men before us dropped their weapons to the ground and sank to their knees. It had been almost half an hour since I had defeated Paer and in that time my plan had worked. The flanks had folded and we had won. Siena was mine.

Epilogue

We stayed in Siena for a month. Paer bought his freedom but it cost him twenty thousand florins. Even more important was the fact that he knew I had the beating of him on every level. Siena was asked for fifty thousand florins as well as ransoms for those who had surrendered. The Perugians who had survived were also similarly ransomed. The Genoese and Florentine horsemen, I let go. Montforte had been beaten by me on two out of three encounters. I wondered if there would be a fourth.

We had lost men but it was the newer ones. I had lost Hugo, but the other three, all of whom were wounded felt that they had earned their place amongst my men. I rewarded them well as I did John. I offered Michael his spurs but he declined, saying that he still had much learning to enjoy. As for Sir Andrew, the humiliation of Perugia went some way to healing the hurt in his heart. With laden wagons, we headed back to Perugia to pick up Otto, his men and the treasure we had left there. We might have made the journey to Perugia quicker but the plunder we had taken meant it took a month and we did not reach Pisa until October where Florentine ambassadors awaited me.

I made them wait for me. I bathed and changed clothes before I saw them in the doge's palace. They were contrite.

"Sir John, we have fought many times and Florence has realised the folly of doing so. You have agreed not to fight Florence for five years. We would go further. We would hire you and your company to be our guardians."

I had not had time to speak to William nor my leaders but I knew that I held the upper hand. There was no need to rush into a decision. I shook my head, "I will not answer yet, I am still engaged by Pisa and I promised my sons that I would be home by Christmas. I promise that I will deliver my answer by Easter. The campaigning season is now over and you will be safe. Is that good enough for you?"

General Malatesta nodded, "It will have to be."

When I had been betrayed at Florence by both friend and foe it had been a low point but I had never questioned myself. Now, with the exception of Naples, I was the ruler of this part of Italy and I knew that if I chose, I could take Naples. A new part of my life was beginning and I would do so with my sons at my side. I had a journey ahead and it would be the end of one life and the start of another.

The End

Glossary

Battle- a military formation rather than an event
Bevor- metal chin and mouth protector attached to a helmet
Brase- a strap on a shield for an arm to go through
Brigandine- a leather or padded tunic worn by soldiers; often studded with metal and sometimes called a jack
Centenar- the commander of a hundred
Chevauchée – a raid on an enemy, usually by horsemen
Cordwainer- Shoemaker
Cuisse - metal protection for the thigh
Faulds - a skirt of metal below the breastplate
Feditore-an Italian warrior
Gardyvyan- Archer's haversack containing all his war-gear
Ghibellines – The faction supporting the Holy Roman Emperor against the Pope
Glaive- a long pole weapon with a concave blade
Greaves- Protection for the lower legs
Guelphs- the faction supporting the Pope
Guige strap– a long leather strap that allowed a shield to hang from a knight's shoulder
Harbingers- the men who found accommodation and campsites for archers
Jupon – a shorter version of the surcoat
Mainward - the main body of an army
Mêlée - confused fight
Oriflamme – The French standard which was normally kept in Saint-Denis
Pavesiers - men who carried man-sized shields to protect crossbowmen
Perpunto- soft padded tunic used as light armour during training
Poleyn – knee protection
Rearward- the rearguard and baggage of an army
Rooking - overcharging
Spaudler – shoulder protection
Shaffron – metal headpiece for a horse
Spanning hook- the hook a crossbowman had on his belt to help draw his weapon

Trapper – a cloth covering for a horse
Vanward- the leading element of an army, the scouts
Vintenar- commander of twenty
Vambrace – upper arm protection

Historical note

John Hawkwood was a real person but much of his life is still a mystery. At the end of his career, he was one of the most powerful men in Northern Italy where he commanded the White or English Company. He famously won the battle of Castagnaro in 1387. However, his early life is less well documented, and I have used artistic licence to add details. He was born in Essex and his father was called Gilbert. I have made up the reason for his leaving his home but leave he did, and he became an apprentice tailor. It is rumoured that he fought at Crécy as a longbowman and I have used that to weave a tale. It is also alleged that he was knighted by Prince Edward at Poitiers. The Duke of Clarence was almost 7 feet tall and Prince Edward was also a tall man. I am unsure when he began to wear his black armour but I chose Christmas 1357 as the date.

The tiny county of Montferrat was hemmed in by both Milan and Savoy. It was The White Company who saved it from extinction.

For those readers who do not like John Hawkwood then all I can say is that all the bad things he did were not made up by me. He did run a medieval protection racket for a while but that just helped him to gather a company which, eventually, became the greatest force in Italy. If you find him flawed then I have done my job and painted a portrait of a real and complex man.

Andrew Belmonte was a real member of the White Company and his exploits are recorded faithfully. He did lead those who left Sir John and he did woo an Italian lady however I have tried to put flesh on the bones I discovered in the eighteenth-century Italian text (badly translated I might add). What I will say is that I have not had to make many things up. Cascina and Perugia were defeats. Cascina was seen, at the time as a heroic failure. The Pisans were well outnumbered but Sir john Hawkwood almost managed to win. He extracted his company, largely successfully, but the Pisans were captured. Baumgarten, Paer and Sterz were leaders of companies. Sterz's death is recorded. The fate of the others was decided by me. The whole Visconti clan should be seen as being similar to Chicago gangsters. We are not yet finished with Bernabò and Galeazzo and Sir john Hawkwood's life has many twists and turns.

Pope Urban did try to, first of all, hire the companies and when that failed, to form a league against them. Such was their success that he failed. In this book, Sir John is in his forties. His greatest victory came when he was in his sixties. The story will continue.

Griff Hosker
February 2022

The books I used for reference were:

- French Armies of the Hundred Years War- David Nicholle
- Castagnaro 1387- Devries and Capponi
- Italian Medieval Armies 1300-1500- Gabriele Esposito
- Armies of the Medieval Italian Wars-1125-1325
- Condottiere 1300-1500 Infamous Medieval Mercenaries – David Murphy
- The Armies of Crécy and Poitiers- Rothero
- The Scottish and Welsh Wars 1250-1400- Rothero
- English Longbowman 1330-1515- Bartlett and Embleton
- The Longbow- Mike Loades
- The Battle of Poitiers 1356- Nicholle and Turner
- The Tower of London-Lapper and Parnell
- The Tower of London- A L Rowse
- Sir John Hawkwood- John Temple Leader

Other books by Griff Hosker

If you enjoyed reading this book, then why not read another one by the author?

Ancient History

The Sword of Cartimandua Series
(Germania and Britannia 50 A.D. – 128 A.D.)
Ulpius Felix- Roman Warrior (prequel)
The Sword of Cartimandua
The Horse Warriors
Invasion Caledonia
Roman Retreat
Revolt of the Red Witch
Druid's Gold
Trajan's Hunters
The Last Frontier
Hero of Rome
Roman Hawk
Roman Treachery
Roman Wall
Roman Courage

The Wolf Warrior series
(Britain in the late 6th Century)
Saxon Dawn
Saxon Revenge
Saxon England
Saxon Blood
Saxon Slayer
Saxon Slaughter
Saxon Bane
Saxon Fall: Rise of the Warlord
Saxon Throne
Saxon Sword

Medieval History

The Dragon Heart Series
Viking Slave
Viking Warrior
Viking Jarl
Viking Kingdom
Viking Wolf
Viking War
Viking Sword
Viking Wrath
Viking Raid
Viking Legend
Viking Vengeance
Viking Dragon
Viking Treasure
Viking Enemy
Viking Witch
Viking Blood
Viking Weregeld
Viking Storm
Viking Warband
Viking Shadow
Viking Legacy
Viking Clan
Viking Bravery

The Norman Genesis Series
Hrolf the Viking
Horseman
The Battle for a Home
Revenge of the Franks
The Land of the Northmen
Ragnvald Hrolfsson
Brothers in Blood
Lord of Rouen
Drekar in the Seine
Duke of Normandy
The Duke and the King

Danelaw
(England and Denmark in the 11th Century)
Dragon Sword
Oathsword

New World Series
Blood on the Blade
Across the Seas
The Savage Wilderness
The Bear and the Wolf
Erik The Navigator

The Vengeance Trail

The Reconquista Chronicles
Castilian Knight
El Campeador
The Lord of Valencia

The Aelfraed Series
(Britain and Byzantium 1050 A.D. - 1085 A.D.)
Housecarl
Outlaw
Varangian

The Anarchy Series England 1120-1180
English Knight
Knight of the Empress
Northern Knight
Baron of the North
Earl
King Henry's Champion
The King is Dead
Warlord of the North
Enemy at the Gate
The Fallen Crown
Warlord's War

Kingmaker
Henry II
Crusader
The Welsh Marches
Irish War
Poisonous Plots
The Princes' Revolt
Earl Marshal
The Perfect Knight

Border Knight
1182-1300
Sword for Hire
Return of the Knight
Baron's War
Magna Carta
Welsh Wars
Henry III
The Bloody Border
Baron's Crusade
Sentinel of the North
War in the West
Debt of Honour
The Blood of the Warlord

Sir John Hawkwood Series
France and Italy 1339- 1387
Crécy: The Age of the Archer
Man At Arms
The White Company
Leader of Men

Lord Edward's Archer
Lord Edward's Archer
King in Waiting
An Archer's Crusade
Targets of Treachery
The Great Cause (April 2022)

Struggle for a Crown
1360- 1485
Blood on the Crown
To Murder a King
The Throne
King Henry IV
The Road to Agincourt
St Crispin's Day
The Battle For France
The Last Knight
Queen's Knight

Tales from the Sword I
(Short stories from the Medieval period)

Tudor Warrior series
England and Scotland in the late 14th and early 15th century
Tudor Warrior

Conquistador
England and America in the 16th Century
Conquistador

Modern History

The Napoleonic Horseman Series
Chasseur à Cheval
Napoleon's Guard
British Light Dragoon
Soldier Spy
1808: The Road to Coruña
Talavera
The Lines of Torres Vedras
Bloody Badajoz
The Road to France
Waterloo

The Lucky Jack American Civil War series

Rebel Raiders
Confederate Rangers
The Road to Gettysburg

The British Ace Series
1914
1915 Fokker Scourge
1916 Angels over the Somme
1917 Eagles Fall
1918 We will remember them
From Arctic Snow to Desert Sand
Wings over Persia

Combined Operations series 1940-1945
Commando
Raider
Behind Enemy Lines
Dieppe
Toehold in Europe
Sword Beach
Breakout
The Battle for Antwerp
King Tiger
Beyond the Rhine
Korea
Korean Winter

Tales from the Sword II
(Short stories from the Modern period)

Other Books
Great Granny's Ghost (Aimed at 9-14-year-old young people)

For more information on all of the books then please visit the author's website at www.griffhosker.com where there is a link to contact him or visit his Facebook page: GriffHosker at Sword Books

Printed in Great Britain
by Amazon